THE IMPENETRABLE SECRET

Also Available from Valancourt Books

GASTON DE BLONDEVILLE (1826)
Ann Radcliffe
Edited by Frances A. Chiu

CLERMONT (1798)
Regina Maria Roche
Edited by Natalie Schroeder

THE ITALIAN (1797)
Ann Radcliffe
Edited by Allen W. Grove

THE CASTLE OF WOLFENBACH (1793)
Eliza Parsons
Edited by Diane Long Hoeveler

Forthcoming Titles

THE MONK (1796)
Matthew G. Lewis
Edited by Allen W. Grove

ZELUCO (1789)
John Moore
Edited by Pamela Perkins

COLLECTED GOTHIC DRAMAS
Joanna Baillie
Edited by Christine Colón

THE VEILED PICTURE (1802)
Ann Radcliffe
Edited by Jack G. Voller

Gothic Classics

THE IMPENETRABLE SECRET, FIND IT OUT!

Francis Lathom

Edited with a new introduction by
James Cruise

VALANCOURT BOOKS
CHICAGO

The Impenetrable Secret, Find it Out!
Originally published in 1805
First Valancourt Books edition, January 2007

Introduction and notes © 2007 by James Cruise
This edition © 2007 by Valancourt Books

Published by Valancourt Books, Chicago, Illinois
http://www.valancourtbooks.com

ISBN 0-9777841-3-4

Library of Congress Cataloging-in-Publication Data

Lathom, Francis, 1777-1832.
  The impenetrable secret, find it out! / Francis Lathom ; edited with
a new introduction by James Cruise. -- 1st Valancourt Books ed.
    p. cm. -- (Gothic classics)
  ISBN 0-9777841-3-4
  1. Nobility--Italy--Fiction. I. Cruise, James, 1949- II. Title.
PR4878.L175I47 2007
823'.7--dc22

                                    2006038120

10 9 8 7 6 5 4 3 2 1

CONTENTS

INTRODUCTION

OF the twenty-one novels that Francis Lathom wrote between 1795 and 1830, only a few of these works—*The Castle of Ollada* (1795), *The Midnight Bell* (1798), and *Italian Mysteries* (1820)—exist in modern editions.[1] With the publication of *The Impenetrable Secret, Find it Out!* (1805), we can now add a fourth. For general readers of gothic fiction and students of late eighteenth- and early nineteenth-century British literature, the "Forgotten Goth," as Arthur Alastair MacConochie characterizes Lathom in an unpublished thesis from 1949, is slowly becoming known—no longer forgotten—in ways that might even surprise an erstwhile dissertation writer.[2] The fate of the forgotten author or the overlooked book is not of course without precedent. In fact it is fair to say that most books published in England by the early nineteenth century and actually include the author's name on the title page probably would draw a blank from most readers. The kind of celebrity status associated with contemporary Anglo-American authorship, whether that author is John Updike or Philip Roth, Margaret Drabble or A. S. Byatt, Joyce Carol Oates or, for that matter, Dan Brown, was in former ages largely unknown. So the act of tracking down the literary effects of the forgotten often takes work: searching bibliographies, pursuing the odd reference from works otherwise well-known, or, in this day and age, getting chest-deep in databases that, with the insertion of just the right search term, yield a long list of titles with which researchers may have had little or no previous familiarity. But in the absence of that kind of scholarly toil, accessible and affordable modern editions are often the master key for unlocking the secrets and mysteries of the past and opening up whole new vistas of literature.

To be sure, general and specialized readers alike already know of a Dickens or a Defoe, in part because printing houses and presses

---

[1] *The Castle of Ollada* and *Italian Mysteries* are available in Valancourt Books' *Gothic Classics* series, both edited by James D. Jenkins. *The Midnight Bell* was issued by Skoob Books in 1993 with an introduction by Lucien Jenkins, and a new edition is forthcoming from Valancourt Books as part of its "Horrid Novels" series.

[2] Arthur Alastair MacConochie, "Francis Lathom: Forgotten Goth" (M.A. thesis, University of Virginia, 1949).

have never ceased publishing their major works—*Great Expectations* and *Robinson Crusoe* are just as available now as they were in ages past. The same is not true for many other—indeed the bulk of—late eighteenth- and early nineteenth-century novels. Novelists such as Charlotte Smith, Mary Hays, Eliza Fenwick, and Charlotte Dacre, to name only a few, are known to us now primarily because of the efforts of presses such as Pandora and Broadview. This rather recent reemergence of the once-forgotten and lesser lights of the literary cosmos, while meaningful, is not, however, easily explained. At moments of weakness and in the case just cited, we can at least imagine that the marketplace did not dictate interest but responded instead to changing attitudes, particularly among literary scholars, that no era or period enjoys full representation if restricted only to those writers who form its "great tradition" or classic core.

Such a core tradition of letters has not looked favorably upon Francis Lathom. The irony here perhaps is that in his own day he did not have to worry about popularity or seek attention for his writing. As a regional dramatist he found both each time one of his plays was staged. Indeed, if we trust what we think we know of his life and personal habits, Lathom's personality was eminently sociable and outgoing; he strikes us, in eighteenth-century terms, as a man of "conversation." Nevertheless, our knowledge of Lathom today essentially draws upon the seeming authority of the *Dictionary of National Biography* and the conjectures of Montague Summers in *The Gothic Quest* (Fortune Press, 1938). James D. Jenkins has, however, uncovered other pieces of factual evidence that add some interesting wrinkles to the fabric of the man.[1] In 1818, when Jane Austen published *Northanger Abbey*, though she does not refer to Lathom by name, she does resurrect one of his novels—a bit of free advertising—and places him, as it were, at the same table with Ann Radcliffe, who has prospered over time better than Lathom ever has. In *Northanger Abbey*, Austen's Isabella Thorpe, positively transported and unwilling to let go of an addiction, encourages Catherine Morland to indulge herself in a reading list of gothic tales that begins with works by Ann Radcliffe and goes on, possibly in descending order, to include Lathom's *Midnight Bell*

---

[1] See the introductions James D. Jenkins has written to two of Lathom's other novels: *The Castle of Ollada*, new ed. (Chicago: Valancourt Books, 2006) and *Italian Mysteries* (Chicago: Valancourt Books, 2006).

(1798). Not for a second, though, should we assume, given the tenor of *Northanger Abbey*, that Austen was intent upon endorsing either the gothic novel in general or the work of Lathom in particular; much the same could be said of Charlotte Lennox's treatment of romance in *The Female Quixote* (1752), which in dusting off anachronous forms of romance ridicules the romantic tendency and extremes of Lennox's principal character Arabella. But no matter how noble-minded their attempts, neither Lennox nor Austen succeeded in dispensing with genres still very much with us today. Mary Shelley's *Frankenstein*, it is worth noting, appeared the same year as *Northanger Abbey*, and Charles Maturin's *Melmoth the Wanderer* was still two years off. And while literary historians may decree that the gothic petered out fairly early in the nineteenth century, around 1820, that assurance is best weighed against the broader age, especially in light of the Victorian fascination with supernatural figures and forms, a matter that Carole G. Silver has amply documented in her *Strange and Secret Peoples* (Oxford Univ. Press, 1999).

Austen's animadversions aside, Lathom, like so many novelists before him, regarded his *The Impenetrable Secret* as serving a moral purpose. In the Preface he remarks, "I should be very sorry to introduce to the acquaintance of society, a book which might leave any of its members more lax in their morals than it found them, especially the younger branches, for whom it becomes the writer to be particularly cautious in drawing praiseworthy examples" (Preface, p. 3). Contemporary reviewers congratulated Lathom on the same grounds. According to one: "we seldom remember to have met with a tale possessing so much to catch the feelings and improve the heart"—and later in the same review: "a work whose doctrines if they be sometimes overstrained, are strained on the side of virtue"; as well as a second: "If the merits of a novel consist, as we have generally been taught to believe, in exciting an interest for virtue and an indignation against vice, till the principal characters are rewarded by that justice, . . . the work of which we speak is entitled to a considerable degree of praise."[1] In fact, the first of these reviewers, *pace* Austen, lauds Lathom for having "travelled through the classic retreats of Mrs. Radcliffe, without stopping us to bait with an Alpine description of the road" (*British Critic*,

---

[1] Respectively, *British Critic* (Dec. 1805), 671-72; and *Critical Review* (Dec. 1805), 435.

671-72). So the thirteen years separating the publication of *Northanger Abbey* in 1818 and a review published in the *British Critic* in 1805 was an interval unlucky enough to prove, for one writer, a fascination with but intolerance for the gothic; and to provide, for all other writers, a durable lesson about the volatility and caprices of literary taste and its marketplace vehicle. Not much has changed between then and now— the end product of novel writing still calls upon the novelist to run a gauntlet of readers, critics, reviewers, and other writers.

Readers of *The Impenetrable Secret* will discover that as much as this novel leans on certain gothic conventions, it also rests on the marriage plot, a feature of the novel as old as the modern or eighteenth-century novel itself. Just as Austen exploited this topic, so too did the eighteenth-century novelist Samuel Richardson. His take on the marriage plot, while not the same as Austen's, shares plot features that depend upon contrivance, suspense, and twists or turns of one sort or another. But even in using the marriage plot, Richardson—the first champion and self-appointed reformer of a genre regarded as debased—managed to exploit the gothic in his first and most sedate domestic tale, *Pamela* (1740/1741). In it the nefarious Mr. B, after the death of his mother Lady B, secrets her one-time maid Pamela to his dark and foreboding Lincolnshire estate, where he keeps the object of his passion in a tortured state under lock and key. Lathom's handling of the marriage plot seems almost tame by comparison. None of these narrative tendencies, either domestic or gothic or their union, met with the approval of Adam Smith, Professor of Moral Philosophy, author of *The Wealth of Nations* (1776), and one of the most formidable intellectuals of the age. In his professorial capacity at the University of Glasgow, Smith delivered a series of lectures between 1762 and 1763, transcribed by one of his students, on matters of rhetoric and belles lettres. Lecture 17 finds Smith bitterly complaining about the novel, during which he isolates its most harmful strain: "As newness is the only merit in a Novel and curiosity the only motive which induces us to read them, the writers are necessitated to make use of this method to keep it up. . . . Even in [ancient] Tragedy where it is reckoned an essentiall part to keep the plot in Suspense this is not so necessary as in Romance. A tragedy can bear to be read again and again, tho the incidents be not new to us . . . ."[1] Read a novel once, if you must, Smith urges, and you are or should be done with it; novelty, curiosity, and suspense, he intimates with a subdued alas, encourage readers of novels and keep their eyes moving across the page. But if suspense, curiosity, and novelty figure in all novels, then the same three figure even more prominently in gothic fiction.

Yet if Smith speaks even a kernel of truth about novels in his characterization of the genre, then his wholesale dismissal of the genre or his wanting to pillory it for some vague moral inadequacy serves no useful purpose. Trying, on the other hand, to understand this cultural need for the mysterious and extraordinary forces readers and students of literature to replace moral outrage with historical understanding. Not irrelevant to any explanation of the origins of this narrative phenomenon is that by the turn of the nineteenth century Britain was no longer the same nation it had been at the turn of the eighteenth century: urbanization, a declining aristocracy, a broader dissemination of wealth, religious controversy and doubt, empire-building, more inclusive forms of cultural life, governmental bureaucracy, increasing literacy rates, and a changing rural landscape had over that interval effectively rooted England in the modern world.

In its darkest forms, the gothic novel seems to have nothing directly to do with any of these concerns, yet no literary work exits a vacuum to position itself in time and space. Ruth Perry, in *Novel Relations*, her recent and exhaustive study of family relations in the novel between 1748 and 1818, concludes that "incest was at the heart of the newly invented gothic novel, testifying to a new fear and a new fixation in English society. . . . Plots feature the predatory desire of an older man determined to possess a beautiful virgin young enough to be his daughter . . . . There is always a dark secret at the center of the mystery . . . . The action is usually set in a time and space sufficiently far from contemporary reality . . . . Old buildings with secret passages . . . , inexplicable rustlings and groans . . . , mysterious personal histories and suppressed consanguineal relations—these elements suggest the incest motif."[2] So in a strange and, perhaps for some, shocking

---

[1] Adam Smith, *Lectures on Rhetoric and Belles Lettres*, ed. J. C. Bryce (Oxford: Clarendon Press, 1983), 97.

[2] Ruth Perry, *Novel Relations: The Transformation of Kinship in English Literature and Culture*, 1748-1818 (Cambridge: Cambridge Univ. Press, 2004), 388-89.

way, Perry effectively shows that the distant and detached world of the gothic is neither distant nor detached at all from period realities, as she knots the domestic and gothic together in a most unholy embrace.

Whether readers or cultural observers from the second half of the eighteenth century and the early years of the nineteenth century were equipped to see the gothic novel as Perry writes about it is up in the air. Even so, enough evidence from the period confirms that acts of reading in general and novel-reading in particular had furled more than a few brows. As is so often the case, cultural acts have political consequences. It was not so long ago in the United States that its then-Attorney General took it upon himself to have drapery placed on an offending piece of sculpture, lest we associate nudity with a man proud to wear clothes. Mercifully, however, most forms of disapprobation are often less staged and operatic, though, if pursued, equally revealing. Consider again Adam Smith's reflections on the novel: he goes out of his way to look over what is so easily overlooked—the novel—in order to indict the genre for its novelty, suspense, and curiosity. On the other hand, this same Smith swims across the waters and explores the depths of easily one of the most morally controversial topics of the eighteenth century, national commercialization, and comes away from that experience refreshed and invigorated. If anything produced novelty, suspense, and curiosity in eighteenth-century Britain, it was the growing economy. Scores of commentators read in this development the moral ruin of the nation and, though helpless to stop it, could not reconcile how self-interest would ever fit the obligations demanded by civic republicanism. Smith, however, emphatically neutralized the moral terror of commercialization by positing in *The Wealth of Nations* something he called the invisible hand, an economic mechanism that is or was supposed to redirect selfish pursuits into state benefits—all unbeknownst to the self-seeking parties. Thus, the material and economic forms of novelty and suspense play a useful role in the domain of "nation"; but take those same principles, render them merely verbal, and gear them only toward the selfish passions of citizen-readers to see how poisonous and debilitating they really are.

It may be a coincidence, though it may not, that Horace Walpole, the originating genius of the modern gothic, recounts to the Reverend William Cole that his inspiration for *The Castle of Otranto* came to him in a dream, this some years before Coleridge's similar experience with "Kubla Khan" (1816). In his dream, Walpole reports, "On the uppermost banister of a great staircase I saw a gigantic hand in armor"—a literal iron fist.[1] It does not take long in *Otranto* for Manfred, Prince of Otranto, to find his "darling," though "sickly" son Conrad "dashed to pieces, and almost buried under an enormous helmet, an hundred times more large than any casque made for human beings" (*Otranto* 17). Manfred's hopes for the future of his line and the transmission of his power lie crushed beneath a diabolical deus ex machina. As Walpole's depiction underscores, the visual effect of the literal imposes terror and amazement; Smith, by contrast, sidesteps moral confusion by rendering his deus ex machina without location and completely invisible. Whether he avoids terror and amazement in the process is not so clear. Seen or unseen, terrorizing or not, those forces that operate upon human affairs and affect states of mind share one undeniable similarity: they perplex observers through the secrets and mysteries of their operations.

By the final decade of the eighteenth century, a crush of novels and plays had appeared before the public that dealt with precisely these concerns: among the novels we can count works such as Eliza Fenwick's *Secresy* (1795), which yokes a stultifying and destructive gothicism to a world of untidy spots. Not so far removed from it or the kind of environment Fenwick crafted was Samuel Pratt's five-volume and controversial monster of a novel, *Family Secrets* (1797); for theater-goers, secrecy appeared as both comedy and tragedy: Matthew Nimmo's *The Fatal Secret* (1792), Thomas Morton's *Secrets Worth Knowing* (1798), or Edward Morris's *The Secret* (1799). Of equal and related importance was the period urban spy narrative, the most famous of which is Ned Ward's *The London Spy* (1703); as a subgenre, the reflections of the urban spy bridged the century, even though these texts remain largely unknown today. Invariably the urban spy narrative summons forth, often from the country, rustics who become shadowy street peregrinators compelled to explore the warrens and back alleys of London, to venture into public haunts of various kinds, or even to make their way into the private homes of fashionable ur-

---

[1] Horace Walpole, *The Castle of Otranto*, ed. W. S. Lewis and Joseph W. Reed, Jr. (Oxford: Oxford Univ. Press, 1990), ix. I subsequently cite from the same edition.

banites to record remarkably like tales of the dark, ominous deeds of the citizenry. In a way, because so many of these narratives focus on the nighttime streets of the metropolis, they carry with them a strong sense of a near-gothic city, at once deep and perplexing. But even if we look in a different direction to survey those novels that carry no apparent gothic associations, we realize that the most celebrated novels of the "great tradition" still depend upon secrecy and mystery. Consider, for example, Fielding's comic-epic novel *Tom Jones* (1749). Were we to know the family secret or the real name of the infant Tom when he turns up at Squire Allworthy's doorstep, we would have a novel perhaps as many as nine hundred pages shorter than its extant form or, more likely, a Henry Fielding known best for two novels rather than three. Of note too is that Squire Allworthy inhabits a "*Gothick* Stile of Building"—who would have thought it?[1] Altogether, then, an ambient gothicism and an atmosphere thick with secrets and mysteries permeated all forms of eighteenth-century literature, well before the emergence of the gothic novel, so that when this genre finally did appear, it merely gave shape to what was already swirling in the wind.

But just as fear, terror, mystery, and creaking superstition filled the minds of readers from expected sources and those less so, these same sensations also filled the minds of those intent upon preserving a putative traditional British life. The great fear of this latter group, as E. J. Clery puts it, was that the common people "were prepared to reverse the course of enlightenment, to laboriously knit together the events of the present with the superstitions of the past, they were prepared to cast doubt on the coherence of treasured institutions, which according to their story could be swept away like sandcastles by the machinations of a handful of plotters."[2] In other words, these fearful keepers and preservers of the status quo viewed a potentially subversive, democracy-hungry citizenry as figures plucked from the pages of a gothic tale. Still, the political machine is forever efficient in its own operations. Beginning in the nineteenth century, according to David Vincent, England began the great work of shaping itself into a "culture of secrecy" through its highest professional and political institu-

---

[1] Henry Fielding, *The History of Tom Jones, A Foundling,* ed. Martin C. Battestin (Middletown, Conn.: Wesleyan Univ. Press, 1975), 42.

[2] E. J. Clery, *The Rise of Supernatural Fiction,* 1762-1800 (1995; reprint, Cambridge: Cambridge Univ. Press, 1996), 163.

tions.[1] The lesson history teaches here is that no one should ever fear, be terrorized by, or find suspicious a government or its vast bureaucracies privileged by secrecy, even when that secrecy itself becomes sanctioned and sealed as Official Acts of the government. The great virtue of this form of secrecy is its utter invisibility and impenetrability, conditions that always preclude enormous helmets from dashing to bits those unfortunately standing beneath them or in their way.

The varieties of gothic experience, as I hope I have suggested in this short space, were many and not at all restricted to what we identify as the gothic novel. Nevertheless, within the framework of that literary genre, Walpole especially and Radcliffe later on served as its exemplars. That Walpole played upon Lathom's literary imagination is clear, as the The Castle of Ollada resonates many things Walpolean, not the least of which is its title.[2] While The Impenetrable Secret owes no apparent debt to Otranto, it may, in an indirect way, draw from another work of Walpole's, The Mysterious Mother, a play first published in 1768. A later edition of this play, published in 1781 and printed by the famous Dodsley, does not bear the name of Walpole on its title page, but in remarks that preface the play, Walpole forewarns his audience that its "subject is disgusting"—though not so disgusting that he would forsake an opportunity of having it published.[3] This play lives up to everything Ruth Perry has said in her epitome of the genre: its "disgusting" subject is in fact incest—to the youthful Frances Burney, "a story of so much horror, from atrocious and voluntary guilt never did I hear!"[4] In the play two friars, Benedict and Martin, more steeped in Machiavelli's The Prince than the holy books, endlessly plot to get the goods on the imperious and, as it turns out, incestuous Countess of Narbonne. Early in the play Benedict tries to catch her with honey before turning later to vinegar. In a private conversation he recommends to the Countess a holy man from a "neighb'ring district"

---

[1] David Vincent, The Culture of Secrecy: Britain, 1832-1998 (Oxford: Oxford Univ. Press, 1998).

[2] For this connection see, Jenkins, ed., The Castle of Ollada, xiii.

[3] [Horace Walpole], Mysterious Mother, A Tragedy (London, 1781), v. In citing from the text of this play, I provide act, scene, and page number parenthetically, since the play is printed without line numbers.

[4] [Frances Burney], The Diary and Letters of Madame D'Arblay, 7 vols. (London: Henry Colburn, 1842-46), 3:235.

as a source for forgiveness and absolution, telling her, "Consult with him. / Unfold th' impenetrable mystery, / That sets your soul and you at endless discord" (*Mother* 1,5:17). With good cause, the Countess contemptuously mocks Benedict's falsely pious proposal as stuff for "Weak minds [that] / Want their soul's fortune told by oracles / and holy juglers" (*Mother* 1,5:18). Walpole's "impenetrable mystery" that grows into a disturbingly dark tale of tragedy may very well be the verbal inspiration for Lathom's "impenetrable secret," a much lighter and pleasingly deceptive tale that turns on the conventions of dramatic comedy. Darker forces lurk, to be sure, in Lathom's story, but the principal of these, the old Conte Roderigo della Piacca, is already dead "many years" before the action of the novel begins. A dissolute man, Roderigo thirsted after money and power and, in the end, was left a broken man unredeemed by the invisible hand. His replacement thugs, Rodovina Maritos and Iago Zincti, lack social stature and, even before the novel begins, inhabit the shadowlands of society and the margins of legitimacy. Their self-interest, while deadly, in the end proves no match for the administration of justice.

It is clear that Lathom experimented with the gothic genre in *The Impenetrable Secret* and in subtle ways, which he mirrors through his courtroom scenes, asks readers to question the truth of appearances, if not the evidentiary foundation for belief itself. Necessary to both is the existence of secrecy. Without it, no fear can be allayed or mistake corrected. His depiction of Averilla, a surprisingly supple female character, proves Samuel Johnson's grave worries about anyone's capacity to keep a secret unfounded—a subject Johnson broaches early in his *Rambler* essays (numbers 13 and 14)—and reaffirms what Susannah Centlivre first showed in *The Wonder! A Woman Keeps a Secret* (1714), except that with Averilla it is no wonder at all. In this novel the good and bad alike have or harbor secrets, sometimes through ignorance and at other times through willfulness and malice. The last and most tender secret of the novel belongs to Rosabella, and that is the secret lying within her heart. Once it is revealed, the blind can see and the stern desires of an autocratic father cease to exist. *The Impenetrable Secret* was a Minerva Press book, the brainchild of William Lane, himself either a Minerva or Hermes of the marketplace, who placed his publications—sentimental, gothic, sensational—in a staggering range of shops and circulating libraries and thereby got his goods in the hands of the people. Revolutions sometimes occur without fanfare or head-lines. In its way, *The Impenetrable Secret* was a part of that revolution and a novel as readable today as it was relevant at the time of its pub-lication two centuries ago.

James Cruise
Natchitoches, Louisiana
August 9, 2006

ABOUT THE EDITOR

James Cruise is Associate Professor of English at Northwestern State University in Natchitoches, Louisiana. His scholarly interests focus on the long British eighteenth century, and his published work has ap-peared in some of the leading journals, including *ELH, JEGP, SEL,* and *Age of Johnson.* He is also the author of *Governing Consumption: Needs and Wants, Suspended Characters, and the 'Origins' of Eighteenth-Century English Novels* (Bucknell University Press, 1999), which examines the eighteenth-century novel in the historical context of British commer-cialization. His current project is a book-length study on the role of secrecy in the long eighteenth century, a section of which will appear in 2007 in a collection of essays published by Rowman and Littlefield.

NOTE ON THE TEXT

THE text of the Valancourt Books edition of *The Impenetrable Secret* is taken from the first edition published at the Minerva Press in 1805. A second edition of this novel was published in London in 1831 by A.K. Newman, as was a second edition of Lathom's *The Castle of Ollada* (1795), suggesting either a renewed or ongoing interest in some of Lathom's earlier novels. The Minerva Press, first under William Lane and later under his successor Newman, published the majority of Lathom's works.

As with any early printed book, inconsistencies and errors turn up from time to time, including printer's errors and orthographic variations and departures. The Valancourt Books edition of *The Impenetrable Secret* preserves, as best as its editor can, the original 1805 text of the novel. Obvious errors have been silently corrected, while the minor variations in, for example, the handling of "della," as in della Piacca, have remained. Variant spelling of words also appear as they did in the first edition, but only those that are either orthographically or, in some instances, phonetically sound. The few modern commentators on this novel have spelled the names of key characters in ways that make an editor wonder whether they consulted the text of the novel as they wrote or, if they did, which edition they used. While I prefer the name Zineti or Zinati to Zincti, as the last of these sounds more like a chemical element rather than an Italian name, Zincti appears so regularly throughout the first edition that there is no wishing it away. In the late stages of the novel, one of the characters, Rodovina Maritos, uses the word "refute," according to Michael Vivane, in the context of an anticipated court proceeding; to my knowledge that word makes little sense as used. Rather than emend it, however, I have let it stand. Contemporary reviewers cited Lathom for stylistic infelicities, but the principal cause for this reaction stems, I believe, from Lathom's use of punctuation. That too remains as it did in the first edition.

Even though more than two centuries have passed since the publication of *The Impenetrable Secret*, the text of this novel remains eminently readable. As a result I have supplied notes only sparingly for the text.

The Impenetrable Secret, Find it Out!

Volume I

PREFACE

"THE Secret!" exclaims a lady, "is it worth knowing?"

"Find it out," hastily replies the Author. But considering, on a moment's reflection, that the lady deserves a little less concise reply, he adds, "if you are a fashionable reader, I fear the pages before you will contain but little interest or amusement for you; for they are written upon the old-fashioned plan of endeavouring to inculcate morality, by shewing that vice is certain to meet its punishment; and that virtue will as infallibly receive its recompense. Now this is a doctrine which so many late publications have given their readers reason to doubt, that I am apprehensive a single individual, like myself, assuring them, that it is still the unalterable law of Providence, will hardly serve to convince them of the truth. However, as I feel convinced myself, I feel it also my duty to endeavour to convince others; and should my readers say, that my morality alone offends them, I shall consider the rebuke as the highest compliment they can bestow on me.

"I should be very sorry to introduce to the acquaintance of society, a book which might leave any of its members more lax in their morals than it found them, especially the younger branches, for whom it becomes the writer to be particularly cautious in drawing praiseworthy examples.

"Nothing shall ever tempt me to become the author of such a work as the mother of a family should blush to see in the hands of her daughters; I would never willingly inflict on another those unpleasant sensations which I should wish to be spared myself; and I have lately seen so many publications of the class of amusement, which, had I found them in the hands of a daughter of my own, I am convinced would have called from my lips harsh expressions against their authors, that I shall be very careful not to place myself in a situation where I may, alike in turn, be condemned for undermining those principles of delicacy which form the greatest beauty and grace of a woman; and must, through their medium, bestow the most perfect happiness on man. The evil owes its first rise to the translations which have been made from the works of some of our corrupt neighbours on the Continent; and the evil is a two-fold one—first, as it has introduced a licentious taste, before unrelished by the English nation; and next, that the fashion for translations is become so great, as to be a stab to the genius, and a material drawback upon the industry of our countrymen and women.

"Thus you perceive, Madam, that—" but the lady is fallen asleep!—No, she wakes again; she only dozed through my sermon, and is going to speak.

"Do tell me," says she, "since you are so communicative, what you write for?"

"Willingly—I write because I am an unemployed man, and find that an occupation of this nature gives to my existence a resort ineffectually looked for in idleness and dissipation; and I publish, because my consumption of pens, ink, and paper, would be inconvenient to my purse, if I had not some remuneration for the expence."

"Oh!" cries the lady, "so much for yourself; and now, pray, if I promise to read your book, is your story a new one?"

"Shall I reply to you with Solomon," rejoins the author, "that there is nothing new under the sun; or will you be better pleased with the words of a modern writer upon this subject?—'He who complains of a want of novelty in these productions,' asserts this modern author, 'complains of Nature herself, from whose stores our materials are derived: And when, to avoid the charge of being trite, or threadbare, an author flies from decent probability, he can at best produce a splendid romance, where human manners, human griefs, and human joys, are displaced by a tribe of sentiments that were never felt, and which Nature disowns and rejects.'

"This tale is not a romance, for I have been faithfully assured, that the incidents contained in it have actually taken place. In action they cannot but have excited considerable interest to the parties who were concerned in them. Should half their interest, with none of their anxiety, accompany them to the closet, the author will judge himself sufficiently repaid for the promulgation of his SECRET."

THE
IMPENETRABLE SECRET

CHAPTER I

ABOUT the beginning of the last century lived, in Genoa, a gentleman named Rossano del Alvaretti. He was a merchant, the survivor of two brothers who had succeeded to their father's business; the elder of whom, Eugenio, had been dead some years. The extent of their commerce and the wealth of their house exceeded that of every merchant, and almost of every noble in the state; they were accordingly universally looked up to, and their alliance courted by all who durst aspire to the honour of forming such a connexion.

Eugenio had been dead about seven years; he had left behind him only one child, who was a daughter, and motherless, at the time we have thought fit to open our history. Averilla, for such was her name, had just completed her nineteenth year. Her person was extremely handsome; her figure tall and striking; and the qualifications of her mind superior to those of most girls of her age; add to which, that she possessed every engaging and benevolent virtue, and that her soul was exquisitely sensitive and tender.

Rossano was the father of two children. Hyppolita, a daughter, whom he had lately married to one of the nobles of the republic; and Felix, a son, who had been blind from his birth. Felix was a few months older than his cousin Averilla, and a year younger than his sister Hyppolita. At the death of her father, Averilla had been left to the sole care and guardianship of her uncle Rossano, who had been empowered, by his brother, to give her hand to any man whose rank and fortune he might judge worthy of a claim to the alliance.

Eugenio was well aware that the disposition of his brother was exactly similar to his own; that it placed the first value upon superiority of condition and the possession of wealth; and that the trust of providing his daughter with a husband, which he had placed in his breast, would be executed as much to his satisfaction, as if he could have lived to have selected one for her himself.

The residence of Rossano was principally in the city, where he

possessed a sumptuous house, and where his directing eye was necessary to the profitable conduct of his trade; but his wife, with his son
Felix, and his niece Averilla, resided principally in a village about four
leagues from the city, and which belonged entirely to Rossano, in the
right of his wife, and where he had built a most elegant palazzo.

The Signora Felicia del Alvaretti had been consigned to the arms
of her husband, by another merchant of the republic, whose daughter she was, with little more ceremony than their bargains in trade
were accustomed to be struck; thus much love could not be expected
on either side; and the Signora finding nothing in the conduct of her
husband to recompence her for having been allied to him, without
any reference being made to her opinion in the business, the solitude
of the country had, from the first of her marriage, been her chief delight: Here she had probably found a species of comfort, from lamenting her lot unseen; and on the birth of her children, her inducement
to remain in the country became stronger, on account of the benefit
they would derive from the opportunities it gave them of enjoying
both air and exercise.

On the birth of Hyppolita her affections were for the first time
strongly called forth; much agony had attended the entrance of the
child into the world, and its sex proving her own, seemed to her a
peculiar recompence for her past sorrows. But the birth of her son, Felix, whose privation of that most useful and desirable sense, his sight,
seemed to call in a particular manner upon his parents to render his
existence as free from regret as it was possible the imperfect state in
which nature had sent him into the world should allow him to exist,
she felt her affections still more forcibly called upon to display themselves; and her conduct towards him gave a most striking proof, that
where nature suffers any imperfection of the functions to be a drawback upon the enjoyment which an individual would otherwise reap
from existence, she never fails to procure for him a superior interest in
the breasts of those to whom he is the nearest allied.

Every surgical aid was called upon, to use its utmost exertion in
attempting to give the infant Felix the blessing of beholding the light
of day, till a physician, in whose knowledge the Signora del Alvaretti
placed considerable faith, pronounced it as his opinion, that it was
impossible for the art of surgery to give him sight; and that every
attempt of the kind would only expose him to suffer much torture,

without the remotest chance of any benefit being derived to him from its use. The mother listened attentively to this advice, and making it her only hope, that her child would never feel the want of a sense which he had never enjoyed, she ceased to subject him to the process of surgical operations.

As Felix grew up, he displayed a heart of the most benevolent and engaging kind; his manners were bland and conciliating; and his memory, which was the only channel through which information could be conveyed to his understanding, of so strong and retentive a nature, that his mind, in the course of a few years, shewed itself to be composed of such materials, that had it been gifted with that only sense of which it was deprived, its possessor must have ranked in the first class of genius and learning.

Instead of mourning that the ability of proving himself so was denied to her son, the sensible mother returned her fervent thanks to heaven, that the light of reason had not been withheld from him who was doomed never to enjoy the light of day; and she continued to make it almost her sole business to amuse and instruct him. All the hours which she could snatch from him, she dedicated to the education of her daughter, who by no means repaid her labours with the delightful recompence of profiting by them, which her unfortunate Felix did. Hyppolita's temper was bad, her talents by no means of the first kind, and rendered still more secondary by her unwillingness to learn, and her obstinacy under necessary correction. But the Signora still resolved to act the just mother, and not to relax in her attentions, because they were so unprofitably received; her conduct was ever the same towards both her children, but her heart leaned in secret towards him who excited her pity as well as her love.

As they advanced in years, Hyppolita became proud, avaricious, fond of arrogating to herself a superiority over her acquaintance, and eager to make a display of her father's wealth; in short, in every respect she resembled him; and at the age of fourteen she had already entered into his ideas of forming an alliance, which should add to the wealth and consequence of her family. This disposition greatly endeared her to Signor Rossano; his hopes of rising to greater wealth and rank, through the means of his son, were greatly damped by the infirmity with which he was oppressed; all his expectations therefore were centered in his daughter; and finding her exactly suited to his intention, he showered on her indulgences, which entirely won him her affection from her mother, and which led her to imbibe and emulate his principles, as a hold upon his heart to ensure to herself a continuance of his partial favour.

When Averilla, in consequence of her orphan state, became an inmate of her uncle's family, she quickly opened for herself a way into the affections of the Signora del Alvaretti, who had known but little of her before. Averilla's manners we have already said were of the most engaging kind, and her heart the seat of every virtue; and more we think need not be said to inform our readers that it became her chief pleasure to emulate her aunt in her attentions to the blind Felix.

With dispositions so unlike, it was impossible there could be any love or indeed friendship between Averilla and her cousin Hyppolita; and the fear which Averilla every day expressed, lest her uncle should compel her into the arms of a man to whom she found her heart averse, excited the strongest ridicule against her on the part of Hyppolita.—"My father will not marry you, depend upon it," said she, "to any man who is not possessed of rank and wealth; and what more can you desire than the happiness which these joint advantages must bring you?"

Averilla shook her head with a smile, which bespoke of how different a nature were her sentiments; and the Signora del Alvaretti sighed, whilst a secret wish passed in her heart, that it were possible for her beloved Felix one day to become the husband of the amiable Averilla.

CHAPTER II

ABOUT three years after the period of Averilla's first becoming one of her uncle's family, chance introduced the Signora del Alvaretti and her children to the acquaintance of a young man named Signor Sylvio di Rosalva. They found him to be the possessor of a neighbouring estate, and as his manners had been such as had prejudiced them in his favour on their first introduction to him at the house of a friend where they had been visiting, the Signora invited him to their villa.

Sylvio di Rosalva was a young man of a most elegant and fascinating address; he appeared about nineteen years of age; in stature near the middle height, perhaps an inch or two below it; his features were regularly beautiful; his eyes blue and brilliant; his silken hair a few shades deeper than the flaxen, and streaked in parts with shades of the most vivid gold; his lips emulated the smoothness and colour of the ruby, and they parted only to display a set of the most regularly white teeth. The qualifications of his mind were equal to the graces of his person; in fact, Sylvio was one of those beings who are a rare instance of perfection in the form of humanity.

The visits of Sylvio to the villa del Alvaretti gave so much pleasure to its inhabitants, that his society was very frequently sought by them; with Felix he was a most particular favourite; it appeared his chief study, whilst with him, to dedicate every moment in producing him amusement or gratification; on this account, it is needless to say how great a favourite he was with the Signora Felicia, the mother of Felix; and in the breast of Averilla, he was almost insensibly creating for himself an interest of the warmest nature.

Hyppolita alone saw him with indifference; he was by no means the man suited to her views, and thus she cared not whether he was absent or present.

About half a year after their acquaintance had commenced with Sylvio, Rossano having selected for his daughter a husband suited to their mutual ideas, she became a wife, and of course retired from the bosom of her family. Her loss could not be much regretted by any one whom she left behind her at the villa, as her conduct towards them all had ever been haughty and repellent; and she had never returned to them, either in her words or actions, any of the interest which they had manifested for her present or future happiness.

His favourite daughter being no longer a part of his family, the Signor Rossano now very seldom visited the villa where his wife continued to reside; his hours of cessation from his mercantile concerns were spent in visiting Hyppolita and her husband. Thus the days of those at the villa passed on uninterruptedly in quiet joys; the Signora Felicia, and Averilla, of whom she became as fond as if she had been her own child, directing all their cares to Felix, and Sylvio di Rosalva continuing to be their constant guest.

Although Sylvio was by no means possessed of wealth adequate to that enjoyed by the Signor Rossano, he was still in a situation of life, which the majority deem enviable; he was the possessor of an extensive estate and handsome mansion, of which the rents were large, and his family was of no immaterial consequence in the republic. After an acquaintance had for some time subsisted between him and the family del Alvaretti, he requested the Signora Felicia to fix a day for suffering him to return some of the numerous civilities ha had received at her hands, by condescending to say when she and her family would visit him.

The Signora taking him apart, replied—"I will not appear so ungrateful for the pleasure we have enjoyed in our acquaintance with you, or for your very kind invitation, as to say we will not accept it; but, my dear Signor, you must not again advance a request of this nature; you see how very little we visit. I do it on account of my son; every new place he goes to must excite in his breast fresh desires of being able to contemplate the scenes he passes through; therefore, on this account, I confine him as much as possible to the house and gardens to which he is accustomed, that these desires may not arise in his mind."

Sylvio perfectly comprehended the argument of the Signora Felicia, and entirely coincided with her in the propriety and tenderness of her conduct to her son. "I knew," said she, "you would see my apology in its proper light, and accept it in the friendly manner you have done. However, this once we shall certainly visit you, to shew you that we have no motive for declining your invitations, but the one I have explained to you; after that, if our society still continues pleasurable to you, you must redouble your visits, to make up for our deficiency."

The visit was accordingly paid, and their reception at the villa di Rosalva exceeded every idea they had formed of it from the elegant manners of Sylvio himself. The mansion was extremely handsome, and superbly furnished; the splendor which it boasted was not injudiciously loaded upon its walls and furniture, but sprinkled with taste over every part. The repast was of the most delicious and tempting kind; and the conduct of their host was such as gave him the air of something more than mortal.

Whatever could be devised to give pleasure to the senses of Felix was prepared for that purpose; the most delicious fruits, wines, and viands were presented to his taste; the rapturous melody of the softest instruments greeted his ear, the perfume of nature's collected flower-garden delighted his scent, and a downy bed of velvet turf was spread for his repose, whilst he partook of the other pleasures dedicated to him by his entertainer. In short, every pain had been taken to make him forget the existence of a fifth sense, in the gratification which was administered to those of which he possessed the enjoyment.

On their return home, their conversation was of course of their entertainer, who had taken a deeper root than ever in the affections of them all. Felix spoke of him in raptures. The Signora Felicia, with a tear of gratitude starting in her eye, praised him for his conduct to her son. Averilla alone was silent; her thoughts were so busily and so intently employed upon him, that she could not find leisure to give them utterance.

The Signora began to rally her niece upon her gravity. "I begin to think," said she, "that Sylvio has stolen further into your heart than that of any one of us. Begun, did I say, that was not exactly correct, I have thought so for some time past."

Averilla blushed deeply, but did not reply.

"Come, come, confess, my dear cousin," said Felix, "is it not so?— I am sure there is nothing to be ashamed of; his person I cannot know any thing about, but I am confident he has a heart of which any girl might be proud of having made a conquest."

Still Averilla continued silent.

"I hope I have not offended you, my dear cousin," continued Felix, laying his hand on her's, "indeed, I hope not; but I must guess I have, because I never before found you reserved on any subject to my mother or myself."

"I am not reserved, dear Felix," returned Averilla; "I only appear reserved, because I have nothing to communicate."

"You mean he has not made you a positive offer of his hand, I suppose?" returned Felix.

"Indeed he has not mentioned love to me at all," said Averilla.

"Perhaps he has called it friendship," said her aunt with a smile.

"Yes, of that he has often spoke to me," replied Averilla. "I feel a wish to tell you all, but I feel also a timidity, an unwillingness. Ah, my dear mother, my dear brother, for such you are to me, do not laugh at your child, your sister, who cannot conceal her thoughts from your affectionate participation."

"My dear girl," replied the Signora, "your confidence in me shall never be misplaced; I rejoice that you feel so tenderly for me as you express yourself to do; repose all you would say in my bosom with security."

"And in mine, my dear sister, since you allow me to give you that title," said Felix; "if I am not so capable of giving you advice as my mother is, believe me that I do not feel less interested in your happiness."

"Speak, my love, speak," said the Signora.

"He has never talked of love to me, as I have already told you," said Averilla.

"You have given me the authority of becoming your questioner," said Signora Felicia. "Do you feel that passion for him?"

Averilla's lips moved, but no sound passed them; she fixed her eyes on her aunt; every feature betrayed the confession through a veil of blushes.

"Be not ashamed, my dear child," said the Signora, "to confess the honourable affections of your heart; it is not in experiencing them, but in the improper indulgence of them, that we are faulty. There is nothing to blush at in feeling a sentiment of affection for Sylvio di Rosalva."

"Perhaps there would not," returned Averilla, "if he had first confessed a passion for me; but he has never done that, he has only talked of friendship."

"Your excessive delicacy, my love," replied the Signora, "may have given so little encouragement to his first advances towards your heart, that he feared to offend you by a warmer declaration of his feelings than that he has already made to you."

"Perhaps I did not understand what he said to me as I ought to have done, or as it was meant," said Averilla.

"What was it he did say?" asked the aunt.

"The first time I ever believed myself not indifferent to him, he said,—'Oh, my dear Averilla, how blest am I in your acquaintance!' He pressed my hand as he spoke, and added, after a short pause,— 'How happy shall I be to become more intimate with you!' Another time, about three weeks ago, when we were alone in the garden, he said—'The greatest bliss I enjoy on earth is the possession of a friend like yourself. Oh Averilla! that our friendship were connected with the strength I desire it should!—Oh that I durst pour out to you my whole soul!' And as he concluded these words, I felt his lips touch my cheek.

I started from him, he started too, and implored my pardon in terms which silenced the rebuke I was about to offer him."

"Dear innocent girl," exclaimed the Signora, "you are happy without being conscious that you are so. The words in which Sylvio has addressed you, are the usual preludes to a declaration of the heart. Your modest reserve has doubtless rendered him fearful of a too hasty confession, lest his ardour to obtain the object of his adoration should lose him the attainment of his wishes. Be easy, be happy, my Averilla; depend upon this, that no man of honour, which we cannot from any cause suspect Sylvio not to be, would have attempted to kiss the cheek of a woman, whose hand it was not his intention to ask in marriage."

The innocent Averilla knew not what to believe from the conduct of Sylvio. The Signora continued to assure her that it could only have the one meaning to which she had attributed it; and Felix breathed a fervent wish to Heaven for the happiness of his friend, and his cousin.

CHAPTER III

On the fourth day after their visit to the villa di Rosalva, was the birthday of Averilla; it was the twentieth anniversary of her entrance into life, and on days of this kind it was the custom of the Signora del Alvaretti to give a treat to the peasantry on the estate, and to indulge them in the evening with a dance to the sound of the merry pipe and tabor, at which time it was her pleasure to sit on the lawn where they danced, and observe their innocent mirth. Her husband would have deemed an indulgence of this kind, both an unnecessary expence to his purse, and a degradation to his wife; but she did not think that unnecessary, by which the rich afford a little recreation from their labours to the dependent, nor consider it a degradation to be a witness to happiness of her own making; and Rossano visited the villa so seldom, that his presence proved no interruption to her benevolent plans.

Sylvio di Rosalva was the only person of degree admitted to be a witness to the mirth of the peasantry on this happy day; and in the afternoon Averilla raised their gratification to the highest pitch by joining in their first dance herself, which they conceived to be a great honour conferred on them; and in this dance Sylvio was her partner.

When the dusk of evening came on, the festivities of the day were, on these occasions, usually concluded with the distribution of small presents to the peasant girls. While Averilla was thus employed, she saw her aunt and Sylvio enter the house with Felix. She continued distributing her birthday gifts, and when she had emptied her basket, she was herself returning towards the house through the garden. In a walk which the overhanging branches rendered particularly dark, she was met by Sylvio.

"Averilla," said he, "I was coming to look for you; do come and join our party; the music to-day has made me melancholy."

"It was very sprightly too, I thought," replied Averilla.

"Yes," returned he, "and I am sure I was happy in my partner; but——" he paused, and at the same time, he lingered in his pace.

Averilla felt herself blush; she knew it to be too dark for him to perceive the emotion of her features. She wished, if ever the confession was to be made, to be released from the suspense of mind she was now in; and still she felt unwilling to stop.

"Oh Averilla!" he again began, "is it not a cruel state of existence, to have a continual burthen upon the mind, a weight upon the heart, which might find relief in sympathy, and yet dreads to confess itself? do you not pity the misery such a wretch must endure?"

They had proceeded some steps while Sylvio said this, and as he ceased speaking, they turned into a less shady walk, where the twilight still cast its influence on the surrounding objects. "Yes, Averilla," he continued. "I will dare to hope you will not spurn me for my avowal"—he fell upon his knee as he spoke—"and in this hope I confess to you——"

At this moment he raised his eyes from the ground, on which they had before been bent, uttered a piercing shriek, sprang from his kneeling posture, and fled hastily away from Averilla.

Greatly astonished at his conduct, Averilla looked fearfully around her on all sides, but could perceive no cause for his flight; he had run towards the house, and she followed him.

On the steps leading to the entrance into the house, she found him leaning for support against one of the pillars of the colonnade.

"Sylvio," she said, "what affected you this instant in the garden?"

"Affected!" he replied, "can you ask that?—Thank heaven we are safe!"

"Safe!" echoed Averilla.

"Why, did you see nothing, then?" asked he.

"Nothing but the usual objects in the garden," said she; "what can you mean, Sylvio?"

"Did you not see a man, who pointed at me a drawn sword from behind a tree?" he asked in low and faltering accents.

"A man!" repeated Averilla, "a man! sure, Sylvio, you dream."

"Oh no, no, no; I am convinced," he replied.

"Indeed you are mistaken," answered Averilla. "You saw only the statue of the Gladiator, which stands close by the spot where we were conversing together."

Sylvio paused, apparently buried in reflection. During the moment of silence, the Signora and Felix, who had been sitting in an apartment of which the window was open, and who had overheard part of the conversation between Sylvio and Averilla, came out to them and joined their enquiries to her's.

"The Gladiator!" said Sylvio; "are you sure it was only the statue of the Gladiator?"

"I am certain of it," replied Averilla.

"Return with me to the spot, and convince yourself," said the Signora to Sylvio.

"No, not now; I cannot return now," answered he. "I feel myself suddenly unwell, and will, with your permission, immediately return home."

He desired his carriage might be got ready without delay; and, with an ill formed apology for his strange conduct, he left the villa del Alvaretti.

The conversation, after his departure, related, of course, to the occurrences of the evening. Averilla repeated all that had passed in the garden, previously to the moment of his flying from her in alarm; and Signora Felicia said, she made no doubt he had chosen that minute for the declaration of his passion. In this idea Averilla readily concurred; but they could not by any means guess on what account he could have been affected as he had by the statue of the Gladiator, even if it *had* been an armed man, as it had appeared, from his own words, he had supposed it, till his error had been explained to him by Averilla; it was unnatural, cowardly in him, unlike his character in every other respect, to have fled from the danger, if there had been any, and have left Averilla alone and exposed to it.

Their conversation was upon the same subject till they retired to rest, and they then parted, without having been able to draw any reasonable conclusion from his conduct.

On the following morning, as Signora Felicia was on the point of sending a servant to enquire after Sylvio, he entered the breakfast apartment. "I am come," he said, "to apologize for my strange conduct, for such it must have appeared to you, last night; and next, to visit the statue of the Gladiator, and convince myself of the error which seized upon my mind."

They all expressed pleasure at beholding him, but no one strove to conceal from him the strange impression which his hasty departure on the preceding evening, and its cause, had left on their minds.

"I cannot be surprised at hearing you make this declaration," he replied; "I must have appeared in your eyes either a madman, or a coward: But indeed I am neither. You are friends, and with you, I trust, my apology will be admitted, when I am convinced the world would laugh at me for assigning it, and judge it a fallacy, and me a fool: I can, however, only assure you that it is the truth. My nerves are weak, excessively so; I am even superstitious. I can only wish that it was not so, and endeavour to combat against the failing, though I cannot conquer it. I was very dreadfully alarmed when a child; I have ever since been timid; and the figure I last night saw brought so strongly to my mind——"

"What you saw in your youth?" asked the Signora.

Sylvio appeared on the point of answering "yes" to her question, but hastily checked himself, and said, "do not on this account discard me from your friendship; bear with my weakness, and I will endeavour to deserve your lenity towards me."

A tear started in his eye as he spoke. His auditors were moved to compassion, and promised to reflect no more on the past.

The breakfast being ended, the Signora Felicia, at his repeated request, walked out with Sylvio to visit the Gladiator.

"I see my folly, I see my weakness," he said, as he observed the statue. "I must nevertheless think, that no one who felt as I did, could have forborne to have acted in the same manner."

The Signora endeavoured to give a turn to the conversation, but Sylvio appeared to wish to continue it. "The moment," he said, "at which this strange error assailed my senses, was one of the most interesting of my life—one on which the future happiness or misery of my days most materially depended."

"You were at the time in conversation with Averilla," said the Signora.

"Yes, with Averilla," he replied. "Dear, excellent, virtuous girl! I was on the point of making to her a confession which has long laboured in my heart. Frequently has it crept upon my tongue, and tempted me to breathe it into your ear; but various emotions have checked my utterance. We are now alone; will you permit me a few moments conversation with you?"

"Undoubtedly," replied Signora Felicia.

"May I trust that you do not esteem me the less for the occurrence of last night?" asked Sylvio.

"It was certainly one which excited my surprise; I did not expect to see you display such timidity; but you have explained it to be rather a distemper than an error of your mind, and as such it merits to be consigned to oblivion."

"Kind as you are to me, I dread to speak my sentiments freely," replied Sylvio. "I dread that you will accuse me of presumption, and drive me from you." He paused, then added—"may I, Signora, proceed?"

"You must be best acquainted yourself how fit the sentiments you wish to declare to me, are for me to listen to; you have too much sense to be able to offend unknowingly," returned Felicia.

"Were I to be sufficiently presumptuous to confess that I aspire to an alliance with your family," returned Sylvio; "were I to declare——"

The sound of footsteps behind them caused Sylvio to break off, and a servant approached, on whose arm leaned Felix. "My father," said the latter, addressing the Signora, "is this moment arrived, and asks to see you, and my cousin Averilla, immediately, on business of importance."

"I am sorry I must leave you thus abruptly," said the Signora Felicia, addressing Sylvio; "but my son will entertain you; he is the same as myself in every respect."

"Oh no, no, not now; I am obliged to depart," exclaimed Sylvio hastily. "I came out only for an hour; my presence is required at home;

I cannot prolong my visit;" and having said this, he wished Felix and the Signora a good morning, and ran towards the stables where he had left his carriage.

CHAPTER IV

THE Signora proceeded to the house, and found Averilla already with her husband. On the countenance of the latter was depicted triumph and pleasure; on that of the former, sorrow and fear. After the first salutation to his wife at meeting, Rossano said, "I come to announce to Averilla, that I have found her a husband, worthy of her greatest pride and exultation. The Count Lorenzo della Piacca has made proposals to me for her hand."

No reply was returned to this information, and Rossano continued—"The Conte is one of the richest men in all Italy; he has vast paternal estates in the neighbourhood of Turin, extensive possessions in our republic of Genoa, and is moreover connected with a mercantile house, which makes the greatest returns in the state. You cannot but see how advantageous an alliance presents itself to your acceptance, Averilla; and I cannot doubt but you will, without hesitation, prove acquiescent to the wishes of the Conte, as soon as you are introduced to him, which will be in the course of a few hours, as I expect him to dine with us here to-day."

"I am fully aware," replied Averilla, "that you are empowered by my father to form for me an alliance which meets your approbation; but I cannot suppose, that if my father had lived, he would have forced me into a marriage with any man who did not equally meet my choice, as well as his own, although he might have withheld me from contracting an union with one whose circumstances did not please him. I hope therefore, that as you represent, in this instance, my father, you will not deny me an indulgence which, I must believe, he would have granted me."

"My brother Eugenio," returned Rossano, "was a man of too great sense to have suffered a child of his to reject an alliance with the Conte della Piacca; his hand is an offer of such honour, as admits no refusal."

"Of that I cannot be a judge till I have seen him," answered

Averilla.

"When you do see him, it is very likely that you will not form a proper judgement of his worth," returned Rossano; "and that it will at last rest with me to force my better judgement upon you. To please your taste, I imagine a man must be a civit cat in perfume, a monkey in capers and agility, a maccaroni in dress, and an Adonis in person. The Conte is none of these, I can assure you; I will sum up his qualifications in one sentence; he is a man of wealth, wise enough to know the value of what he possesses."

The Signor Rossano continued firm in his resolution that his niece should become the wife of the man he had selected for her husband; and Averilla retired, in tears, to her own apartment.

When Signora Felicia was left alone with her husband, she endeavoured to soften his determination with respect to their niece.—"Permit her, at least," said she, "to see him, to become acquainted with his manners and his mind, before she gives an answer to your demand."

"She already knows his inclination," replied Rossano; "and if she is not sensible how to treat the honour conferred on her, it becomes me to show her what is her duty, and exact the performance of it. As to an answer, I require none; I command her, in the person of her father, and she has only implicitly to obey."

The Signora sighed; in the same manner had she been consigned to the arms of Rossano. "It can be no honour to a woman," she returned, "to have proposals of marriage made to her by a man who has never seen her; on the contrary, such an offer must cause her to regard him, at his first introduction to her, in a contemptible light, as it plainly bespeaks that an image, with her possessions, would be equally welcome to his heart. What woman, who is possessed of any soul, could marry a man on such terms?"

"She is to be guided by the senses of those who are better able than herself to discern what is for her good," replied Rossano.

"To make her rich, at the expence of her peace of mind, can never be for her good," answered Signora Felicia. "To compel her into the arms of one man, while her heart is devoted to another, ought never to be the act of one who is placed in the situation of a parent towards her."

"And what handsome peasant has caught her foolish heart?" exclaimed Rossano, contemptuously.

"No peasant," returned Signora Felicia; "her esteem is fixed on one who has, I doubt not, as many claims to be considered a gentleman, as the Conte you vaunt of—a man of her own age, possessed of handsome means, the most engaging of manners, a heart of such universal benevolence, as compels those who are acquainted with him to admire and esteem him."

"Has this Phœnix no name?" asked Rossano, the satyrical sneer, with which he had before spoken, still hanging on his lips.

"You are here so seldom," replied the Signora, "that you do not know your neighbours; his name is Sylvio di Rosalva, the possessor of the adjoining estate to your own."

"Sylvio di Rosalva!" echoed Rossano; "and have you the effrontery to place him in comparison with the Conte Lorenzo, whose annual income could buy the entire inheritance of Rosalva. Let me not hear of him again;" and with these words he indignantly left the apartment.

Felicia sought her niece, and found her reposing her sorrows in the bosom of Felix. To them the Conte Lorenzo was an utter stranger; they did not even recollect to have heard his name before that day. However, there was no doubt that the wary and avaricious Rossano had made a cautious investigation into his *merits*, before he had acquiesced in his proposal for the hand of his niece; and, on this conviction, they all feared that the die of Averilla's fate was irrevocably cast.

"Oh Sylvio!" exclaimed Averilla, "why didst thou not confess thyself to me? why hast thou not, ere this, avowed me the possessor of thy heart? I could then have advanced thee as my apology for refusing the Conte, whose addresses I have now no means of avoiding." She paused an instant, then added, "But, perhaps, I am still deceiving myself, and that Sylvio never thought me otherwise than as an esteemed friend; if it be so, if he never did regard me in a tenderer light than that of friend; if I am never to be Sylvio's, and must still become a wife to swell my uncle's pride, the Conte Lorenzo is as welcome to my person as any other man would be." Another pause ensued, which Averilla again broke: "Tell me, I entreat you tell me, my dear aunt," said she, "whether you still believe Sylvio ever entertained more than friendship for me."

"Since you compel me to a confession of my sentiments," replied the Signora, "I cannot now hesitate to tell you, that every doubt of his love for you is removed from my breast. At the moment your cousin

Felix came to me in the garden, this morning, to announce to me the arrival of your uncle, he had requested my attention to a matter of importance, which, he said, he wished to communicate to me; and had already asked me if I should think him presumptuous, if he confessed a wish to be allied to my family."

"Oh heavens!" exclaimed Averilla, "and am I, at this moment, doomed to the arms of a stranger? a man whose indelicate mode of proposing for my hand, betrays him to value me only as an intermediate step towards the increase of his wealth and interest. Oh, my dear mother, how wretched is your Averilla!"

The Signora knew not in what shape to offer her comfort, conscious, as she was, that no arguments would move her husband from his purpose. She besought her to dry her tears, and to meet the Conte with pretended firmness and composure at dinner, however remote those feelings might be from her heart. Averilla promised to exert herself to the utmost, according to the advice of her aunt; and Felix sought his father in order to try the effect of argument, in favour of his cousin's happiness, upon his mind. But words produced no alteration in the purpose of Rossano; he had formed his own opinion, and he considered it the only one in the world worth attending to.

About an hour before the time of dinner, an elegant carriage, attended by numerous servants, rolling rapidly towards the villa del Alvaretti, announced the approach of the Conte della Piacca.

From the description which Rossano had given of the man whom he supposed his niece would approve as a husband, and the contemptuous manner in which he had spoken it, she judged that she should find the Conte Lorenzo exactly the reverse of that description: consequently old, unengaging in his manners and unqualified in his mind; a man who would regard her merely as an article in trade.

But the Conte Lorenzo's first appearance proved to Averilla that she had formed a mistaken opinion of him. He entered the room with the address and manner of a gentleman, fully acquainted with those graces which are the happiest passport through polished society. His age appeared at most thirty-five; his person was good, although not strikingly handsome; and his conversation of the most agreeable kind. In short, he was a man who, from what Averilla could judge of him upon the acquaintance of a day, she believed it would not have caused her a very great struggle with her heart to have received him as her destined husband, had she never beheld Sylvio; but having known Sylvio, and known him to esteem him as she did, she felt it impossible that the Conte Lorenzo should ever supplant him in her heart. Nay, her passion grew even stronger for Sylvio, on finding the Conte more agreeable than she had expected he would have proved. If the rival of Sylvio was thus tolerable, when considered alone, how infinitely perfectioned must Sylvio be, thus to surpass him in comparison!

Throughout the day the Conte displayed a desire to render himself pleasing, particularly to Averilla; but neither his words nor actions seemed to indicate that he considered himself as her received admirer: This the Signora Felicia perceived, and hoped that it might still be possible that her husband had not made an absolute promise to the Conte of Averilla's hand; or even if he had, that the Conte might be of too generous a disposition to enforce the performance of it, in opposition to the happiness of her niece.

The Conte Lorenzo, and Rossano, remained at the villa del Alvaretti that night. On the following morning when Averilla arose, she saw the Conte and her uncle in conversation together in the garden; and when she went down into the breakfast room, she found the Conte alone in it. She was again retiring, but he sprang from his seat, and hastening towards her, requested her to honour him with a few moments conversation.

She could not do otherwise than comply; the Conte took her hand, and leading her back into the room, he thus addressed her—"It has for some time past, Signora, been my ambition to ally myself to the family del Alvaretti; in consequence of this wish, I have requested of the Signor Rossano to introduce me to you, his niece, the graces of whose person, and the charms of whose mind, have been poured into my ears by every tongue in Genoa. On being admitted to your presence, I find that rumour, which usually exaggerates, has, in this instance, fallen so far short of the truth, that astonishment almost awes me into silence, and makes me timid of confessing the passion that warms my breast. Believe me, that I speak the sentiments of my heart, when I declare myself to be dazzled by your charms from all recollection of my first desire of an alliance with your uncle's family; and that were I at this moment to know you only as a simple peasant, I would throw myself and my fortune at your feet, as I do now; though Rossano's niece, the wealthiest heiress in Italy, were offered to my arms in any shape but yours."

"The elegance of your compliment, Signor," answered Averilla, "demands a reply far beyond the talents of eloquence which I possess; I must therefore trust that you will accept the candour with which I shall answer you, as an equivalent for it. I cannot but confess myself honoured by the sentiments which you have this moment expressed for me, perhaps more so, from a man who had proposed himself as my husband, before he had gained a knowledge of me, as you have done, than from any other. But I have not the power of returning the passion you profess; my affections being already irrevocably bestowed."

This declaration, on the part of Averilla, appeared a most unexpected blow to the promised happiness of the Conte; his countenance fell, and he maintained a silence of a few moments; at the expiration of which, he said—"But, Signora, your uncle Rossano assured me that your heart was without a prepossession in favour of any other object, and promised me that your hand should be mine, before he invited me hither."

"I throw myself upon the generosity of your heart," replied Averilla, "in confessing to you that such is not the case, and trust, that as you are a gentleman, you will not join with my uncle in tearing me from that heart for which I can alone ever feel stronger esteem than that of friendship. Plead my cause for me to my uncle, and you will ever be considered by me as my worthiest, my noblest friend."

"Surely," replied the Conte, with some degree of hesitation, "I may be allowed to doubt a prepossession having place in your heart; surely if it were so, the Signor Rossano must have known of it."

"Of this I do not perceive the necessity," rejoined Averilla, "but I can nevertheless assure you that it is a truth."

"Have I not rather had the misfortune to inspire you with some disgust?—to commit some action, which has resolved you not to hear my suit?" asked Della Piacca.

"No," replied Averilla, "I give you my word, that I have yet seen nothing in you to disapprove; and that nothing but your persisting to continue your suit to me, can make me alter the favourable opinion I have of you."

The family now assembled at breakfast, and their conversation was thus broken off for the present.

CHAPTER V

ROSSANO had first become acquainted with the Conte Lorenzo della Piacca at the house of his son-in-law, the Marchese di Bivelli, where he was a constant visitor. The Conte was lately arrived at Genoa from Turin, to which city he had come on account of a connection he had formed with one of the first mercantile houses in it. Hyppolita's husband Di Bivelli, had himself originally been of Turin, and well acquainted with the Conte Lorenzo in his youth; thus their intimacy had immediately been renewed.

Here Della Piacca had first heard Averilla mentioned; the Marchese di Bivelli had spoken of her, as she really was, possessed of a most amiable mind, a very considerable fortune, and great personal charms. Like most of his countrymen, the Conte Lorenzo added to the pride of rank, that kind of economy which desires an increase of its wealth. He had also enough of the finished Italian about him, to be an admirer of the perfections of mind and charms of person of the softer sex; and were we to add to this, that he had, for some time past, resolved on matrimony, and was merely awaiting the moment when a good alliance should present itself to his acceptance, for putting his resolution into effect, it can create no surprise that, in a country where marriages are usually contracted by parents or guardians, the Conte Lorenzo and Signor Rossano should have proceeded as far as we have already seen they had done, in their matrimonial negociation, without the knowledge or consent of Averilla.

It is true that the Conte Lorenzo had made enquiry of Rossano whether the heart of his niece was free from any prepossession; and Rossano had boldly replied, that it was; and for two reasons he had pronounced it so; the first, because he really believed it to be the case; and the second, because he had decided within his own mind, that whether it were so or whether it were not, she should still become the wife of the Conte Lorenzo; and therefore considered it most advisable to tell him her heart was free, at all events.

When breakfast was ended, the Conte sought Rossano, and informed him of what had that morning passed between himself and Averilla. Rossano smiled, and said he supposed some transient folly had taken possession of her mind, which would die away the moment she became his wife.

The Conte replied in a sentence which bespoke him doubtful whether it became him in honour to persevere in his suit, as he had found the heart of Averilla placed on some other object; and even, whether he should not be committing an imprudence, in the point of his own happiness, as well as her's, not to desist from it.

Rossano replied, that as Della Piacca had made proposals to him for an alliance with his family, and as he, who was the regulator of its actions, had agreed, and still did agree to give him her he sought to wife, he would consider the contract dishonourably broken on his side, if he receded from his agreement, on account of the foolish fancies of a girl, whom he considered it his duty to compel to the acceptance of such happiness, as he was pleased to compliment the Conte, by saying, she must enjoy in an union with him.

The Conte Lorenzo, for various reasons, did not at all wish to give up the idea of a connection with the family del Alvaretti; all he feared was, that if he persisted in obtaining it, by rending asunder the first affections of Averilla, the tongue of slander might attack him for his conduct, and therefore he had resolved to be cautious how he proceeded; but now Rossano had taken the whole weight of the burthen upon his own shoulders, by intimating that he should consider it dishonourable in the Conte to retract from his agreement, he felt satisfied that he was the destined husband of so beautiful a woman, on any terms whatsoever.

After his conversation with the Conte, Rossano called apart his wife, and, in terms of no very delicate nature, he upbraided her for having suffered Averilla to form any acquaintance without his approbation, and insisted on her informing him of the exact state of affairs between his niece and the Signor Sylvio di Rosalva. His reason for this enquiry, he said, was, that if he found things had proceeded to such an extremity as had given the Signor reason to believe himself her destined husband, he should immediately take measures for informing him of the fallacy of his expectations.

Not less from the awe in which the Signora Felicia stood of her husband, than her apprehensions that a concealment of the truth might prove of much worse consequence than a frank avowal of all she knew, she informed him of such particulars as she was acquainted with.

As soon as the Signora had done speaking, Rossano ordered Averilla to be summoned to him. When she appeared, he said—"You have, I am sorry to say, acted in a manner which I think extremely reprehensible; this Rosalva has made you no positive offer of his hand, and still you have the indelicacy to declare yourself attached to him. It is, methinks, well for you that a husband of merit has presented himself to save you from ruin; for the steps you were pursuing could, in my opinion, have led to nothing else. I therefore, now, inform you, that it is my final determination that you give your hand to the Conte Lorenzo. As for Rosalva, your aunt shall address him by letter, saying, that the interruption which was given to the conversation with him yesterday morning, having then prevented her from informing him how impossible it will be for him to contract an union with this family, she thinks it becoming in her thus to give him the intelligence."

In vain did Averilla remonstrate with her uncle upon his cruelty, in not only withholding from her the affections of the only man she could love, but compelling her into the arms of another, of whose claims upon her love she was allowed no investigation, before he was admitted to her acquaintance as a destined husband.

Rossano was deaf to every argument she advanced; and it was with difficulty that the Signora Felicia prevailed on him to suffer their son Felix to be the bearer of such intelligence, as he had wished her to have communicated on paper to the Signor Sylvio di Rosalva.

His consent to this change being procured, the carriage was ordered, and in a quarter of an hour's time Felix was arrived at the villa di Rosalva.

He was received in the garden by an old lady named Bianca, who was Sylvio's grand-aunt, but whose circumstances, it was generally understood, were indifferent, and compelled her to live in a dependant state upon her nephew, whose kindness to her was extremely great. She never visited with him, nor was present when he received company; she appeared averse to emerging from that humble sphere to which misfortune had reduced her, and returned to her nephew the benevolence he exercised towards her, in regulating the economy of his establishment, and superintending, with a most creditable conduct, his concerns, for which task she was fitted both by her natural sense, and the good education she had received in her youth.

The family del Alvaretti were considered such particular friends by Sylvio, that the good lady Bianca had been introduced to them, on the visit they had paid to the villa di Rosalva; she accordingly received Felix with the utmost tenderness and complacency, and placing him in a garden chair, she went herself in quest of her nephew.

In a few minutes Sylvio advanced—"This is very kind of you, Felix," said he; "I am very happy you have been tempted to come and visit me."

"I know not, my dear Sylvio," replied Felix, "whether you will think my visit a kindness or not, when you know the cause that brings me hither."

"Indeed!" rejoined Sylvio, "what can it be?"

"Lend me your arm," said Felix, rising as he spoke: "Let us walk a little way from this spot, lest your aunt should return; I have something of importance to communicate to you."

Sylvio drew the arm of Felix through his, and they walked on a few moments in silence; at last Felix said, "Are we now quite alone? can no one overhear us? you know I cannot perceive whether we are observed, and what I have to say to you, I wish, for your sake, to be said in secrecy."

"There is nobody at all near us," answered Sylvio.

"I come commissioned to you from my father and mother," said Felix. "When you called yesterday morning at the villa del Alvaretti, you mentioned something to my mother of an alliance with our family. You know, I am sure, that my mother, Averilla, and myself, all esteem you, love you exceedingly; but not withstanding that, you must lay aside all idea of being more nearly related to us than in esteem and friendship."

Sylvio did not reply, and Felix felt the arm on which he rested his, tremble violently.

"My mother," continued Felix, "could not avoid understanding the inclination of your heart, in the alliance for which you expressed so fervent a wish; she begs me to say, that she pities you; for your conduct has been so engaging towards us all, that she loves you. Averilla too, yes, Sylvio, I will confess it to you, Averilla also loves you—tenderly loves you."

"Loves me!" exclaimed Sylvio, "Does Averilla love me?—Oh God! Oh God!"

"Call resolution to your aid, and abate these ecstacies, I entreat you," returned Felix. "I have made the confession of her love to you, that you might not condemn her for having acted a fickle part towards you, and believe it her act to give her hand to another, when it is that of her uncle, on whom her will is entirely dependant."

Sylvio sobbed, as if in the act of weeping, and drawing his arm away from that of Felix, he heard him blow his nose violently, as if endeavouring to dispel the strength of his emotion.

"Oh Felix!" he, after a pause, exclaimed, "I am the greatest wretch this earth contains! If you knew what passes at this moment in my heart, you would pity, and——Oh, Heavens, what have I said!—I entreat you to remain here an instant—do not stir—I will return to you directly;" and so saying, he placed Felix on a bank of velvet turf, and ran hastily from him.

Felix called upon him loudly to stay, and hear him. Never before had he so anxiously desired his sight as at that moment; he dreaded lest the disappointment of Sylvio's passion was driving him to some act of desperation. To the grounds he was almost an utter stranger; it was therefore impossible for him to attempt to follow him; and the repeated calls which he made brought no one near him, to whom he might impart his apprehensions for his safety.

After about ten minutes passed in the greatest possible anxiety of mind, he heard footsteps approaching him, and these were followed by the sound of Bianca's voice. "Signor Felix," said she, "I am sorry to inform you that my nephew is taken suddenly so ill, that I must excuse him from having the pleasure of seeing you again this morning; he entreats that you will not attribute his conduct either to disrespect or want of inclination to converse longer with you, but to the real cause of sudden indisposition; and he moreover begs you to convey that note to the Signora Felicia, your honoured mother."

Unwilling as the humane Felix was to depart without the opportunity of administering further consolation to his friend Sylvio, upon his recent disappointment, still as Sylvio continued resolute not to see him again that morning, he was obliged to return to his carriage, and suffer it to convey him away from the villa di Rosalva.

CHAPTER VI

ON his return home, his father met him in the hall, and led him into his mother's dressing-room, where she was sitting with Averilla. According to the injunctions of his father, Felix repeated, with faithfulness, all that had passed between himself and Sylvio; it was accepted by all as a confirmation of what had been his wish with regard to Averilla, and her grief gathered strength from the recital.

The Signora Felicia now opened the note addressed to herself; her eyes wandered over it a few moments in silence, whilst an emotion of the greatest astonishment was visible in her features. At length she spoke—

"This is very strange," said she, "wonderfully strange!"

"Read, read!" exclaimed Rossano impatiently.

The Signora obeyed, and read these words:—

"DEAREST AND MOST REVERED LADY,

"Favour me by presenting to your amiable niece Averilla, those wishes for her happiness which proceed from my heart; deliver them to her in the most expressive terms of friendship; tell her that I ever was her friend, and hope ever to be considered as such by her—but that I was never *more* than her friend. In my conversation with you in the garden yesterday, you misunderstood my meaning. Tell Averilla this—tell her that Sylvio *never was her lover*. Farewell, most honoured lady; that every blessing may attend yourself and your family, is the fervent prayer of the unhappy

"SYLVIO DI ROSALVA."

The astonishment with which Averilla heard these lines read, produced so great a shock on her frame, that she sunk into the arms of the Signora her aunt. Surprise tied the utterance of Felix; and Rossano found, in this declaration, the greatest cause for triumph, in the exposure, as he judged it, of the indelicate hopes and ideas which his wife and niece had entertained with regard to Sylvio's having a passion for Averilla. His remarks upon the discovery were short; he merely said, darting as he spoke a significant glance at his wife, "You now perceive whose intentions, with regard to Averilla, do most justice to the head and heart that conceived them; and I trust that Averilla herself now sees the folly of the passion she so lately nourished. I shall therefore make it my immediate business to inform the Conte della Piacca, that there no longer exists any obstacle to his becoming her husband."

Having said this, Rossano left the apartment.

However averse Averilla felt to his conveying this intelligence to Della Piacca, still she had now no motive, except what her uncle might indeed deem an indelicate one, for withholding him from his resolution; and accordingly she was constrained to suffer him to leave the room without contradicting his intention.

When left alone with her aunt and Felix, a flood of tears came to the relief of her full heart, and as soon as she regained the power of utterance, she began to call upon her aunt to justify her in those ideas, which she had so long entertained, of the Signor Sylvio possessing a predilection for her; and to give her the candid opinion of her heart concerning his letter.

Signora Felicia replied, that she could undoubtedly justify the opinion which her niece had entertained of Sylvio's sentiments with regard to her; she had received from him every attention that could lead her to believe he had entertained for her an honourable passion. The question that he had advanced to herself in the garden, had, in her idea, confirmed it; and she could now only judge, that being put to the test of his passion by the discovery of his possessing a rival, if not in her affections, at least in her train, he had found his heart too uncertain of its passion, to make her an offer of immediately becoming her husband; and therefore had pretended that he had never considered himself as her lover. "As such is the fickleness of his heart, my love," continued the Signora, "I am extremely thankful he has thought fit to act as he has done, rather than to have deferred a display of his mutable temper till after you was become his wife."

In reply to this, Felix urged, that he must consider Sylvio to have felt too strongly on receiving the intelligence of Rossano's intention of uniting Averilla with a husband of his choice, to have been undetermined in his passion.

"Many men," replied the Signora Felicia, "feel very strongly, who have not the fortitude to act so; and many likewise love very passionately, without any intention of immediately becoming husbands. I am convinced of my Averilla having too much pride, too much good sense, to wish to force herself upon the heart of a truant; she will therefore, I am sure, very soon consign to oblivion the ill-requited passion which has heretofore inhabited her breast; and as she has already confessed the Conte della Piacca to be a man to whom an unprejudiced woman could raise no solid objection as a husband, I hope she will experience, in an alliance with him, all the happiness her virtues deserve to be rewarded with."

"You both know," returned Averilla, "that Sylvio had insinuated himself very deeply into my heart; but this proof of the error in which I had fallen with regard to his sentiments of me, or of the deceit he has practiced towards me, in suffering me to believe them of a different nature to what they were, appears an appeal to my pride, to conquer every latent, lingering feeling of affection for him, which may still be lurking in my breast. Give me your kind encouragement in this instance, as you have done on every other occasion, and I will endeavour not to suffer the image of one who has proved himself unworthy of my affection, to corrode a moment of my future peace."

Averilla's determination was praiseworthy and such as reflected honour on her sense to have formed; but she wanted resolution to put it perfectly into effect. It was true, that she now received the attentions of the Conte Lorenzo, in a manner that gave satisfaction to her uncle, delight to her destined husband, and a kind of soothing revenge to her own heart; but there were still moments, when she would seek the solitude of her chamber, and indulge in weeping; and at these moments there could be no doubt that the image of Sylvio was present to her thoughts.

The Conte Lorenzo della Piacca had indeed found Averilla's person to be beautiful beyond the idea he had formed of it, and the declaration he had made to her of the violent passion with which she had inspired his heart, was no more than the truth; his attentions to her, it may therefore be easily imagined, were now of the most rapturous kind, since a decided affirmative in his favour, from the lips of the object of his adoration, had chased away the cloud, which had obscured the prospect of his bliss, on his first introduction to her.

Averilla had, undoubtedly, not forgotten Sylvio di Rosalva, but while she remembered him, she remembered also how ungenerously he had treated her, in the most delicate instance, where the honour of man stands concerned in his intercourse with the weaker sex; the Conte Lorenzo gained additional interest in her heart every day.

About a fortnight had now elapsed, since the Conte della Piacca had been publicly declared the destined husband of Averilla del Alvaretti. The Conte had, during that time, passed his hours entirely at the Palazzo of his future uncle Rossano; but some affair of business calling him for a short time to Genoa, he was constrained, for one day, to quit the object of his admiration. He accordingly left the Palazzo one morning, and was to return to it on the next day.

No sooner was he gone, than the spirits of Averilla began to sink; at the moments when his attentions were employing her thoughts, the fervency with which he paid them, caused her to regard him as deserving of every mark of gratitude she could bestow on him in return; and thus, by keeping her anxious not to appear deficient in her conduct towards him, kept her ideas from wandering to any other object; but when he was absent, they naturally returned to the point on which they had been accustomed to rest, and melancholy sensations always attended them to it.

At an early hour, Averilla retired to rest; for the reflections of her pillow produced a soothing calm in her mind, which was unequalled by any balm but the influence of religion. Educated in the strict tenets of the universal religion of her country, Averilla never failed to pay the devotions of the morning at the shrine of Saint Francis, her tutelar saint, in a chapel dedicated to him, in the village of which the Palazzo del Alvaretti formed a part.

The Signora Felicia and her son Felix, were equally regular in their morning devotions, but as they did not address the same saint, their worship was performed in another chapel.

When Averilla returned home on the morning of that day on which the Conte Lorenzo was absent from the Palazzo, on meeting the Signora Felicia at breakfast, the latter perceived a more than usual emotion expressed on the countenance of her niece, and immediately enquired the cause of it.

"Ask me no questions, I entreat you," replied Averilla, in a gayer tone of voice than she had been heard to speak in for some considerable time past; "I confess I am agitated, but I must not reveal the cause."

The Signora and her son could not forbear expressing sentiments of surprise; and Averilla only replied to them in the same words which she had before spoken in, of—"Pray do not question me; I am infinitely happy, but am withheld from disclosing the cause."

Felix smiled in silence. The Signora watched the countenance of Averilla, anxious, if possible, to gather from her features the information which her lips refused her; but she could only read in her face the appearance of perfect happiness and composure.

They had not been long seated at the breakfast table before a servant entered the room and announced the Signor Sylvio di Rosalva. Felix started—the Signora Felicia looked surprised—and Averilla pleased. With the greatest diffidence Sylvio entered the apartment. Averilla rose, and advancing to meet him, took him by the hand, and leading him towards the breakfast table, said—"Dear aunt, and cousin, receive Sylvio di Rosalva again as your friend:—We are reconciled."

"May I hope," said Sylvio, "that the entreaty of my fair pleader will prosper with you?"

"You both surprise me so much," returned the Signora, "that I scarcely know how to reply to you."

"I wish you to believe," rejoined Averilla, "that we are fully reconciled—that Sylvio is more my friend than ever; and that he greatly merits to be re-admitted to the friendship of you both."

"Then why make his merit an enigma?" asked the Signora Felicia.

"Let all the blame which arises from the concealment of the cause, rest with me," returned Averilla; "I am certain, at least I will say I trust, that you think too justly of me, to imagine that I would myself stoop to any meanness of conduct, or would require of you an improper act of lenity towards one, who had offered an offence to your family. But I am so thoroughly convinced of Sylvio's innocence of any intention to wound my feelings, or to act a double part towards any one of us, that I have forgiven him; and rest much of my happiness, on hearing you pronounce his pardon likewise."

Still no reply was made on the part of the Signora, or her son.

"If you love your sister Averilla," continued the niece of Rossano, addressing Felix, "believe that she never would tempt you into bestowing your friendship on any one whom she did not know to be worthy of the gift; such she *does* know Sylvio to be, and she therefore once more entreats you not to refuse her petition;" and with these words she put the hand of Sylvio into that of Felix.

The hands of both had been too much accustomed to meet in cordiality, to be able to refuse each other the pressure of friendship, especially when joined by those of Averilla, and they greeted the touch with the fervour they had been accustomed to do—"We are friends! we are friends, Sylvio!" said Felix. "Averilla's interference succeeds; she would not deceive us."

The Signora now extended her hand towards Sylvio, but accompanied her action by saying—"You do not treat us quite like friends, to withhold from us the cause which claims our assent to a re-union of friendship."

"My dear aunt," said Averilla, "the time probably will come, and shortly too, that you will know all; at present I am bound by a vow; do not therefore any more distress me with questions which I am not permitted to answer."

That the Signora Felicia could not immediately divest herself of some degree of distrust and suspicion at this unexpected re-introduction of the Signor Sylvio into her family, after the strange instance of his conduct just past, and by the very woman to whom that conduct had been particularly reprehensible, may be easily imagined; she however constrained herself to do all the justice she was able to the asseverations her niece had made of his innocence, and claim to a reconciliation. Some degree of embarrassment hung upon Sylvio, but he took his accustomed place in the apartment, directed his attentions once more to Felix, and Averilla appeared still happier than when she had considered her union with him secure.

The Signora judged it to be as great an act of duty in her to discover what was the nature of the mysterious bond by which her niece and Sylvio were re-united in friendship, as she judged that she should be reprehensible in using any means for tempting her to break the vow by which she had declared herself bound to secrecy.

In a short time she left the apartment, and having satisfied herself, from the information of the porter, that Averilla had not corresponded with Sylvio since her acquaintance had commenced with the Conte della Piacca, she could only suppose that they must have met, at the hour of her going to mass, and some explanation, of which it was impossible for her to guess the nature, have then taken place between them.

She recollected that Averilla had come home later than usual on that very morning. To question a servant on the conduct of her niece, was a step very foreign to the inclination of the Signora Felicia; she judged herself not to be justified in making any concealed enquiries into the actions of one, who had never yet deceived her, or acted contrary to her advice and direction. However, the uneasiness of her mind furnished her, in the present instance, with an apology for summoning into her presence, the servant who had attended her niece to the chapel of Saint Francis.

"My niece went as usual to mass this morning, did she not?" the Signora began her enquiries by saying.

The man replied in the affirmative.

"She was out beyond her usual time," rejoined the Signora; "did any accident happen to the carriage? I have a particular reason for wishing to know from what cause she was detained."

"The Signora Averilla did not come out of the chapel till full a quarter of an hour after every body else," answered the man.

"And did she come out alone?" asked the Signora.

"Yes, quite alone," was the reply.

"You do not know on what account she remained there," rejoined the Signora, "after every one else had left the place?"

"Oh, no," the man returned.

"And did you see no one follow her out?" enquired the Signora.

"After the Signora had been returned to the carriage some moments," answered the man, "I saw the Signor Sylvio di Rosalva come out of the chapel; but I do not know whether they had seen each other in the chapel or not."

Signora Felicia motioned with her hand to the servant to leave the apartment, and going up to her own dressing-room, she sent to request Averilla would come to her there.

CHAPTER VII

THE moment Averilla appeared, the tears gushed into the eyes of the Signora Felicia, and advancing to meet her, she threw her arms around her neck and said—"My dear child, you must be sensible that I love you as tenderly as if I really was your mother. Thus, it is impossible for me to express to you how anxiously I feel on your account, when I fear that any shade is about to fall on a character hitherto spotless; and this anxious apprehension must plead for me to your heart, to hear me with indulgence, and to reply to my enquiries with that gentle sweetness of which it has hitherto been my pride to behold your disposition composed. Think not, dearest girl, that I am about to urge you to break that vow by which you have this morning informed me you are bound to secrecy upon the events which are at this time filling my mind. Think not a mother, as I feel myself to you, will ever urge you to commit a sin towards your own conscience, and towards Heaven. You saw Sylvio di Rosalva, my love, this morning at the chapel of Saint Francis, did you not?"

"Yes, dearest mother, I did," replied Averilla.

"This point avowed," returned Felicia, "I may naturally conclude that your vow was made at his instigation, and probably to him; have you any reluctance to satisfy me in this question?"

"None, none," replied Averilla; "it was made at his instigation, and to him, at the altar of that saint who has been my protector from my cradle——"

"And upon whose ear, your conscience would doubtless have restrained you from breathing a vow to the concealment of any weakness, any immorality," returned the Signora, fixing her eyes on Averilla, as she spoke.

Averilla smiled, and replied, "Do you think, my dear Signora, that guiltless as you have ever known me, I could at once become so in love with vice as not only to have yielded to its temptation, but to have offended the ear of Heaven by pronouncing an oath of secrecy upon my crime? for, conscious as I am, how very strange my conduct must appear to you, and understanding, as I cannot forbear doing, by what apprehensions your enquiries are dictated—for I plainly perceive that you dread lest the explanation of this day's enigma should prove that I have not been able to conquer a personal attachment to Sylvio, and have contracted an intimacy with him to the dishonour of my intended husband—I here declare to you, by all my hopes of blessed eternity, that Sylvio di Rosalva is of all beings the last, if my present love of virtue were to desert me, whom I would suffer to be the spoiler of my own or my husband's honour."

"I cannot doubt the innocence of your heart after this asseveration," answered the Signora; "and it relieves my mind from a weight of heavy anxiety; nor can I suffer you to leave me, till I warn you still to beware of your conduct; for free from error as I now believe your heart to be, you are not aware of the straits into which a vow of secrecy, upon any point, may lead the most innocent and best designing of hearts."

"I thank you, from the very bottom of mine, for your excellent caution," answered Averilla, "and only wish it were in my power to communicate to you what now appears to you a mystery, that I might convince you how incapable is my past action of ever producing to me any regret of its having taken place; and, likewise, because if it were consistent for me to reveal it, many more than you would be much happier than it is now possible they should."

"I have still one apprehension," returned the Signora. "I dread that you will not find it so easy to convince the heart of the Conte della Piacca of your innocence, in thus mysteriously granting your friendship a second time to the man who appears to have deceived you, in raising false hopes of his affection in your breast."

Averilla paused a moment upon this idea; then said—"Yes, my dear aunt, I *shall* be able to convince the Conte of my innocence; no woman would willingly introduce to her intended husband a rival; the very candour of my conduct must cause him to see it in a guiltless point of view."

Signor Felicia expressed her doubts whether the Conte, however generous in his disposition, would in this instance think exactly as Averilla supposed, and doubtless desired he should; and again entreated her to act with caution; but Averilla still smiled at her aunt's apprehensions relative to the jealousy of the Conte being inflamed by the reconciliation which had taken place between her and Sylvio.

Signora Felicia was much easier in her mind in consequence of this conversation with her niece; she judged that whatever the mystery which imposed upon her silence, relative to her hasty reconciliation with Di Rosalva, still the ease of mind which she displayed must be proof of her innocence; no heart conscious of error, at least one, of which the snow-like purity had, till within the few last hours, never for an instant been darkened by the cloud of suspicion, could be so gay, so self satisfied, as her's now appeared; and from what she knew of her unacquaintance with dissimulation, she doubted not that the appearance was real.

Sylvio was still below when Averilla and her aunt returned to the apartment. Like Averilla, he appeared more cheerful than he had done for weeks before, and his greatest joy seemed to be placed in his renewal of friendship with the family Del Alvaretti, appearing to produce gratification to his friend Felix. For whatever, as an author, we may know of good or evil in the conduct of Sylvio, and for the interest of our tale choose for the present to hide from the reader, we must in justice declare, that his friendship for Felix was from the heart.

Averilla told Sylvio, that she must introduce him to her intended husband: "the man who is to bear that happy title," said she, smilingly, "will return hither to dinner; I must entreat you to remain with us today, and become acquainted with him."

Sylvio accepted the invitation readily, although the Signora Felicia did not second it; she chose in this instance that Averilla, who was alone acquainted with the motives from which she was acting, should herself regulate every point wherein the Conte could possibly feel himself offended at her conduct; she had given her the best advice which she was capable of bestowing, and more it was not in her power to do.

On the preceding day Averilla had received a letter of complimental congratulations on her approaching marriage with the Conte della Piacca, from the Marchesa Hyppolita di Bivelli, and judging that she ought to lose no time in replying to it, lest the writer should deem her neglectful, she in a very short time retired to her own apartment for that purpose, telling Felix and Sylvio that they would see her no more till she was dressed for dinner.

The Signora Felicia also retired to her private apartment; and the newly-reconciled friends remained below in conversation.

About the time that Averilla expected the Conte Lorenzo, she went down with her aunt into the garden; they passed the window of the apartment where they had some time before left Felix and Sylvio; Averilla looked in, and saw Felix, who was amusing himself with his flute—"Where is Sylvio?" she said.

"I supposed him with you," replied Felix; "he has left me some time—nearly an hour, I dare say."

Averilla judged it probable that he was gone home to dress, and communicated the idea to her aunt, who enquired of a servant passing near them, if the Signor di Rosalva had ordered his carriage? The servant replied in the affirmative, and Averilla now regarded her conjecture as confirmed.

"The air is extremely pleasant, Felix," said his mother; "will you come and take a turn with us?"

Felix consented, and Averilla ran into the house and led him out.

The soul of Felix was of too generous, too noble a nature, to condescend to pry into any secret which was not voluntarily imparted to him; thus so far from having led, in his conversation with Sylvio, to any explanation of the unknown cause of their reconciliation through the means of Averilla, satisfied that he had regained his friend in a manner creditable to them both, and particularly so to Sylvio, who was thus acquitted by the very individual towards whom he had been judged faulty, if not criminal, in his conduct; he forbore to touch on the subject, even in the slightest manner; and Sylvio had equally avoided the making it a part of his conversation.

When Felix, accompanied by Averilla, had joined his mother, he said—"I wonder Sylvio did not mention to me that he was going to return home before dinner; I did not even know that he had left the apartment, till some time, I imagine, after he had quitted it. Just after I had replied to a question he had advanced to me, I put my flute to my lips and played a short melody, at the end of which I addressed him; he did not answer me, and supposing he had not heard me the first time of my speaking, I repeated my question; he still did not reply; I then said—'Sylvio, are you in the room; tell me if you are?' No answer was returned to my address, and I found that he was gone."

"I see nothing very unaccountable in this," remarked Averilla; "and I am inclined to think you would not either, if there was not at this moment a degree of mystery hanging over poor Sylvio."

"There is some truth in your observation," replied Felix; "we are always apt to attribute motives to the actions of a man thus circumstanced, when in any other person they would pass unnoticed."

In a few minutes a servant met them, who put into the hand of Averilla a note, which he said had just been brought by a domestic of the Signor Sylvio di Rosalva.

"Read it without reserve, my love," said Signora Felicia; "I will retire for a moment from your side." Upon saying which, she immediately led Felix away a few paces from his cousin.

Almost instantly Averilla called out, "Stop, pray stop, it is addressed to us all."

The Signora returned to the side of Averilla, and beheld the note to be superscribed, "To the Signora Averilla, and her amiable friends, Signora Felicia and Signor Felix."

Averilla broke it open, and found the contents to be these:

> "Farewell, dearest, best of friends! In a few hours, I shall quit the Villa di Rosalva for a considerable length of time—perhaps for ever. You are not, any of you, the cause of my abrupt departure; nor can I explain to you what the cause is. If I durst declare to any one the place of my retreat, it would be to you; but prudence commands me to conceal it. As I am sure you are my real friends, you will not want to be told more, than that any attempt at discovering it, or stopping my departure, will but add to my unhappiness. Once more, farewell! Truly, I am the friend of you all.
>
> "The unhappy
> "SYLVIO DI ROSALVA."

These words called forth fresh emotions of suspicion in the breasts of Signora Felicia and her son; and Averilla appeared more astonished than they were, by the unexpected information which the paper in her hand had brought: "What can he mean by this unaccountable conduct?" she exclaimed.

"If you cannot explain the mystery, my dear cousin, who are so much more in his confidence than we are, how is it possible that we should divine it?" returned Felix.

"That he is unhappy, I can with truth vouch for him," said Averilla; "but how he is actuated in the step he here informs us he is about to take, I assure you, upon my word of honour, such particulars as I *do* know concerning him give me no clue for imagining."

"Surely," said the Signora Felicia, "the very many instances of an extraordinary line of conduct which we have been witnesses of in him, may excuse a supposition that he possesses a weakness of temper, of which he spoke on the morning succeeding his alarm at suddenly beholding the statue of the Gladiator, that must have a nearer connection with the brain than he told us, or is perhaps aware of himself."

"I am very glad, as he forbids our interference in his case," rejoined Felix, "that he is possessed of such a friend as the good Bianca. It is impossible that any thing which occurred since his arrival here this morning could drive him to this resolution; nothing but commonplace conversation passed between himself and me; and it is on affairs only of the most immediate moment, that men form determinations of this nature."

"You said," rejoined Averilla, with some degree of agitation marked on her countenance, "that the last words which passed between you, previously to your discovering that he had left the room, were spoken by you in reply to a question he had advanced to you."

"Exactly so," answered Felix.

"Can you recollect what that question was?" asked Averilla.

"Not immediately," replied Felix, "but I will endeavour: Let me see—he had been enquiring into the age and person of your destined husband, and I had been giving him such information on these points as the remarks of others had furnished me with; his last question was something regarding him."

A momentary silence ensued, which Felix broke by exclaiming, "I recollect now what his last question was; it was the name of him you were destined to espouse."

"Have you any idea that he fled upon being told the name of Conte della Piacca?" asked Averilla.

"Pardon me returning the question upon you," said Felix.

"No indeed," replied Averilla; "neither his name, nor the name of any one else, is concerned in the mystery of which I am a party."

"It is very strange," said Signora Felicia.

"Indeed it is," returned Averilla; "I pity him extremely; and so would you, Felix, I am sure, if I were at liberty to interest you in his fate, as I very much wish circumstances permitted me to do."

"It certainly was immediately on my informing him that your destined husband was the Conte Lorenzo della Piacca, that he left me," repeated Felix.

"His departure is to me equally an enigma, as it is to either of you," rejoined Averilla, "as I have already told you." She hesitated a moment, then added, "As he will in a few hours leave this part of the country, and leads us to believe it possible that we may never see him again—which possibility I, from my soul, desire Heaven to avert—favour me, my dear Felix, my dear aunt, by not mentioning to my uncle, or the Conte, my reconciliation with him. I am averse to their becoming acquainted with it, now I have not Sylvio here to introduce to their knowledge; had he been here, it had been a pride and a pleasure to me to have done so."

The Signora and Felix promised to acquiesce in her wish; they had already so far placed confidence in her conduct regarding Sylvio, that they could not, without being guilty of the greatest inconsistency, refuse still to act under her guidance in such points as referred to their late reconciliation.

CHAPTER VIII

WITH the hour of dinner arrived at the Palazzo del Alvaretti, the Conte Lorenzo and Signor Rossano: the latter informed his wife that the marriage of Averilla would be solemnized in Genoa; and as he intended it to take place in the course of three weeks, or a month, he wished her to move to that city without delay, and superintend the necessary preparations for its celebration.

The Conte Lorenzo brought with him a casket of beautiful jewels, which he presented to Averilla, as the first gift of his passion; and the pleasure with which she received them, and the complacency with which she now listened to his addresses, gave with every hour additional strength to his love.

The Conte, we have already said, really loved Averilla upon his introduction to her, although he had solicited that introduction previously to his having seen her, and trusted to chance to reward or punish him for his temerity.

Of Averilla we have also said, that had she never seen Sylvio at the time of her first introduction to the Conte Lorenzo, she would not have felt much reluctance in giving him the promise of her hand; and it is but now proper to inform our readers, that since her reconciliation with Sylvio di Rosalva, her affections were entirely given to the Conte Lorenzo, and that she looked forward with satisfaction to the idea of becoming his wife.

In the course of a very few days the family del Alvaretti, in compliance with the wish of Rossano, repaired to the city of Genoa. Previously to their departure from the Villa, Felix had taken measures for informing himself whether Sylvio di Rosalva had indeed left his villa, and he found that he had set out from thence on the afternoon of that day on which he had last visited the Palazzo del Alvaretti, attended only by the good Bianca, and one man servant; and that no one knew the cause of his departure, whither he was gone, or when he intended to return.

The hours of Averilla were now passed in a continual round of feasts, dances, concerts, and, in short, every amusement which could be deemed a compliment in those who gave them, to her and her family, on her approaching union with the Conte Lorenzo.

A few days previously to her marriage, and about a month after the family del Alvaretti had left the country, they visited at the house of a gentleman of distinction in the republic, named Della Bagua, who being a widower, his only daughter Virgilia, now eighteen, had been educated in a convent, from the protection of whose walls she was just returned to her father's house.

New to the world, every common incident of life appeared to Virgilia both surprising and delightful; she had been educated at a convent in the city of Milan, and her journey from thence to Genoa was now her favourite topic; in crossing some of the mountains in the more barren parts of Tortona, the carriage in which she traveled had been overturned, and she was now eager to communicate to every one the history of her escape.

To Averilla and Felix she had but just gained an introduction; the story of the danger she had escaped was consequently new to them, and she took the first opportunity of detailing to them her narrative. They heard her account with patience, and not without some degree of interest; and Averilla easily discovered that the pleasure which Virgilia received from the repetition of her accident, was that of dwelling upon the services she had received at the hands of a handsome young peasant, who, it was no difficult matter to discover, occupied her whole heart.

"You can form no idea," said Virgilia, "of the elegant, the engaging, the benevolent manners of this young man; his attentions to me were indescribable. You cannot think how anxious he expressed himself in discovering whether I was hurt or not; and with what tenderness he invited me into his cottage, and brought me refreshments."

"How long did you remain the tenant of his hospitality?" asked Averilla.

"Only a few short hours," returned Virgilia; "the carriage was quickly repaired, and my governante hurried me away. Heigho! I assure you she was in a much greater hurry to be gone than I was."

"I am afraid you are in love with this peasant," said Averilla, half smiling.

"No, not in love; not absolutely in love," answered Virgilia; "but I think he merits my esteem for the very kind attention he shewed me. And he was, besides, the handsomest man I ever saw in my life—indeed, I never beheld any body at all like him; his eyes so soft and blue, and still so full of animation; his teeth so regularly white and beautiful; and his hair of the most delightful flaxen, striped, as it were, with locks of a brilliant gold colour! Did you ever see any body with such hair?"

"Averilla can tell you of one who has always been described to me to have exactly the same eyes and hair you mention," said Felix.

"You mean Sylvio di Rosalva," returned Averilla.

"Sylvio di Rosalva!" echoed Virgilia. "You know him then; Sylvio di Rosalva, the peasant I have been telling you of informed me was his name."

"No," replied Averilla, "they cannot be the same person; the Sylvio di Rosalva, with whom we were once acquainted, was a gentleman of considerable fortune."

"But how strange a coincidence!" returned Virgilia.

"The name is not an uncommon one," answered Averilla; "and is, I dare say, borne by many more persons in Italy than the two we happen to know."

"But it is certainly singular that their persons should so strongly resemble each other," said Felix.

"In the description we find a resemblance," replied Averilla, "which would probably be entirely lost in the comparison."

"But that hair of so extraordinary a colour should be found exactly the same on the head of two men of the same name, is astonishing, I am sure," rejoined Virgilia.

Felix enquired how long it was since Virgilia had seen this peasant on the mountains of Tortona? She replied, little more than a week. He then asked, whether she knew how long he had lived on those mountains? Of this she was ignorant. Whom she had seen in the cottage besides himself? he next enquired. Nobody, was the reply. Felix decided in his own mind, that either from some concealed necessity of retiring from the neighbourhood of Genoa, from some eccentricity of character, or flightiness of brain, it was the same Sylvio di Rosalva whom he had so lately called friend, that was now become a peasant on the mountains of Tortona.

Virgilia was at this instant called upon to attend to some of her father's guests; and Felix took the opportunity of saying to Averilla, "What is your opinion? do you not think this peasant to be our Sylvio di Rosalva?"

"Believe me, Felix," returned Averilla, "that I cannot form the remotest idea whether it is or not."

"I am, however, glad," said Felix, "that if it is himself, he does not attempt to conceal his name, as it appears from the account of Virgilia he does not; it seems to imply, that whatsoever the cause of his unexplained conduct, he has no apprehensions about revealing himself; which is a knowledge that cannot but give pleasure to those who have once called themselves his friends."

Averilla agreed with him in this declaration; and they then joined in the general conversation.

The day was now arrived on which Averilla was destined to become the wife of the Conte Lorenzo della Piacca. Previously to the performance of the ceremony which was to bind her his forever, she called him apart, and thus addressed him—"As I am about to become your wife, I consider it conducive to the happiness of us both, that I should become so under the most favourable impression. I therefore feel it my duty to repeat to you, that although I laboured under a prepossession for another when I first saw you, that passion is entirely eradicated from my breast, and my whole heart is now your own. I have had convincing proofs that my affections before were improperly placed; from you I have received the most flattering testimonies of esteem and love; and I am henceforward your's alone, and for ever."

The Conte received with rapture this voluntary confession from the lips of Averilla; her dazzling beauties appeared in his eyes to gain, if possible, additional lustre from the avowal; and he led her triumphantly to the altar, from which she returned his wife.

The feasts continued with equal fervency and splendor for many weeks after the celebration of the nuptials of the Contessa Averilla, as they had previously been given with. At length, every due compliment having been paid to the family del Alvaretti, during their stay at Genoa, the Conte proposed a journey to Turin, in order to introduce his newly-married lady to his own relations.

With regret Averilla bade farewell to her beloved friends, the Signora Felicia and her son Felix. "I shall see you soon again," she said, for the Conte had assured her, that his stay at Turin would not exceed a year, if it were even so long; and in this hope of soon meeting again, she bade them farewell with very tolerable composure.

She believed the Conte really to love and respect her; he had hitherto given her every reason to believe him sincerely attached to her; but still she considered that he was as yet hardly more than her lover; that she had as yet only seen him under the eye of her own family; she did not doubt that he would every where continue an equally affectionate husband, as he had hitherto proved himself; but still there was a possibility of the contrary, and it threw a momentary damp upon her spirits at leaving Genoa.

A very short time, however, reassured her; every confidence she found to be due to the Conte; he was uniformly kind, attentive, good humoured, and affectionate; and it was her pride to deserve the happiness she enjoyed in her union with him.

On their arrival at Turin, at the elegant Palazzo of the Conte, of which the establishment was of the most sumptuous kind, Averilla received every flattering attention from the family to which her marriage had allied her; and the same round of festivities which had taken place at Genoa, were instantly set on foot at Turin.

There were even now moments at which Averilla's thoughts would return to Sylvio di Rosalva; she would then wonder where he was, and wish that she could hear he was more happy in his mind than when she said seen him last; but she now thought of him only as a friend.

She corresponded constantly with Signora Felicia, who becoming at times the amanuensis of her son Felix, who did not consider it a sufficient remembrance of his cousin to send her only a postscript to his mother's letters, would then dispatch to her niece a double packet of friendship and intelligence, which differed only in the signature, as they breathed equally warm expressions of their joy at her felicity, and assurances of their love for her not being diminished by absence.

In one of Averilla's replies to these letters, she had enquired of her aunt whether she had ever learnt any intelligence of Sylvio since her departure from Genoa? to which question the answer of Signora Felicia was, "that she had never heard him spoken of by any one; and that she knew him never to have returned to the Villa di Rosalva, since the day on which he had so hastily, and so unaccountably, left it."

CHAPTER IX

WHEN Averilla had been resident about five months at Turin, those festivities which had been held in honour of her began to subside, and leave time for the more tranquil pleasures of domestic enjoyment. She had hitherto been so much occupied with the inhabitants, that she had scarcely seen anything of the city; and she now took great delight in walking with the Conte on the ramparts, and in those delightful and extensive gardens along the margin of which runs the meandering Po. But her favourite amusement was an evening visit to a beautiful spot called the Corfo,[1] where it was fashionable for all persons of condition to ride or walk, and to spend an hour or two, in strolling about, in conversation, or in taking lemonades and ices in the surrounding cassinos.

In one of her evening walks at the Corfo, while in conversation with some ladies of her acquaintance, the eyes of Averilla fell on a male figure, handsomely drest, whom she immediately recognised to be Sylvio di Rosalva; as soon as she could catch his eye, she bowed, or rather nodded to him her head; as he did not return it, she judged that he did not instantly recollect her; she accordingly turned aside her veil, and at the same moment kissed her hand to him.

He returned her salutation with a bow of so formal a nature, that she judged still he could not have recognised her. "Do you know that gentleman?" asked one of her companions.

"I have known him so intimately," replied Averilla, "that the formality with which he now greets me, leads to suppose he does not recollect me; I cannot possibly be mistaken in him:—it is—it must be the Signor Sylvio di Rosalva."

"Yes, that is his name," returned one of the ladies. "You knew him then, before he came to Turin?"

---

[1] "Corfo" is not an Italian word; it should probably read "Corso", Italian for a wide avenue or main street. However, whether Lathom's mistake or a typesetter's misreading of his manuscript, the spelling occurs repeatedly and is retained here as in the first edition.

Averilla explained where he had resided, and the terms of intimacy he had been upon in the family of her aunt.

"He is almost a stranger here," returned one of the ladies; "a man of a very genteel address, and apparently of good fortune; but he has very few acquaintance, and tells, as I have understood, a very different story of himself from what you do; he gives it out, that he has till very lately lived with an uncle, an aged man, who loved retirement, and inhabited an humble dwelling somewhere in the mountains; that this old man is now dead, and having left him a handsome property, he is come to enjoy himself upon it in the society of this city."

Averilla recollected Virgilia's account, and asked her informer if she remembered whether the uncle he had spoken of had lived in the mountains of Tortona?

"Now you mention it, I recollect they were those mountains," returned the lady.

They were now joined by the Conte Lorenzo and a large party; and as they saw Sylvio no more in the course of their rambles, he was not again spoken of by them.

When the hour for leaving the Corfo arrived, the Conte choosing to return home on horseback, Averilla, in the solitude of her carriage, had time for reflection; she considered that the only motive which could have withheld Sylvio di Rosalva from approaching her on the terms of intimacy he had been accustomed to do, must have been an idea that his presence, as the man who was once supposed to be seeking her hand himself, would be disagreeable to her husband—"This opinion, on his part, must not be suffered to curtail us to the pleasure of his friendship!" exclaimed Averilla. "I will explain to the Conte the conviction I received while at the Villa del Alvaretti, of Sylvio never having regarded me as an object of passion, but merely of friendship; and request him to invite him into our family as an occasional visitor."

Conscious herself how pure was the motive from which she acted with regard to Sylvio, she believed no unjust imputation could be put upon it by the world. But in this opinion Averilla deceived herself:—it is not sufficient that we know our motives to be free from impropriety ourselves, we should also be careful that they appear so in the eyes of others.

When the Conte returned home, he brought with him some gentlemen to supper; and their presence prevented the Contessa from putting her design, relative to Sylvio, into execution that evening.

During supper a letter was brought to the Conte; he read it twice with apparently great attention, and begging pardon of his guests for rising from table, he went out to give a verbal reply to the person who had brought it. When he returned to the table, he affected cheerfulness, but it was very evident to perceive that it was forced, and a visible agitation was at times depicted on his countenance.

As soon as the guests were retired, Averilla besought him to confide to her what it was that gave him uneasiness; he fixed his eyes upon her with an expression of extreme tenderness, and said, "How kind, how good a wife, is my Averilla!" and upon these words he paused.

"You do not give me a just proof that you think me so, in not confiding to me your sorrows," returned Averilla. "No good wife is ever so happy as when she can participate in her husband's griefs."

"It is late to-night," said the Conte, "and I am not very well. In the morning you shall know all; and perhaps I shall put your affection for me to a greater trial than you imagine."

"You cannot put it to any one it will not bear for you with pleasure," returned Averilla. "But I shall not sleep easy in this ignorance of the cause of your anxiety," she added.

"Believe me," replied the Conte, "I have none which it is not in your power to remove."

"In that assurance I am easier," rejoined Averilla; "for whatever it is, you will wrong me, if you do not conclude it already done."

Upon these words they retired to rest. In the morning Averilla first renewed the conversation of the former evening—"Come," she said, "I am all impatience to know how I can add to your happiness."

"Tell me Averilla," replied Della Piacca, taking her hand as he spoke, "if I had ever had a wife before yourself, should you be angry with me for occasionally taking pleasure in contemplating her picture, heaving an accidental sigh to her memory, or now and then speaking of her to you in terms of praise?"

"Oh no," answered Averilla, "I could not be offended at seeing that your affection for one to whom you had devoted your heart, was not as transient as her life had been; I should also be taught to hope, that *my* memory would receive the same tribute from you, if you were my survivor."

"And if I were the father of a child by that wife, could you bestow on it any portion of your affections, as being mine?" asked Conte.

"Undoubtedly I could," replied Averilla.

"And if you had children of your own, should you not be jealous to see it stealing away some part of my love from them?"

"Jealous of seeing a child of yours beloved by its parent!" exclaimed the Contessa della Piacca: "If I could for any thing dislike that parent, it must be to see him neglect one descended from himself. But what mean these questions? Only to banter me, I believe; for I think you already know my heart too well to ask them in earnest."

"No, indeed; I have a motive for advancing them," returned the Conte.

"Am I to understand, then, that you have already been married?" said Averilla.

"No, no," returned Della Piacca; "I have not been married."

"But you are still a father; is it not so, my husband?" asked the Contessa.

"Yes," replied the Conte, "I am the father of a little innocent cherub, who, I will not blush to confess to you, possesses a considerable share of my affection; and"——he paused.

"And what?" said Averilla tenderly.

"She is at this moment without a home, or a protector," he added, fixing his eyes on his wife as he spoke.

"A child of your's without a home, without a protector!" exclaimed Averilla. "Bring her hither instantly! If you are her father, doubt not that she shall find a mother in me. Oh, Della Piacca," she added, in a softened tone, "I fear I must, after all, quarrel with you, either on my account or your own. Did you conceive all this prelude necessary to the acquainting me how I might perform an humane action, or were you ashamed of confessing yourself interested in the fate of one who owes to you her existence? In either case you were wrong, and can only make amends to me and yourself by bringing her hither immediately."

"Dear, generous, beloved Averilla!" exclaimed the Conte; "how transcendent is my happiness in possessing a wife like yourself! never shall I be able to repay to you the gratitude I owe you for this disinterested kindness."

The Conte then proceeded to inform Averilla, that the child of whom he had spoken was a girl of eight years old; the hour of her birth had been the date of her mother's death. Ever since that period, the child had been under the protection of a distant relation of the Conte's, where he had constantly visited her, and where she had been taught to know him as the author of her being. The letter he had received on the preceding evening, while at supper, he proceeded to say, was from a physician of the city, informing him of the sudden death of his relative; by this accident he was entirely deprived of an asylum for his daughter; and the very great affection he had for her, and the anxiety he felt for the proper regulation of her conduct and morals, were so great, that they had given him resolution to make known to his Contessa his desire of her becoming one of his family; in which wish she had so generously, so enchantingly met his thoughts.

Perhaps my more nice and less humane female readers, may condemn the conduct of Averilla; but let such remember, or rather learn, that the man whom they select as the partner of their lives, never can appear to them in a light more deserving of their love, than when in the performance of benevolent and affectionate actions towards those who have a claim upon his heart and his services; and that when they neglect to assist him in the performance of these duties, they are not only culpable themselves, but guilty also of having suffered their influence to lead him into sins of omission. They are equally enemies to themselves, for in loving those to whom he is attached, they will find the strongest hold upon his affections; and in the estimate of merit, those will doubtless be considered as greatly deserving, who have stretched out their hands to rescue the innocent from falling the victims of such evils as usually attend on those who are driven from the bosoms of their natural protectors.

The Conte ordered his carriage without delay, and proceeded to the house of his deceased relation, in order to bring home to his wife her new charge. During his ride thither, he passed some of the happiest moments of his life; he had ever been extremely fond of the child, and he had besides suffered many scruples of conscience, respecting the injustice of a parent's refusing his personal protection to one whom he acknowledges his own child, on account of the neglect of such ceremonies previous to its birth, as the unhappy infant can have no concern in, but is through life doomed to feel the omission of, on the part of its parents. For both these evils he had now found a remedy; he should have the child continually near him to caress at pleasure, and the child would enjoy the immediate protection of her father. Nor did his greatest joy arise from these reflections; it was with ecstasy that he contemplated the virtue, the benevolence, and the attachment of the Contessa to himself.

At the sight of her father, the little Flavia flew into his arms, with an exclamation of delight; and the rapture with which she received the intelligence, that she was henceforth to live with him, could only be equalled by the sorrow in which she had passed the night, with an old nurse of her deceased protectress for her only companion.

When they arrived at the Palazzo della Piacca, Averilla came out to meet them, and imprinted a kiss of welcome on the lips of Flavia. "You cannot, my dear Flavia," said the Conte Lorenzo, "shew your love for me in any way that will please me better, than by doing every thing in your power to oblige this lady."

"I am sure I shall love her," returned Flavia, "she looks so good tempered."

"I am glad to hear you say you think you shall like me for your mother," returned the Contessa.

"Are you my mamma?" asked Flavia; "I thought she had been dead a great many years."

"So she has, my love," returned the Conte; "but this lady is my wife, and is so kind as to become your second mother."

"I am sure she is very good," cried Flavia; "and I promise to be very good too, and love her very much. I am sure she is very fond of you, and therefore she ought to be good to me on account of my mamma."

"Why so? What do you mean?" asked her father.

"Because, much as she loves you," replied Flavia, "if my poor mamma had not died, she could not have been your wife."

Averilla and the Conte both smiled at this remark of the innocent Flavia, and the Contessa again clasping her in her arms, said—"I now hold you to a bosom in which you may place the confidence you would in a real parent, and which will ever consider itself most blest when it can add to your happiness."

CHAPTER X

When Flavia was for the first time retired to rest beneath the same roof which covered her parent, and Averilla was left alone with her husband, she said, "My dear Conte, I never before felt unwilling to make a request to you. I wish it had so happened that you had not mentioned the dear little Flavia to me till to-morrow; for I have at this moment a request which I have been wishing for an opportunity to advance to you ever since yesterday afternoon; and I now feel a reluctance in doing it, lest I should appear to be arrogating to myself a supposed right to your indulgence, in consequence of the transaction that has marked this day."

"If so mean a motive could ever for an instant be supposed to be the inmate of so noble a breast as yours, the open and generous manner in which you express your delicate apprehension, is at once sufficient to declare you entirely innocent," replied the Conte. "I am much pleased, my dear Averilla, to find that there is any circumstance by which I can repay your exalted conduct towards me."

"Don't say repay," returned Averilla; "you are making me fall into the very error I wish to avoid. If you talk of repaying, I shall never tell you what it is at all; if you will hear what I have to communicate to you, for itself alone, and give me your reply, entirely unbiassed by any idea of *repaying* any point in my conduct, I shall have much pleasure in making my wish known to you; but if you do not promise this, I must keep it to myself."

"There is no condition," replied the Conte, "in which I shall not feel a happiness in promoting a wish of yours."

"I have never seen you jealous of me yet," said Averilla, smiling; "is jealousy your disposition?"

"Your question," replied Della Piacca, smiling in his turn, "is the most perplexing one a woman can put to her husband: if he says 'yes,' she immediately augurs that he suspects her fidelity; if 'no,' she is equally displeased on the score of indifference."

"Then you won't answer the question," said Averilla.

"Not exactly so," replied the Conte; "but I must remember that we are in Italy, and had any woman but my Averilla, with the delicacy of whose sentiments I am so well acquainted, proposed the question to me, as her husband, I should undoubtedly have expected, that if

I had said 'no,' she would directly have said, 'Then I'll introduce my Cicisbeo to you.'"

"And that, I hope, would immediately have made you change your answer to 'Yes,'" replied Averilla; "for I am as capable of discovering the vices and follies of my own country as of any other; and I think that if there can be a more despicable character than the woman who entertains such an acquaintance, it must be the husband who tamely submits his honour to be insulted, upon the example of other fools who have gone before him."

"Excellently defined!" exclaimed the Conte. "No, Averilla, I am not jealous; the man who is jealous of his wife must either know her undeserving of his love, or devoid of sense; neither of these cases, I am certain, is chargeable upon you, and therefore I am *not* jealous. And now what is your request?"

"That you will receive a friend of mine as your friend likewise," answered Averilla.

"A male friend, of course, by your scruples?" returned the Conte.

"Why, they are usually males, I believe," replied the Contessa, "who wear boots and a sword; and such is the friend whom I wish to introduce to your acquaintance."

"If he will esteem my acquaintance a pleasure," answered the Conte, "I make no doubt but we shall be happy in his. Pray who is he?"

"It shall be fully explained to you," returned Averilla; "and if you then feel the slightest repugnance to admitting him as an occasional visitor at your house, believe me, that your candidly confessing your objection will not in the least render me dissatisfied with your conduct."

"Your preface is all I can desire," returned Della Piacca: "now come to the subject; what is the hero's name?"

"Signor Sylvio di Rosalva," answered Averilla.

The Conte gave an involuntary start.

Averilla continued—"I know what you are going to say, that he is the man on whom my affections were placed, previously to their becoming yours."

"The man," replied the Conte, "who, if I may be allowed the expression, slighted the preference you confessed for him."

"The man," returned the Contessa, "who opened my eyes to the very great happiness I am now enjoying in being your wife."

"If it is only on this account that you wish my friendship to be extended towards him, I must indeed be flattered by the excess of your gratitude," said Della Piacca.

"We are, my dear Conte," returned Averilla, "bordering upon jest, in the discussion of a subject to which I wish to fix your serious attention, in the hope of making you feel the same interest in it that I do myself. I was, as you have already had explained to you, entirely mistaken in the opinion I had formed of the attentions which the Signor Sylvio di Rosalva paid to me; I have, since that time, had my mistake explained to me by himself."

"Indeed!" said the Conte; "where have you met?"

Averilla instantly informed him, that they had seen each other one morning in the chapel of Saint Francis, in the village of Alvaretti, and that there he had given her a full explanation of such circumstances, as had not only proved to her how great had been her error in supposing that he had ever felt for her any passion except that of friendship, but had also convinced her that it was not his intention to marry at all.

"You present me with an enigma," replied the Conte; "but I suppose you mean to give me its solution."

"I am bound by a vow," returned Averilla, "never to reveal what he that morning entrusted to my confidence; and I now give you the greatest proof in my power, of the faith which I believe you to place in my veracity and my honour, when upon these obscure terms I still urge you to admit him to your friendship."

"Believe me, my dearest, my best beloved Averilla," returned the Conte, after a short silence, "that you cannot consider the confidence which I place both in your veracity and in your honour, to be more unbounded than it really is; and when I for a moment hesitate to acquiesce in your undoubtedly extraordinary request, it is, that I dread lest your unsuspicious, your susceptible heart, should have been the dupe of some concealed villany in those who tempted you to take the vow you mention; and if I have a wish to know the secret upon which it fixes a seal, Heaven is my witness, that no selfish interest inspires me with it, and that it arises out of my anxiety for your welfare and security."

"I am, I dare say," answered the Contessa, "very unfit to cope with such beings as have sufficiently evil dispositions to wish to creep as serpents into the hearts of those whose peace it is their aim to destroy; I feel an inexpressible gratitude for the interest you express for me, in wishing me to avoid all the specious arts which are daily held out by the designing, to allure the innocent and inexperienced to their ruin; and the only motive which I, in my turn, have for wishing that my conscience would allow me to reveal to you the only secret it has apart from you, is, that I might thus be allowed to ease you of any doubt on my account, by shewing you how impossible it is, that either my vow, or that Sylvio, for whose sake it was taken, should ever cause me one moment of repentance or of pain. Sylvio di Rosalva is one of those beings on whom fate has frowned with peculiar sternness from the hour of his birth; he is one to whom it becomes the duty of the individual trusted with the secret of his misery, to administer such consolation as he is capable of receiving; he has a heart which is the seat of every virtue; an understanding which spurs him on to their practice; he is one whom you will one day commend me for having won you to bestow the services of friendship upon, although the object of that friendship is condemned to receive them from you through a veil of mystery."

"Thou art a most insinuating pleader, Averilla," said the Conte; "it would be double heresy to neglect the performance of a good action, recommended by thee; and my actions have of late taken so much delight in being the reflection of thine, that they will not easily be shaken from regarding thee as their mirror. Let Sylvio, therefore, be invited to visit us; and doubt not, if it be a virtue to bestow soothing friendship on him, that I shall become insensibly virtuous by following thy example."

Averilla fell upon the neck of her husband; and with the tears standing in her eyes, she kissed his cheek, and said—"I perceive that I have inconsiderately been guilty of an error of conduct. At the time I knew myself about to become a wife, I should not have bound myself to the keeping of any secret, with which my husband was not to be made acquainted. I knew my vow to be a positive virtue, and I did not consider, at the moment I took it, the partial evil which arises out of it. I cannot now, without the most material injury to my peace of mind, swerve from a vow taken in the name, and at the altar of the Saint who protects me; but I now, for the first time, perceive that any necessary concealment which I practice towards you, it is my duty to keep the recollection of from rising to your thoughts as seldom as possible; I am, therefore, unjust in asking your friendship for one, whose presence will but keep awake in your mind that I have a secret from you. Di Rosalva must not be introduced to this house; give me your pardon for not seeing the error of my request before I advanced it."

"No, my Averilla," returned Della Piacca, returning her kiss with the tenderest affection, "my own conscience would become the constant monitor to me of an error in *my* conduct, if I were not to insist on a husband's right, for compelling my wife to the performance of such actions as she knows to be virtuous, and yet, from delicacy of sentiment towards him, would forego the performance of; nor shall I be satisfied with knowing *you* not to be omissive in this point of friendship—*I* must participate with you in that conduct which shall gain us both the gratitude of your friend."

A few moments were now passed in the indulgence of that happiness which arises from the discovery, that those we most esteem are possessed of such qualities as are congenial to the feelings of our own hearts, and render us additionally happy in the sensation of our having already placed on them our affections.

Perhaps there may be minds which will think that, had they been placed in the situation of the Conte della Piacca, no idea of any good which the action might confer on a suffering individual, should have induced them to have permitted a wife to renew her acquaintance with a man on whom her affections had once been placed; but we must beg leave to say, that we think such a mind must be a weak one, and that the man who will not do it, must be sensible that his conduct towards his wife is not what it ought to be, when he fears that her's should, from situation, become faulty; and that where a man is suspicious of the faith which a woman has pledged to him, till he has actual cause to believe her deserving of his censure, he merits to suffer, as he dreads, for the meanness of his heart.

In the instance, also, of the Conte Lorenzo, the conduct of Averilla, with regard to his natural child, had given him proof that her mind was possessed of that strong sense, which shewed her too well acquainted with the nature of virtue, not to be shielded against the attacks of vice. Had her conduct, in other respects, been weak and trifling, he might have suspected the exercise of a single excellent action, to be the veil of one of an opposite nature; but where the regular habit of a female is steady goodness, without parade in its exercise, base indeed must be the heart of the man who is not satisfied that, for her own sake, she will preserve her purity, if she has not even the consideration of his unspotted honour adding a lustre to her's.

The Conte proposed to seek out the residence of the Signor di Rosalva on the following day, and invite him, without delay, to visit the Palazzo della Piacca; but Averilla, with many expressions of gratitude for the liberality of his conduct, entreated that the introduction of the Conte to him should rather be left to the chance of the first time when they should meet him in the Corfo, or some other place of public amusement.

"The circumstances of his life," she said, "have imposed on him a restraint of manner, which has induced upon him a natural timidity, an apparently unaccountable conduct, which appeared formerly as strange to me, as it will, doubtless, now strike you to be; but which, now I understand the motive of it, I only pity, and cease to be surprised at."

And as a confirmation and example of her account, she mentioned the circumstance of Sylvio's alarm at suddenly turning his eyes upon the statue of the gladiator in the garden Del Alvaretti; recounted his sudden departure from his own villa on the day of his reconciliation with her aunt, with Felix, and herself; and then spoke of his having been seen living as a peasant on the mountains of Tortona, by Virgilia della Bagua.

"These circumstances," added the Contessa, "must appear mysterious to you, my dear Lorenzo; nor can I myself comprehend the exact cause of each immediate action; but I know sufficient to be convinced that they are not only excusable, but deserving of pity, and they might be easily explained, and their mysterious actor still be proved to be in his senses."

The Conte smiled; he did not advance to his wife a single remark which bore the appearance of a wish to tempt her into giving him the slightest information which could infringe upon a letter of her vow: What she was at liberty to relate to him, and which were only such particulars of Sylvio as our readers are already acquainted with, he listened to with apparent pleasure and interest; and when they ceased speaking of him, which was not till they retired to rest, the Conte said—"No one can have pursued the mysterious conduct which the Signor Sylvio has done from choice; it is impossible that any individual would place himself in suspicious points of view, if he were able to avoid it, by submitting the motives of his actions to the inspection of his friends; the very circumstances, therefore, which excite surprise, ought equally, in the mind of reflection, to awaken pity. Believe me, Averilla, I now desire to become acquainted with him, and extend the sympathy of my words and actions towards him."

CHAPTER XI

THE greater part of the week which followed this conversation proved very rainy and unfavourable to visiting the banks of the Po, or mixing in the gaieties of the Corfo. At length an afternoon came, which tempted the Contessa to say she would ride to one of the public gardens, which were, at that season of the year, the resort of fashion, on the margin of the Po, from whose refreshing streams a cooling breeze was wafted upon the spot of enjoyment.

"Shall you not like to see those beautiful gardens?" said the Contessa, addressing Flavia.

"Oh yes, that I shall," exclaimed Flavia, her heart bounding with delight.

"Do you intend to take her with us?" said the Conte, his eyes beaming gratitude towards his wife for her attention, as he spoke.

"Have we not both acknowledged her as our daughter?" asked the Contessa; "and shall I confer on her the tenderness of a mother by halves?—treat her with kindness at home, and blush to have her seen with me abroad? Oh no—no! I shall think it no sacrifice to give up the acquaintance of such as would like me less, because I bring this picture of loveliness and innocence in my hand with me. If I have any such fastidious beings amongst those who have hitherto called themselves my friends, I shall not be sorry that this beloved one proves the touchstone of their sincerity."

"Fall on your knees, Flavia, before her who now supplies to you the place of a mother, and return her those thanks which I have not words to express to her for you!" exclaimed the Conte.

"I knew she was very good, the first moment I saw her," replied

Flavia; "but you can thank her much better than I can: When I stand smiling before her, she looks very kind, and very much pleased; but when you smile at her, she looks so delighted, and so happy, that I am sure you can thank her much better."

Flavia received an embrace from each, as the reward of her discernment, and the present of a new hat to ride to the gardens in, from her dear second mamma, as she delighted to call the Contessa.

They had not been long in the gardens before sudden clouds arose, which brought with them a heavy rain, and obliged the company to retreat precipitately to their carriages: unfortunately, that of the Contessa Averilla having no top, presented her with no prospect of comfort, on entering it, but that of being speedily conveyed to the shelter of her own house; but before she reached it, both she and Flavia, although they had wrapped themselves up in their cloaks, were wet through all their clothes.

Flavia had the good fortune to escape with merely the inconvenience of the hour; but Averilla found, on the succeeding morning, that she had caught a cold of such severity as threatened to confine her to the house for a considerable time: its effects, however, were more troublesome than dangerous, and a few days relieved her from every apprehension but that of catching cold afresh, if she ventured out again too incautiously.

While she was in this state, a day arrived on which the celebration of an annual *fête*, which was held on the Po, was to take place. The Conte della Piacca possessed an elegant gondola, in which it had been his intention that himself and his Contessa should join the festivities of the day.

On an excursion of this kind, Averilla was apprehensive of venturing, on account of her health; and as she was to be absent, the Conte had changed his design of going himself; but the Contessa requested him, as an indulgence to her, to go upon the water, and take Flavia with him, as she had promised her a share in the amusements of the day, and wished her not to be disappointed of her frolic.

The Conte acquiesced in her request without hesitation; and Flavia, dressed in her new hat, of which she was extremely proud, as being the first gift of her dear second mamma, continued to dance about the apartment in which the Contessa was sitting, in ecstacies at the approach of the hour which was to present to her a sight, to the nature of which she was an utter stranger, and of which she could, consequently, form no idea, but that it must be delightful, because every body was anxious to visit it.

At length the expected hour of pleasure arrived; and Flavia having taken leave of the Contessa, seized hold of her father's hand, which was to lead her to the spot of joy.

As the Palazzo della Piacca was situated near the extremity of the city, some gardens only, which belonged principally to the Conte, separated it from the river, and through these they went to the gondola.

Flavia was delighted with the scene; it was by no means devoid of charms for those of riper years, and more mature understandings: alternately her notice was attracted by the beauty of the gondolas, the richness of their colours, the elegance of the Signoras they contained, and the novelty of the motion she was experiencing; and each, in turns, drew forth her warmest admiration—till, at an unlucky moment, as her head was stretched out of one of the windows of the cabin, pursuing with her eyes a more than ordinary rich vessel, which was rowing ahead of the gondola on board of which she herself was, her highly-prized hat fell from her head into the water, and in a sudden effort which she made to recover it, she plunged head forwards into the river.

The Conte, who was at some distance from her, but who heard her fall, uttering her name, accompanied with a cry of the utmost affliction, darted towards the spot, and was on the point of throwing himself in after her, doubtless with the vain hope of being able to act towards her preservation, and forgetting, at the moment, that he was a stranger to the art of swimming, which his servants remembering, withheld him from his purpose.

Meanwhile several gondoliers from other vessels, who were acquainted that the gondola from which the child had fallen belonged to a man able to reward their services, had jumped in to her rescue; but their endeavours were all secondary to those of a gentleman, who had sprung into the tide from an opposite gondola, on seeing the joint distress of the father and child, and who now replaced her in her parent's arms, and was then lifted by the gondoliers into the Conte's vessel.

In those wild exclamations of joy and gratitude, which the sight of a child suddenly snatched from death naturally drew united from the lips of the happy parent, the Conte poured forth the ecstacies of his soul, snatching only a single moment from his bliss, to order his gondoliers instantly to row back to his Palazzo.

The unknown Signor who had been the instrument of Flavia's preservation, requested to be allowed to return to the gondola from which he had sprung to her rescue; but Della Piacca would admit of no refusal to his going with him to his Palazzo, and having immediate attention paid to the changing of his clothes, and the administering of such comforts as were likely to preserve him from becoming himself a sufferer from his humanity.

Averilla was still alone, reading, in the apartment where the Conte and Flavia had so lately left her, when a servant, who had accompanied them on their voyage, ran hastily into the room, and begged the Contessa would not be alarmed, on account of his Lord and the dear little Signora Flavia being returned so soon, for that they were both well now; only the dear little Signora had had the misfortune to fall into the water, from which she had been drawn out by a Signor, a stranger.

On hearing this account, Averilla immediately flew out of the apartment, to order another dress of Flavia's directly to be warmed, which she might, with all expedition, change for that now upon her.

As she passed a window of the corridor, which looked into the garden, she saw the Conte running towards the house with Flavia in his arms, and a gentleman following him, whose dripping clothes, left no doubt that he was the rescuer of the Conte's daughter, and whom, to her surprise, she immediately recognized to be Sylvio di Rosalva.

So greatly astonished was she at beholding him, that, anxious as she was to provide for the safety of Flavia, she could not forbear stepping back to take a second look at him, and assure herself that she had not been mistaken in his person: she was now convinced that she had not, and moved on towards Flavia's chamber.

Hither the Conte almost immediately followed her, with Flavia still in his arms. The child had been greatly alarmed; and from terror and cold united, she still wept. On being received to the arms of Averilla, her anxieties suffered a very material abatement.

"Have I not cause, my Averilla, to praise God for the rescue of my child from an untimely death?" exclaimed the Conte.

"Blessed be heaven, that she still lives to us, my husband," replied the Contessa. "Fear not that I will, with every possible care and tenderness, attend to her welfare. Do you, meanwhile, issue your commands that every attention be shewn to her preserver."

"Can you doubt that I should be deficient in active gratitude to the man to whom I owe the life of my child?" asked the Conte, leaving the apartment.

"Do you know who her preserver is?" asked Averilla, in a tone of voice that, for an instant, stayed his steps.

"Do you?" he hastily returned.

"No other," replied the Contessa, "than the Signor Sylvio di Rosalva, of whom I spoke to you the other evening."

"Merciful heaven! can this be possible?" exclaimed the Conte.

"It is he, indeed," replied the Contessa; "and an opportunity now presents itself to you, for entering into friendship with him on your own account."

"Is it possible!" again ejaculated the Conte, and hastily left the chamber of his child, to visit his guest.

In a very short time, the physician, who was in the habit of attending the family of Della Piacca, arrived, in compliance with the summons of the Conte, that Flavia, whether she required his assistance or not, might have the benefit of his advice, as a preventative against the effects of the water.

The physician ordered her to be put to bed; and said, that if she could be induced to sleep, and compose herself after the fright she had undergone, no danger was to be apprehended from her recent accident.

Averilla having left Flavia to the care of her own female attendants, went down with her husband and the physician into the apartment to which she was informed Sylvio had just been conducted, from the chamber where he had exchanged his own wet clothes for a suit of the Conte's.

On entering the apartment, Della Piacca said—"I need not, Signor Sylvio, introduce you to my wife; I bring her hither to be a witness to my telling you, that every hour which it can give you any pleasure to pass in this house, will be an addition of happiness to us."

"And I," added Averilla, "can only repeat, that if it were possible for any occurrence to strengthen the friendship I before entertained for you, it is the service you have this day rendered him, whom it is my pride and felicity to call husband, in the preservation of his child."

Sylvio replied with courtesy to these acknowledgements, and said—"That the act of humanity he had just had an opportunity of performing, was one of which the self-satisfaction was increased, by its having contributed so materially to the felicity of persons who so condescendingly acknowledged the obligation, and that he should very soon do himself the pleasure of calling at the Palazzo, to enquire after the health of Flavia;"—and with these words he took up his hat from the table.

"Nay, nay," said the Conte, "we cannot so immediately suffer the minister of our happiness to leave us; favour us by giving us your company this evening—I can admit of no ceremonious excuses. Our introduction was such as must be allowed at once to remove all the distance of formality between us."

"I should, with much pleasure, accept your invitation," returned Sylvio; "but I have an appointment about this hour, which I cannot break."

"If it is with a lady, I can have nothing further to say, than to hope the service you have rendered me has not curtailed you of many moments of happiness," replied the Conte.

"But if I were to venture to say, that I think the appointment is not with a lady," said the Contessa, smiling, "would you, Signor Sylvio, indulge a lady, by deferring your attendance till another evening?"

"My appointment, Contessa," answered Sylvio with gravity, "I candidly confess to be with a lady; and that one of no other nature should make me seem thus reluctant to improve my acquaintance with those in whose society I have now the pleasure of being, at this first opportunity which presents itself to me for so doing."

"Not a word more can be said then," rejoined the Conte. "I hope some other means than words will quickly present themselves to me, for repaying your disinterested action; meanwhile, let us see you as often as it does not interfere with your pleasanter pursuits to visit us. Farewell, dear Signor!—give me your hand at parting."

"And me too," added Averilla. "You know my husband desires us to be friends; therefore, you will pay me a very ill compliment in not attending to his invitation. So farewell—all happiness attend you till we meet again."

Sylvio returned their compliments with expressions of the utmost politeness, and then left the Palazzo della Piacca.

When he was gone, the Conte said—"The Signor Sylvio is a man of the most engaging manners: I am certain that my first acquaintance with him would have prejudiced me in his favour, had I never heard his name mentioned before I had seen him; or had we met with any other feelings than those which arose out of humanity on the one side, and gratitude on the other."

"Indeed I think so," said the physician; "and yet, if report speaks true, we see him to disadvantage at present: a man cannot appear in the most favourable point of view, whose thoughts are absent, as are those of every lover; and I have heard it very confidently asserted that he visits the daughter of a merchant named Eldorado."

"As her suitor?" asked Averilla.

"Yes, Contessa, so it is said: it is certain that he goes a good deal to the house; and Eldorado is a man in such a situation in life, that it must be honourable love which forms the motives of his visits."

"He deserves happiness, in whatever shape he can meet it," replied the Contessa.

The conversation was here interrupted by one of the attendants whom Averilla had left with Flavia, coming into the apartment, and saying that her young Lady had fallen asleep.

"That is well," said the physician; "you need now entertain no further fears for her safety; she will, I doubt not, wake in perfect health and composure;" and with this consolatory prophecy he took his leave.

CHAPTER XII

THE Conte and Contessa conversed together till a late hour, upon the accident which had so unaccountably introduced Sylvio di Rosalva to the acquaintance of the former; and the Contessa said—"That if it was allowable to find delight in the good which arose out of evil, she could not but express herself pleased, that the Signor Sylvio had been introduced to the Conte in a manner which must interest him in his favour on his own account, and take off from her the weight of the prejudice with which she had wished, still had felt averse, to inspire him, for the object of his gratitude."

They both visited the chamber of Flavia before they retired to rest, and found her buried in the lap of peaceful slumber.

On the following morning Flavia was so much recovered, that about noon the Contessa, who was tempted by the fineness of the day to believe that the air would be of service both to her and her adopted daughter, ordered her carriage, for the purpose of a ride.

During the period of her absence from home, the Signor Sylvio di Rosalva called to enquire after the health of Flavia, and was received by the Conte, who with all the rapture with which his sight really inspired him, presented to him a ring of gold, in which a beautiful antique was set, and which he begged him to wear in remembrance of her whose life he had preserved.

Signor Sylvio replied, that he accepted the ring with pleasure, not as deeming the merits of his exertion on the preceding day to have been equal to a reward of that costly nature, but as a token which would constantly remind him that he was honoured with the friendship of the Conte della Piacca.

After about an hour passed in social conversation, the Conte said—"I cannot admit this call as a visit; neither have you today seen the Contessa, a circumstance which I am sure she will regret. Will you dine with us to-morrow? I will invite a few of my particular friends to meet you."

"To-morrow," replied Di Rosalva, "I am engaged; will you accept of me on the following day? I make this offer, that you may not judge me unwilling to accept the invitation, which it gives me great happiness to have offered to me."

"The next day," the Conte said, "I shall expect you."

On the return of the Contessa from her ride, her husband informed her what had passed in her absence; and invitations were immediately dispatched to some of the nearest relatives and most intimate friends of the Conte, to meet the Signor who had signalized himself by the courage and humanity he had displayed on the day of the fête upon the water, in the cause of the little Flavia.

The Contessa believed herself to have gained more strength since her late indisposition than she really had done, and her morning ride had so much fatigued her, that the moment the dinner was removed, she was obliged to retire to a couch which stood in a recess at one end of the apartment; as she had said that she did not feel inclined to sleep, but merely wished for the relief of a reclined posture. The Conte had taken Flavia upon his knee, and was reading to her the marvelous history of the famed Riquet with his Tuft. Suddenly he was interrupted by the Contessa's uttering a deep sigh, which almost approached to a shriek; he ran hastily to her, and found that she had fainted.

He directly called for assistance, and in a short time Averilla was restored to sense, but complained of being ill, and desired to be led to her chamber. Her wish was instantly complied with, while the Conte sent to seek the physician.

On his arrival he found her already undressed, and in bed; after a few moments passed in observation, he pronounced that the fright which she had received from Flavia's accident had produced a very powerful effect on her spirits, which were at the time weakened by her late illness, and that her relief would consist in a premature release from a burden of nature, which she had borne nearly four months.

A couple of hours verified the physician's prediction, and in two more he pronounced, that if the Contessa was kept perfectly quiet, and every care taken to restore her strength, not the slightest danger was to be apprehended on her account.

When the Conte entered her chamber, she called him to her bedside, and said—"Fear not for me; I feel that I shall not sink under my present illness; and console yourself with the idea, that your daughter lives to repay to you your present disappointment of an heir."

"Believe me," dearest Averilla, replied the Conte, "I feel no concern but for the re-establishment of your health."

"And do you, in turn, believe me," she said, "that nothing will so much conduce to the re-establishment of my health, as knowing you to be happy, and not curtailed of any pleasure by my confinement; promise me, therefore, that you will receive the friends whom you expect to visit you the day after to-morrow, exactly the same as if I were able to divide with you the pleasing task of giving them welcome; indulge me by not letting them know any thing of my indisposition till they arrive; and then attribute my not appearing among them to a return of the cold under which they know I have for some time laboured."

"You have so kind, so irresistible a way of persuading me to be happy," replied the Conte, "that I am convinced it must constitute some part of your felicity to see me won to your wishes; it shall therefore be as you desire."

The Contessa was on the third day so well, in her own idea, that if she had followed her inclination, she would perhaps have mixed for an hour or more with the Conte's guests; but her physician strongly enjoined her not to attempt leaving her chamber for several days, and she willingly agreed to comply with his advice; as she dreaded to incur any danger which might give a moment's unnecessary anxiety to a husband by whom she was so tenderly beloved.

At the appointed hour the company assembled; Averilla received from the Signoras messages of their grief at not beholding her one of the happy party; and from the Signors, the most well-dressed compliments for her speedy recovery; and with these, and the accidental visits of Flavia, she consoled her solitude.

In the evening, before the guests were yet departed, a letter was brought into her chamber by one of her attendants. She inquired whence it came, and was informed, that a young man, apparently a servant, had just brought it to the Palazzo.

It was directed to the Contessa della Piacca; the hand-writing was one which Averilla remembered to have seen before, but could not immediately recollect where, or whose it was. The impression of the seal was one she was not acquainted with. Having once more looked at the direction, she broke open the letter. Some large letters at the top of the paper immediately attracted her attention: They expressed these words:—

"Remember your vow to Sylvio di Rosalva. *If any one be near you at the moment you open this, forbear to read it till you are alone.*"

Averilla was alone, for her attendant was gone into the adjoining apartment, and she therefore went on perusing the contents; they were these:—

"Dearest Averilla, single friend of the care-worn bosom of Sylvio di Rosalva, with how great anxiety do I desire the conversation of an hour with you! Much have I experienced since I saw you last at the Villa del Alvaretti, much of sorrow, much of pain, and one solitary sunbeam of hope has now shed its influence on my hitherto dreary path of life. But much still remains to be weighed and considered, before I dare venture to place faith in what may only prove a delusion to

my senses. I have already borne so much calamity, that a disappointment in this last hope would, I think, deprive me of the power to feel
any more. This you will perhaps think I ought to consider as the most
acceptable alleviation of my miseries—to close them to death. But the
greatest wretch still clings with eagerness to life; a hope of something
better still to come, cheers the most desponding, and makes unwel-
come the approach of death, if even they are sufficiently unacquainted with their own real sentiments, to have prayed for him in the hour
of trouble. Certain as I feel myself, that from the interest you have
already displayed in my fate, you will afford me the best of counsel
in my present state, between doubt and hope, I ask to see you. I dare
not approach you with the knowledge of your husband; I am, as you
know from circumstances, nervous, weak, and perhaps foolish; you
must therefore grant me this conference unknown to him. Indulge
me, dear Averilla, in this my request, I entreat you, by the friendship
you have declared yourself to feel for me. Name where, and at what
time, I may see you, as I shall not remain in this city longer than till I
have conversed with you. Direct your answer for me at the Hotel of
the Holy Virgin, where my servant will be upon the watch to receive it.

"Farewell, dear Averilla! and believe me most gratefully yours,

"SYLVIO DI ROSALVA."

As Sylvio had been told from the Conte's own lips, that he ap-
proved of his friendship for his wife, and as he was at this moment
a guest of the Conte's, in his own Palazzo, Averilla could only guess
that something more than she was acquainted with in his fate had
occurred to him since their interview in the chapel of Saint Francis,
in the village del Alvaretti, upon which he had no one to advise him
but herself; and that he might still be afraid lest a conference held
in private with her should excite the jealousy of the Conte Lorenzo,
and thus rob him of his friendship, and of such opportunities as he
should now frequently enjoy of being in her society;—she accordingly
returned him an answer in these words:—

"DEAR SYLVIO,

"Whatever benefit you may conceive it possible that my advice is
capable of conferring on you, or whatever consolation you can gain
in your misfortunes from the sympathy of my heart, shall ever be at

your command. Till I leave my chamber, where I am now confined by indisposition, I cannot, however, grant you the conference you require; in the course of a few days, I hope to be again at liberty, when I will appoint a time for you to call on me during the absence of my husband from the Palazzo; and sincerely do I desire that our interview may realize the shadow of hope which now plays upon your senses.

"Farewell, dearest Sylvio; believe me your sincere and constant friend,

"AVERILLA DELLA PIACCA."

Fearing that from some mistake of the servants, this note might be given to Sylvio in the presence of her husband, as the messenger employed to take it to the Hotel of the Holy Virgin might deem his walk an unnecessary trouble, when he to whom it was directed was in the house from which he was going to carry it, she waited till she had learnt that all the guests were departed, and then ordered somebody to be sent with it to the place whither Sylvio himself had ordered it to be brought.

"The Signor Sylvio is undoubtedly in love," said the Conte to Averilla, when he came into her apartment, "as our friend the physician informed us; he has throughout the day been very thoughtful, and when I occasionally rallied him upon his absence, he started into fits of assumed gaiety, which served but to expose the real state of his heart."

Averilla smiled in silence at this conclusion on the part of her husband.

"When the wine was circulating," continued the Conte, "he sat next to me, and I whispered in his ear, that the passion which it had been hinted to me he entertained for a certain fair one in this city, would cause many a sigh to a female friend of mine."

"Indeed!" he replied, "pray who is the Signora who, in your opinion, will so far honour me?"

"Do you not remember," said I, "a pretty girl, whom you relieved from the embarrassment of her carriage breaking down with her, upon the side of a mountain in the chain of Tortona?"

"I recollect the lady's accident," he returned.

"And she," said I, "remembers nothing of it but your coming to her assistance. Her name is Virgilia della Bagua."

"Fate smiles upon me," he replied, "and causes my slender benefits to be too highly rated by all to whom I have the good fortune to be serviceable; you are yourself," he added smiling, "the very example of the rest."

"And this said, he gave a turn to the conversation. So that I find," continued the Conte, "our fair friend, Virgilia, must submit to the disappointment of her first love, if, with a giddy girl like her, it is her first, which I much doubt; for the Signor di Rosalva appears immoveably attached to the planet he worships."

"Did he speak of her?" asked Averilla.

"No, he did not," replied the Conte; "nor did I more than hint at my knowledge of his having become the captive of love's fetters; but he bore those hints with a complacency and composure which gave me no reason to suppose that they were otherwise than pleasing to him."

"I hope, amidst all his forgetfulness, he did not omit to enquire for me," said Averilla.

"No, no, be assured he enquired for you in the most particular terms," returned the Conte.

"Did he leave you before the rest of your guests?" asked the Contessa.

"Oh no," replied Della Piacca; "why do you imagine he did?"

"I only supposed he might do so, in order to pay a visit to the planet of his devotions, as you are pleased to term the lady he visits," returned Averilla.

"There is time for half an hour's chat with her yet," rejoined the Conte, "it is not so late."

Averilla believed him to be very differently employed, and could only suppose that as he had not known of her indisposition till he had arrived at the Palazzo to dinner, and his letter had been brought to her during the time of his visit, he had intended that it should be given her while he was a guest in the house, in order that no idea might be entertained by the Conte of its having come from him.

CHAPTER XIII

SOME days passed on, during which the Contessa heard no more of Sylvio di Rosalva. It was still judged prudent that she should not quit her chamber, and the Conte went alone to pay a visit to a nobleman in the vicinity of the city.

On his return home, the Contessa enquired whether the Signor di Rosalva had made one of the party?

"No," replied the Conte; "but I have seen him to-day; I caught merely a glimpse of him this morning, in a carriage which mine passed upon the road; and I do not even believe he saw me at all, on account of the rapid rate at which my horses were moving; for he did not return my bow, or at least not till I was out of sight, if he did at all; I perceived that there was an old lady in the carriage with him."

"Describe to me the old lady who was with him," said Averilla eagerly.

The Conte replied, that the hasty view he had caught of her was very unfavourable to a description; but still he gave one of her, to the best of his ability.

"You have told me enough," replied the Contessa, "for me to understand that his companion was a most amiable old lady, who lived with him when he resided in the neighbourhood of Genoa; her circumstances are indifferent, and she owes the comforts of life to his kindness: but she must, on that account, not be entirely overlooked; I must invite her to pass a day with us, when I am sufficiently recovered to call upon her for that purpose."

"I am surprised," said the Conte, "that if this old lady, whom you mention, resides with him, he is not in private lodgings; he lives at an hotel."

"That of the Holy Virgin, is it not?" asked Averilla.

"No," returned the Conte Lorenzo; "it is at the hotel of the good Samaritan that he resides."

The Contessa made no reply, but felt inwardly surprised at the direction which she had received, to send her letter to the hotel of the Holy Virgin.

Three days more restored Averilla so perfectly to her usual strength, that on the fourth she met her husband in the breakfast apartment; and hearing from him that he should pass his morning in riding to an estate which he possessed at some distance from the city, she resolved to send to Sylvio, and acquaint him that she should be alone till dinner time.

While they were yet at breakfast, the Major-domo of the Palazzo entered the apartment, and addressed his master by saying, that a few minutes before, as he was going into the city, he had met the servant of the Signor Sylvio di Rosalva, who was running with all possible speed towards the Palazzo della Piacca, to request the Conte would so far honour his master as to come to him immediately, if in his power.

"What is the matter?" hastily enquired the Conte. "What has happened to him?"

"That I have not had time to learn," replied the Major-domo; "all I know is, that the Signor di Rosalva is summoned to appear before the court of justice which is now sitting."

"Whatever his case, my services are his due," said the Conte, "I will lose no time in going to him."

He took up his hat, and with a hasty farewell to Averilla, departed.

The Contessa called back the Major-domo, as he was following his master out of the room.

"Are you indeed ignorant, Bernardo," she said, "what is the occasion of the Signor di Rosalva's being called before the tribunal of justice?"

"I am, indeed, Contessa," replied Bernardo.

"Do me the favour to learn as quickly as you possibly can. I have a most material reason for wishing to know," rejoined Averilla, "Pray use expedition."

Bernardo promised he would do so, and left the room.

In about half an hour he returned. "I have discovered the cause of the Signor di Rosalva's summons," he said.

"Explain! explain!" cried Averilla.

"He is going to be tried," returned the Major-domo, "for a breach of a promise of marriage."

"A breach of a promise of marriage!" echoed Averilla. "Impossible! Bernardo, impossible!"

"Indeed it is confidently affirmed to be so, Signora," replied the Major-domo.

"And with whom was this promise contracted?" asked Averilla.

"I have not heard the name of his accuser, nor her rank," answered Bernardo.

"It cannot be," said Averilla, suppressing a smile.

"I am told his own hand-writing, signed to the promise, will be brought in evidence against him," returned Bernardo.

"Try what more information you can gain, and bring it to me," said Averilla.

The Major-domo bowed, and was retiring.

"But I am sure it is impossible!" again exclaimed Averilla.

The Major-domo stared, bowed again, and left the room.

When the Conte della Piacca arrived at the apartments of Sylvio, he found him in conversation with a gentleman whom he knew to be a practiser of the law; the moment he entered Sylvio approached him, and said—"Do you, Signor, pardon me the liberty I have taken?"

"I can pardon you for any thing," returned the Conte, "but calling that a liberty which is your right, by the law of gratitude; my services belong to you, and I am never so happy as when my friends account my exertions worth their seeking."

"The only assistance which it is in your power to afford me," replied Sylvio, "in my present dilemma, is that of granting your countenance to me, and allowing me to shew to the world, that stranger as I am here, and indeed almost every where else, from the peculiarity of circumstances which have attended me from my birth, I am not entirely without friends."

"What, my dear Signor," asked the Conte Lorenzo, "is the nature of the dilemma in which you stand?"

"One," replied the lawyer, "in which I hope the villany of those who have led him into it, will meet a due exposure and punishment; but I must confess that it is a case of which the event cannot be guessed till it is tried. I do not wish to flatter those who seek my advice—it is my maxim always to tell them exactly my sentiments; and I own that, where a man's hand-writing can be produced in evidence against him, as in the case of my client, however innocent his friends may know him to be, it is a very difficult matter to substantiate his innocence, in opposition to such an apparent proof to the contrary."

"You have not yet told me," said the Conte della Piacca, "of what nature the accusation preferred against him is."

"That of a breach of a promise of marriage," replied the lawyer.

"Which promise, I suppose, was never made," returned the Conte, addressing Sylvio.

"Not to the woman who now claims its performance," replied Sylvio. "I have, I freely confess, signed my name to a promise of marriage; but she who would now exact from me the performance of it, is not——"

The door opened, and Sylvio's servant entering, said the messenger from the court was arrived, to say, that the cause which had preceded Sylvio's was ended, and his presence immediately required.

Sylvio and his friends directly obeyed the summons: in their way thither, Sylvio continued in conversation with his lawyer, from whom he was receiving directions for his conduct; and the Conte Lorenzo was, therefore, obliged to await the formal procedure of the court for gratifying his excited curiosity.

They entered the court, and repaired to their appointed stations; and the rank and character of the Conte della Piacca were so universally known and respected, that no opposition was made to his accompanying Di Rosalva to the bar, at which he was to be arraigned.

In the course of a few minutes, the forms necessary to the opening of the cause were gone through: from these it merely appeared that Rodovina Maritos was about to sue for reparation to be made to her daughter Vitellia, a minor, by Sylvio di Rosalva, for having refused to fulfil towards her, a promise of marriage which he had made to her.

This done, Rodovina Maritos was first called upon to substantiate her charge, and she immediately entered the court.

To the eye of a common observer, Rodovina would probably have appeared to have exceeded her sixtieth year; but one better skilled in those physical causes which produce the appearance of age, would easily have discerned that she had not passed her fiftieth. Her figure was tall and thin; her bones were large, and, from the scantiness of the flesh which covered them, the grey veins were remarkably conspicuous both on her neck and arms. It was evident that she had once been handsome; her countenance was a wreck of charms, to the preservation of which no attention had been paid. In her eyes, which were black, and to which long eye-lashes gave a peculiar character of darkness, were alike discernable cunning, frailty, and ferocity. Her dress was that of a person in the middle rank of life, but put on in a manner that bespoke her to have been accustomed to display her person to the best advantage.

"Are you Rodovina Maritos?" asked the judge.

"I am," she replied, in a firm tone of voice, which bordered as much upon the masculine as did her person.

"And you appear here," said the judge, "to sue for reparation to your daughter Vitellia, from Sylvio di Rosalva, for his refusing to perform a promise of marriage, which you say he has made to her?"

"I do," replied Rodovina.

"But," returned the judge, "before you can attempt to demand reparation for his neglect to perform this promise, you must first prove that the promise was made. Can you do that?"

"Most satisfactorily," answered Rodovina. "I have the marriage promise, in writing, about me, to which his name is signed with his own hand."

She was ordered to produce it, and it was given to the judge. After some moments, during which he had cast his eyes in silence over the paper, he read aloud the contents.

"We, the undersigned, do solemnly bind ourselves to become united to each other by the holy bond of matrimony, immediately after the death of Henrico Eldorado; and if we do either of us secede from this agreement, we declare ourselves willing to abide by such penalty as the laws may have the authority of imposing on us.

(Signed) Sylvio di Rosalva.

Vitellia Maritos.

Witness, Rodovina Maritos."

March 13, 1707.

"Do you allow this to be your handwriting?" asked the judge, addressing Sylvio.

"I do," Sylvio replied.

"If you also allow that it was not extorted from you by threats or force, I have nothing further to do but to enquire in what degree the daughter of the plaintiff is a sufferer by the failure of your promise, and to pronounce what reward the law adjudges her."

"I do also allow," replied Sylvio, "that my signature was not extorted from me, either by threats or force; but still I trust, that my cause is not yet deduced to the moment of pronouncing sentence. Arts of the most reprehensible nature have been used to draw me into a connection, at which the heart of a man of honour would shrink back with horror. I believed myself to be addressing a woman of virtue, of family, and of perfect manners: on the contrary, I discovered myself to have been duped into a connection with an acknowledged courtezan, the daughter of one by whose example she has been led to infamy, and whose conduct to me has, throughout, been that of the most skilful hypocrisy! As a man, I stand in the world upon an inequality with my fellows; I have no relation whom I can call upon to speak in my defence—for so peculiar has been my fate, that it is but a few months that I have known my own name; who were my parents, I shall perhaps never be able to learn. Thus situated, it is but natural to conclude that my friends must be few, as I could have no means of attaching any one to me but by such acts of my conduct as I have accidentally, during my short acquaintance with the world, been able to gain the favour of strangers by. Thus circumstanced, I think you will perceive that I have more claim upon the protection of the law, than those who do not stand equally alone in society. Permit me, therefore, to recount to you, every circumstance of my acquaintance with this woman and her daughter; and let her then, if she can, controvert the charges which I shall throw upon her."

Rodovina cast a glance of malignity at Sylvio, and then turned her eye, with an insolent security of expression, to the paper in the hands of the judge.

The judge spoke thus:—"As you have no relatives to appear in your cause, and as the opinion of the law is always materially governed by the repute which any individual, who comes under its inspection, bears in the world, you must, in this instance, become your own historian; and from the apparent artlessness, or duplicity of your tale, I must endeavour to gather my judgement, upon your innocence, or culpability, of the charge now brought against you."

"As the retirement in which I have lived from the world, till within the last eight months of my life," replied Sylvio, "must materially plead in my favour, for not having earlier discovered the arts to which I have been a dupe, I must request permission to preface my account of such transactions as are immediately connected with the charge now brought against me, with a few sentences relative to the former years of my existence."

The prepossessing countenance of Sylvio, added to the manly and open manner in which he spoke of himself, interested the judge in his favour; and he directed him to begin his account, promising that he should not be interrupted in his narrative.

CHAPTER XIV

"THE twenty-two years of my life," Sylvio began, "previously to my coming to Turin, were marked with less adventure than has signalized each day since my arrival here.

"The first I can recollect of myself was, that I lived on the mountains of Tortona, with an aged man, whose manners and education were of a far superior nature to that of the peasantry amongst whom we resided. His almost constant employment was to impart to me, through the medium of such books as he possessed, some part of that knowledge with which his own mind was stored. He seemed to be extremely fond of me, and, at times, regarded me with a rapturous expression of countenance, which usually sunk, after a few moments indulgence, into an evident anxiety, and lowness of spirits, which I at the time saw without reflecting upon, but which has caused me some thought since his death.

"A few hours before his departure from life, as I sat by his bedside, he addressed me, by saying—'I am not the good man you believe me to be; my youth was vicious, my maturer age far otherwise than free from error; and the only act upon which I found my hope of eternal pardon from the Distributor of Justice, is, that I have omitted to perform the nefarious deed against you, for which my services were bought. I was hired to murder you. I received, as my reward, an immense sum of gold; and at the moment it was paid to me, I entertained the idea of being faithful to my employer: But the interposition of Heaven preserved me from the horrid act; and you from the weapon of your destined destroyer.

'Poverty was the spur which goaded me into the promise of performing the vile deed; but no sooner was the sum, adjudged me as the recompense of the crime, paid to me, than the mercy of Heaven inspired my breast with the consideration, that the sum I had received for your death was sufficient to ensure a comfortable existence both to you and me, to the end of our days; and that, by preserving you to enjoy with me, the little independence I had become possessed of, I should be making my peace with Heaven for my past misdeeds.

'If I have not suffered you to live to the extent of such enjoyment as the ability of my purse would have enabled me to have permitted you to do, believe that it proceeded from motives of kindness to yourself, in order that I might have the larger sum to bequeath you at my death, at which moment I had ever resolved to impart to you the secret of your birth.'

"But, alas!" said Sylvio, interrupting himself in his narrative, "my kind old friend had too long delayed the disclosure of my history. He had, for many days, been very ill, when he addressed to me the words I have just recounted to you; and he had become so considerably weakened by the exertion, that when, after a short pause, he endeavoured to resume his story, the power of utterance was lost to him: he immediately pointed to a pen, which I brought him, with some paper that lay upon the table. With a trembling hand he wrote down—'Your name is Sylvio di Rosalva—your father is——.' A deep groan expressed him lamenting his inability to write more; the pen fell from his hand; and although his existence was protracted several hours, his power of speech did not return to him. He died on the following morning in my arms."

Sylvio here paused a moment, while he wiped away the tear which had sprung from his heart, as a tribute to the memory of his deceased benefactor; it was an offering of gratitude to the ashes of the merciful, in which almost every one present joined him.

To the Conte Lorenzo alone, there appeared a mystery in his account of himself, which had the appearance of a deviation from truth. It was true that Virgilia della Bagua had seen him living as a peasant on the mountains of Tortona; and that Averilla herself had not been surprised at this account of him, as it was after his departure from the Villa di Rosalva: but previously to that time it had not appeared, from Averilla's acquaintance with him, that he had ever lived any where but at the Villa di Rosalva; and he now declared his whole existence, with the exception of the few last months, to have been passed on the mountains. It was undoubtedly strange, the Conte considered; but still this contradiction might be only a necessary part of the mystery, in which Averilla had so often declared he was doomed to live; and he, therefore, resolved, that, in order to preserve a due regard for the promise he had made to his Contessa respecting Sylvio, it became him not to remark on this incongruity to any one but herself.

Sylvio continued speaking thus:—

"About a month after the death of him whom I shall ever consider in the light of a parent, I collected the sum of money which he had bequeathed to me at his decease; and coming with it to this city, I placed it in the hands of a banker, from whom I found that it was sufficient to support me in a comfortable state of independence. Previously to my coming to Turin, I had held many debates with my own mind, whether I should pass by my real name, or adopt a feigned one. I had, doubtless, enemies abroad—at least I must have had, as my deceased friend had himself been hired to become my murderer: but this was twenty-two years ago; all those to whose interest my removal from the stage of existence might then have been, were now, perhaps, no more. At all events, I was at an age to defend myself against villany; the concealment of my real name might, in my intercourse with the world, prove to me a material detriment; and, therefore, I resolved boldly to confess myself for the person I was.

"A few weeks after my arrival here, as I was one day at my devotions in the church of Saint Luke, my eyes fell on a countenance which pleased me more than any set of features I had yet beheld. I visited the same church on the following day, and the day after. On the third from my first beholding her, she appeared at vespers, on the same spot where I had before seen her. I resolved, if possible, to learn who she was; and as I saw no very easy means of conversing with her, I determined on watching her home, in the hope that an acquaintance with the place of her abode might let me into the secret of her name.

"She was accompanied by the old woman who appears here as my accuser, on whose arm she leaned, and who frequently turned back her head, as I supposed, to observe whether I was following her. As they moved on at a very quick pace, I began to fear my pursuing them was objected to, and I was often on the point of turning back, or stopping; but my curiosity got the better of every other feeling, and I still continued to walk within a few yards of them.

"At length they entered a handsome house in the street of Saint John, and I saw no more of them that day. The next morning, when in conversation with some of my acquaintance, I enquired who lived at the house I had seen them enter, and was told that it belonged to an old merchant, named Signor Eldorado, one of the greatest misers in all Italy, whose family consisted of one son and one daughter; that the son was gone to reside in Naples, on some property which had devolved to him in the right of his deceased mother; and that the daughter, Lucia, was kept the close prisoner of her father's house, with the exception only of being allowed accidentally to go to church, as he did not choose she should be seen, lest any one should fall in love with her, and propose for her hand in marriage, as he had resolved not to portion her off during his lifetime.

"I did not feel dismayed by this account; I judged that, if we could by any means find an opportunity of becoming acquainted, if she thought as well of me as I did of her, we might easily reconcile ourselves to the necessity of waiting till the death of her father for the completion of our wishes, as we should, meanwhile, be kept happy in the security of each other's affections.

"It must be almost unnecessary to say, that having, till within the few last months, known nothing of the world but from such accounts of it as I had received from my deceased preceptor, I was as unequal to cope with its inhabitants as every one must be, who has not had the benefit, either of observation upon its manners, example of the conduct necessary to be observed on its stage, or of experience in treading its winding paths.

"I never omitted going regularly to vespers in the church of Saint Luke, or of passing frequently, every day, the house of Signor Eldorado. At length, I one day met the old woman, whom I had constantly seen at vespers with the object of my passion, coming out of the house. I bowed to her, and muttered some incoherent words as a first introduction, to which she dropped me a low courtesy; and I then said—'Does your beautiful lady go to vespers this afternoon?'

'I can't exactly say, Signor,' she replied, 'whether my lady and I shall be there to-day or not.'

'I am very sorry for that,' I returned; 'I had hoped to feast my eyes by beholding her there. Do me the favour to express to her the regret of the Signor Sylvio di Rosalva, at his disappointment, and accept this piece of money for yourself—and I put into her hand a zechin as I spoke.

'Is your name Di Rosalva—Sylvio di Rosalva?' returned the old dame.

'Yes,' said I, 'does it surprise you?'

'Oh no,' replied she, 'I am only thinking you are a very handsome man, with a very handsome name; and that if my lady sees you with the eyes I do, she must love you as much as you love her.'

'I am infinitely obliged to you for your compliment,' returned I, laughing; 'but when do you think she will again go to mass or vespers?'

'Not to-day, nor to-morrow,' replied she; 'but I'll tell you what— meet me here to-morrow, about this time, or an hour later, and I will let you know at what time you may expect to catch a glimpse of her.'

'I will certainly be here,' I returned; 'but tell me, my good woman—I know you saw me, both at vespers, and in the street, after they were concluded—did your lady see me too?'

'Now you want me to make a confession of all my lady said, about your face, your shape, your teeth, and your well-made leg!' exclaimed she; 'but don't think you shall get all that out of Rodovina at first acquaintance—no, no, Signor!'

"Which words she spoke in a tone that fully convinced me that Lucia had thought of me as I had done of her, but had not wished me to know that I had made an impression upon her heart, before we either of us had heard the sound of the other's voice.

'Well, Rodovina,' replied I, overjoyed at this discovery of her mistress's sentiments—for this was my first love, and therefore nothing need to be said of its warmth—'depend on it, I will not repeat your confession to your mistress; do all you can to represent me in an amiable light to the divine Lucia, and you shall find me an excellent friend.'

'Lucia!' returned Rodovina.

'Yes, Lucia is the name of your master's daughter, of the divine Signora I saw with you at vespers—is it not?' I asked.

'Oh, to be sure,' replied Rodovina.

'But you seemed to repeat the name after me in surprise,' said I.

'And might I not well be surprised to hear you call her any thing but an angel, or a divinity, or something of that kind?' returned Rodovina.

"I smiled, and agreed with her in her remark.

'Well, farewell, Signor; be true to your appointment to-morrow, and see what I will do for you, if I can, between this and then.'

"With this promise Rodovina went her way, and I went mine, sufficiently pleased that my first advances towards the heart of a woman of character had met with so flattering a reception.

"I was punctual, the next day, to my appointment with Rodovina, and waited for her but a few minutes at the place of appointment, before she came to me.

'Your servant, Signor,' said she; 'but you know not what risks I run in coming out to speak to you: should your Lucia's father discover our meetings, I know not what would be the event of it; but she is as earnest, I must confess, as you can be, that I should be true to my word, and therefore I have ventured.'

'Well, then,' said I, 'when may I hope for the happiness of beholding her again?'

'To-morrow morning,' she replied, 'she will go to mass, and you may see her as she leaves the church of Saint Luke; but I should almost advise you not to address her for some time; but if you do, I must charge you, on no account, to repeat to her my foolish confessions about her having avowed an affection for you—for she is delicate in the extreme; a word too much on the score of love is more likely to offend her than a volume too little; and if you once disoblige her, you will find it a more difficult matter than you imagine, to reinstate yourself in her favour.'

'Depend on it that I will be careful, for my own sake,' rejoined I, putting, as I spoke, a second piece of gold into her hand.

"She received it with a courteous smile, and something like a nod, and said—'Believe me, Signor, I feel more interested in your happiness than you may perhaps imagine, or can have any just reason for believing, now I tell you so; and this it is that makes me so open with you, as to confess to you the real state of my lady's heart, which she would be angry enough to have divulged at present, as I have already told you. But I speak out to you, because I really think that you were designed for each other by Heaven, and that it is a pity any human obstacle should appear to present itself, for a moment, to the happiness of either of you. I met with a disappointment myself in my youth, which was the event of my being too bashful to speak out my mind boldly, when I was first addressed in the way of love, and I have since that time, done all in my power to prevent others from suffering by the same cause.'"

A smile here ran through the court at the expence of Rodovina, who exclaimed—"How long am I to be detained here, listening to this foolish tale? Can all he may say have the power to efface his signature from the paper I gave the judge? Thus, of what use can attending to him be?"

"In order to enquire under how just an impression he placed his name to that paper," returned the judge: "therefore, if you know yourself innocent of all fraud towards him, every word he speaks will be to the advantage of your suit, and your character. Meanwhile I command you to be silent till he has done."

With a sneer indicative of the most violent anger and discontent, Rodovina let herself fall on a seat behind her.

"We parted as before, after a little farther conversation," continued Di Rosalva; "and on the following morning I was in the church of Saint Luke some time before the celebration of mass commenced. At the moment the organ was pouring forth its first burst of harmony, I saw the object of my passion enter the church, with Rodovina by her side; they took their usual places, and it was nearly half an hour before the eyes of Lucia encountered mine; at the moment they did so, I made her a profound salutation, and she returned it in a complaisant but distant manner.

"On leaving the church I ventured to approach, and for the first time to address her; her replies verified Rodovina's account of her extreme delicacy and diffidence; and when we had reached the extremity of the cloisters through which she passed in her way home, she bade me good morning, and I durst not, at this first interview, disobey what I judged a hint to me to leave her for the present; I accordingly returned her compliment, and withdrew from her.

"As I had made no further appointment with Rodovina, I was constrained to await the next appearance of Lucia at the church of Saint Luke, for gaining any information of her; she came thither again on the third day from our late meeting, and I again joined her as I had before done, as she was leaving the place.

"Our acquaintance was thus carried on for above a month, during which we had never enjoyed the opportunity of conversing together for above ten minutes at a time; the strangeness of her father's disposition was such, she said, that she durst not ask me home with her; nor durst she venture to pass an hour in walking with me in any of the public gardens about the city; as he was well acquainted at what exact time the service of the church ended, that he calculated with equal exactness what time it took her to walk home, and always flew into a most outrageous passion if he thought her half a minute beyond her time. I was glad of enjoying as much of her society as possible, and therefore never missed those opportunities of seeing her which her visits to the church of Saint Luke presented me with; but I had much more that I desired to say to her than those few scanty moments allowed me time for, and I proposed to her the commencement of a correspondence, to which she, with little reluctance, agreed."

CHAPTER XV

"We continued to communicate by letter for full four months, each writing a letter alternately every day, and had bound ourselves, most unequivocally, to become united, on the death of her father, the Signor Eldorado, when I was surprised at not receiving any answer, for three successive days to a letter of mine; during which time, I saw neither Lucia nor Rodovina at the church of Saint Luke, nor the latter any where in the streets, which I had lately very frequently done.

"On the third night of my not receiving the usual intelligence of Lucia's health and welfare from her own hand, I wandered, almost mechanically, towards the spot which contained all I held dear upon earth, the street of Saint John, in which was the house of Signor Eldorado.

"As I stood under the piazza of an adjoining building, I saw two men come out of the house of Eldorado, who, in descending the steps into the street, I could hear conversing in these terms:—'Since you think he cannot live long,' said one of them, 'I shall certainly write the letter I was mentioning to you.'

'I desire you, by all means, to do it,' replied the other. 'If there is nobody of authority upon the spot when he dies, that shameless woman will, in spite of his daughter, rob the house at least.'

"I heard no more—but this was enough to inform me, as I imagined, that the old miser was approaching to his last struggle with death; and that some one, unknown to me, a female, from the expression of my unconscious informer, would practise injustice towards my Lucia.

"I believed her silence now to be accounted for, in her time being spent in attention to the expiring flame of her father's life, whom she judged it her duty to console and comfort in his hours of sickness, whatever had been his conduct towards her heretofore.

"I longed to ring at the door of the house and ask for Rodovina, but I was withheld from putting my wish into execution, by a fear of offending Lucia; accordingly, after having loitered some time longer in the street, and not seeing any one more come out or go into the house, I retired to my own lodgings, in the hope that a letter might have reached them since my departure from home.

"I found my hope to be a vain one. I passed the evening along with some of my acquaintance, whose society I sought merely for the sake of making enquiry amongst them, relative to the female whom I had heard the unknown persons mention as they left the house of Eldorado. I did not choose to make them acquainted with those particulars, which I had heard myself, so merely enquired who was the other female that resided in the house of Signor Eldorado, besides his daughter?

'There are probably more than one in that situation,' replied the gentleman to whom I had more immediately, than any of the rest, addressed my question. 'Eldorado, though the greatest miser in Turin, if not Italy, in every respect but in the indulgence of his passion for women, is in that one instance perhaps as great a prodigal and dupe, as he is in every other respect wary and cautious of incurring even necessary expences. He has constantly one courtezan living with him in his house, and she as absolutely rules him during the time she keeps in favour with him, as he sways the sceptre over the rest of his family.'

"This account of Lucia's situation gave me great uneasiness; I did not tremble lest her being exposed to behold a woman of this description one of her father's household, should contaminate her mind; I believed it too firmly in love with virtue to be shaken from its adherence; on this score I had no anxiety; but I dreaded what influence such a woman might not in other respects exert, in alienating the affections

of the father from his child, more than they were already estranged
from her happiness, to the gratifying of his own unruly passions.

"My night was a very uncomfortable one; the morning, to my
great joy, brought me a letter, although not from Lucia, but from
Rodovina. In it she appointed me to meet her in the evening, in the
street of Saint John, opposite to the house of Signor Eldorado; she
had much, she said, to communicate to me, and would, at our meeting, fully satisfy me respecting what I perhaps might deem the neglect
of her young lady, in having been four days without answering my last
letter to her.

"I was in the street of Saint John at the hour of appointment, and
in a short time Rodovina came out to me.

'Well, Signor,' she said, 'I fear you have been forswearing my
young lady for false hearted; but you are unjust to her if you have. She
has been very unhappy of late, that is, within the few last days; her old
father is on his death-bed. You cannot suppose that I mean she will be
so very sorry to lose him, as he has been so unnatural a father to her,
as you must know he has; but there are other causes that depress her
spirits very much.'

'What are these?' I asked.

'I am almost afraid to speak here,' answered Rodovina, 'for fear
we should be overheard; there is no knowing who may be passing by
in a dark night.' She paused, then added, 'I have a good mind to take
you into the house; we should be safer there awhile; and then you
might just see my lady too, and that you would like, no doubt.'

'Exceedingly! I should, of course, like to see her,' I replied, 'if
you think no danger can accrue to her from my introduction into the
house.'

'There is none to be feared from her father,' returned Rodovina;
'he has not been able to get out of his bed for two days past; he cannot
come down stairs now to see who is in the house. No, it is somebody
else that I am afraid of; a vile courtezan, whom the old fellow keeps
in the house; she is ever upon the watch, and carries to him every
bit of intelligence she can pick up in the family, to curry favour with
him, and make mischief for others. Thus, if I do take you in, and you
should see any other woman besides my lady or myself, conclude it
to be her, and on no account speak to her; and if she should happen
to speak to you, and ask you who you are, say your name is Morelli,

Rodovina's nephew, and that you are come to speak to your aunt. Do you understand me?'

'Perfectly,' I replied, 'and will you now admit me for a few minutes to the presence of my angelic mistress?'

'I will venture,' replied Rodovina; 'follow me up the steps into the house in silence.'

"Implicitly I obeyed; she let herself in, and I followed her into a marble hall, where a candle stood burning on the floor; she took it up, and pointing to me to enter an apartment, of which the door was open, she shut me in, saying—'Nobody will come to interrupt you; don't be uneasy, I shall soon be back.'

"In this apartment there was no light, but that produced by the blaze of a wood fire, which fell immediately on the portrait of a robust, handsome-looking man; and as this was the only object I could distinguish, I stood observing it.

"In a few moments Rodovina brought me a light;—I enquired of her whom the portrait represented?

'It is,' she replied, 'the Signor Charino Eldorado, your Lucia's brother;' and again left the room.

"Long before my patience was exhausted, the door opened, and Lucia appeared, conducted by Rodovina, who, entering first, said— 'Her father is asleep, so you may chat a little while without interruption; I will watch by him the while;' and this said, she retired.

"The present moment was the first at which I had ever been left alone with the object of my love, and it appeared a peculiar blessing. Lucia, as on every former interview, and likewise in her epistles, was all feminine delicacy and reserve; she told me that her father was, beyond all doubt, on his death-bed, and that her brother Charino had been summoned from Naples; she said, that she considered herself equally responsible for seeing every attention paid to his last moments, as if he had been to her the very reverse in conduct to what he had proved himself; and therefore spent almost all the day by his bedside, which must apologise for her apparent neglect, in not having answered my last letter, and for her requesting me to excuse her, saying that my visit must be a short one, as she intended to return to her father's chamber the minute he should awake.

"I esteemed her more than ever for the proof I had just received, that she did not deem herself justified in discarding from her heart the filial duties, because her parent had been neglectful of those which he owed to his child; and in a short time took my leave, having previously gained her permission to see her again on the following evening.

"Rodovina let me out, and said she would come and look for me on the same spot on the morrow where she had found me that night.

"Rodovina was true to her promise, and for a second time led me into the house of Eldorado; she followed me into the room where I had before been, and shutting the door, said—'I fear, Signor, it will not be possible for you to see my lady to-night; her father is not asleep, as he was when you were here before, and she does not like to come out of the room when he is awake; nor indeed would it be commendable that she should, for in such case that filthy courtezan of his, that I spoke to you of the last time I had a word with you, would be left alone with him; and she uses every moment to cant him out of something away from his children. She has got enough from them as it is, I can promise you.'

'Her depredations must now soon come to an end,' said I, 'that is one comfort to them, as her friend is so near the termination of his existence.'

'Yes, yes, true enough, as you say,' returned Rodovina; 'it can't be for long, and that is the only good we can say of it; but it is praiseworthy in my lady to take care, as well, on her brother's account as her own; is it not, Signor?'

'Undoubtedly,' replied I; 'it is a justice she owes to him and herself.'

'Aye, indeed,' rejoined Rodovina; 'he has a wife and four children, to make it of consequence to him; and on my young lady's part, you have no doubt ever believed that she will have a great fortune; and she is miserable lest your hopes should be disappointed, and you abandon her for some other woman.'

'Good Heavens!' I exclaimed, 'is it possible that my Lucia can entertain such an opinion of my love? Oh no, no, you only do this to prove whether my passion is sincere or not. Will not her fortune, at all events, far exceed what I have to offer her? She cannot think thus of me!'

'If she does, it only shews how sincerely she loves you, and how worthy she thinks your person and qualifications of all it may be in her power to bestow on you,' returned Rodovina. 'I should not indeed have exactly said, that she fears you should abandon her in such a case, but that she considers that she should feel herself unworthy of becoming your wife, except she became so as the mistress of such a fortune as she thinks you deserving of.'

'Oh, that she were here,' cried I, 'that she might hear me declare it is for herself alone I love her; and that it is not in the power of the fickle goddess Fortune, to rob her of a grain of my affection, or to give her one more than she possesses.'

'She shall see you, if it be but for one instant,' said Rodovina; 'she will go to bed the happiest woman in all Italy, if she hears you pronounce these words herself.'

'Often might she have heard them from my lips, which have ever been desirous of expressing to her the full conviction my heart entertained of her charms, her perfections, but that she has forbidden me to make herself the theme either of my letters or my conversation,' said I.

'It was all her modesty, the meekness, the humility of her disposition,' returned Rodovina. 'Oh, she is a treasure indeed! It will take you years to discover all her good qualities—She is all over an angel—I must bring her to you, if it be but for one instant.'

"She left the room, and shortly returned with Lucia. She approached me with downcast eyes; I met her, took her hand in mine, and repeated those sentiments I had already declared to Rodovina; she thanked me, with a most diffident smile, and begged me to forgive her those apprehensions of my fidelity which her regard for me had occasioned her.

'You were born for each other,' exclaimed Rodovina; 'all marriages are made in Heaven, and your's is registered there, I am certain. But you should sign a contract—it makes every thing so sure and comfortable.'

'But that is impossible,' I replied, 'without making some lawyer acquainted with our attachment, which might be a most imprudent step while Signor Eldorado lives.'

'I do not want a lawyer's contract,' returned Rodovina, laughing, 'I only mean a marriage promise, as it were, just an agreement between you two, drawn up on a bit of paper, and signed by you both.'

'If it will be any satisfaction to my Lucia,' I said, 'it shall be done immediately.'

"Lucia looked as if it would be a satisfaction to her.—I repeated my question—she replied faintly in the affirmative; and I directly asked Rodovina to provide us with a pen and paper for the purpose.

"Rodovina undertook to write what was necessary for the satisfaction of her young lady; and in a few minutes she read, as nearly as I can recollect, the following words:

'We, the undersigned, do solemnly bind ourselves to become united to each other in the holy bond of matrimony, immediately after the death of Henrico Eldorado; and if we do either of us secede from this agreement, we declare ourselves willing to abide by such penalty as the law may have the authority of imposing upon us.'

"These," said Sylvio, interrupting himself in his narrative, and addressing the judge, "are, I think, the words of the marriage promise which Rodovina Maritos has just produced with my signature."

"The very same," replied the judge.

Sylvio proceeded thus:

"Without hesitation I took up the pen and signed my name at the bottom of the paper; Lucia received the pen from my hands, and wrote something under my signature, which I could not doubt to be her own name; and beneath this, Rodovina said she would write down hers, as a witness of the transaction. Lucia looked infinitely happy, and put the paper into her bosom; I could not at the time forbear smiling myself; little did I then imagine how great a dupe I actually was at the moment of my imagined felicity.

"Lucia almost immediately returned to her father. When Rodovina was again left alone with me, she said, 'You are a most excellent man, just the Signor to make a woman happy; and I am sure I wish you joy, from my heart, that your felicity is so near at hand, for the physician says our old miser cannot live out the month; and for my part, I say he will die this day fortnight.'"

CHAPTER XVI

"I CONTINUED now regularly every evening to be admitted into the house, and frequently had the pleasure of passing an hour or more with Lucia, who told me that her father grew worse everyday. I asked no questions relative to his courtezan, as I thought my enquiries might be suspected to have a mercenary view concealed in them; and neither Lucia nor Rodovina mentioned her to me.

"About five weeks after my first introduction into the house, going as usual to my appointment, when Rodovina had conducted me into the apartment where I was always received, she said—'It is all over at last—the old fellow is dead.'

'And how is my Lucia?' I asked.

'As well as can be expected,' replied Rodovina, with a satirical smile. 'I must leave you,' she added, 'and it may be some little time before either she can come to you, or I return; for the breath is but just out of his body.' She left the room, and I sat me down contentedly; for the frequency of my visits to the house had given me a kind of security in it.

"Half an hour elapsed, during which I heard no sounds but what appeared to me persons moving about over my head: at the expiration of this time the door opened, and a gentleman entered, who carried in his hand a wax taper, an inkstand, and some paper; he placed himself hastily at a table, and was dipping his pen into the ink before he perceived me;—the moment his eyes met mine, I discovered, by his resemblance to the portrait hanging in that very room, that he could be no other than the Signor Charino Eldorado, the brother of Lucia. He started at seeing me, and rising from his seat, as I did from mine, he said—"I have not the pleasure of knowing you, Signor; have you any business in this house?'

'I think, Signor,' I said, 'from your likeness to that picture, you must be the son of the late Signor Eldorado; am I not right in my conjecture?'

'Undoubtedly I am he,' replied the Signor.

'My name,' said I, 'is Di Rosalva; have you never heard your lovely sister, Lucia, mention me?'

'No, Signor,' he returned, 'never; nor can I guess what you mean to insinuate.'

'As your father is no more, Signor,' I replied, 'I have no reason for wishing to conceal the motive of my visits to this house—your sister honours me with a partiality, which forms the greatest happiness of my existence.'

'Honours you with a partiality, Signor!' exclaimed Charino: 'you are an utter stranger to me, and therefore the surprise I express at what you advance does not proceed from my deeming you unworthy of her affections; it is impossible I should know any thing of your pretensions to an alliance with her; what astonishes me is, that I should be told that she entertains two suitors at the same time.'

'Two suitors, Signor!' echoed I in my turn.

'Yes,' replied he; 'you say you are one, and I expect a friend of mine from Naples, to whom my sister has long been privately contracted, to meet me here to-morrow; and he hopes, in a very short time after, to receive her hand in marriage.'

'There must be some mistake in this,' I replied. 'I am so very positive that the sentiments of your sister are in my favour, that your account of her being contracted to any one else, appears to me the greatest enigma I ever heard.'

'Your account appears equally mysterious to me,' replied Charino. 'There is but one way of deciding who is in the right, and that is, to propose the question to herself. I will call her down, for that purpose, immediately.' He directly left the room, and I remained standing up in the middle of it, hardly convinced that I was awake.

"In a very few minutes he returned, leading in an elegant and beautiful female, whom he addressed by saying, 'Do you know this gentleman?'

'No, brother, I do not,' was the reply of the Signora.

'What am I now to think of finding you here, and the false account you have given me of the cause of your being here?' asked Charino, advancing a step towards me.

'Signor,' replied I. 'I stand here in amaze; my faculties seem all to be bound up by the strangeness of the events which have marked the few last minutes of my existence; but I am still sensible that the lady now present is not the Signora Lucia, the daughter of the late Signor Eldorado.'

"The lady's countenance indicated emotions of the greatest surprise; and Charino said—'Not Lucia! Do you affirm that I do not know my own sister?'

'It is certain,' replied I, 'that one of us cannot know her, if you assert that this is the daughter of Eldorado.'

'Signor,' returned Charino, in a haughty tone of voice, 'you are either a madman, or have some motive which must be enquired into, for your unaccountable conduct. Sister, call some of the servants hither, to secure this man.'

"The Signora immediately left the room, and I heard her calling out, 'Pietro, Sancho, come to my brother instantly.'

'Great God, Signor!' exclaimed I, 'you will drive me from my senses, by the conduct which you observe towards me. Do not condemn me without a hearing—be assured that one of us is the dupe of some gross imposition; condescend to enquire coolly which of us it is.'

'Well,' said he, waving to the servants, who appeared at the door of the apartment, to keep back, 'what explications can you give?'

'Permit me,' said I, 'to see Rodovina, and to refer my case to her.'

'More enigmas,' exclaimed he contemptuously; 'pray who is Rodovina?'

'Can you possibly ask that question?' I returned. 'You must know that Rodovina is the name of an ancient female, who is in the service of your sister Lucia.'

'No indeed,' he answered; 'I cannot allow that I know any thing of the kind; my sister's attendant is called Laura; I just now left her in my sister's apartment.'

'Signor,' cried I, 'I will stake my life upon there being a woman of that name in this house.'

'Pietro!' exclaimed Charino. Pietro came into the room. 'Is there any old woman of the name of Rodovina in this house?' asked Charino.

'Yes, Signor,' replied Pietro; 'and a terrible old hag she is; it were good she was burnt for a witch.'

'No comments,' returned Signor Charino; 'send her hither.'

"The silence was unbroken till Rodovina made her appearance.

'Do you know this gentleman?' asked Charino.

'Bless his heart, know him, Signor!' cried Rodovina, 'he is my nephew, Morelli; he called to speak to me on an errand of duty, just about the time our poor dear old gentleman died, and I put him in here, and never thought of him since, Heaven help me!'

'Your nephew Morelli!' exclaimed Charino; then turning to me, he said, 'I thought you told me your name was Di Rosalva. Am I correct?'

'Perfectly so,' I replied; 'my name is Di Rosalva; I have never yet blushed to speak it, and I feel no necessity for doing so at this moment. I recollect that when that woman first introduced me into this house, to an interview with the object of my affections, she told me, that if I by accident should see any other lady besides the Signora Lucia, and she should question me who I was, to call myself her nephew, and say my name was Morelli; as there was a courtezan of your father's in the house, who was always on the watch to carry intelligence to him, and would for ever mar my happiness with the Signor Eldorado, if she discovered me to be his daughter's suitor.'

'Jesu have mercy! Nephew, do not stand talking nonsense, and telling rigmarole stories there, but go away peaceably,' said Rodovina, 'and leave me.'

"Signor Charino interrupted her—

'Whose attendant do you call yourself in this house?' he asked.

'I am a servant here,' replied Rodovina; 'a servant of the household.'

'But whom, I ask, is it in particular your office to attend upon?' asked the Signor, in a decisive voice.

'I shan't be in the house an hour longer, and therefore it cannot signify to you who or what I am,' returned Rodovina, pertly, and sliding towards the door as she spoke.

"Charino caught her by the arm:—'I am now the master of this house,' he said, 'and have therefore a right to inspect into the conduct of such as I find in it. Are you not the servant of Vitellia?'

'Here is usage to your father's old servants, the moment the breath is out of his body,' replied Rodovina, counterfeiting weeping as she spoke.

'Are you not the servant of Vitellia?' repeated Charino, loudly. 'Answer me.'

'And what of that?' exclaimed Rodovina. 'I do not owe my wages to you; nor am I any part of them in your debt, haughty Signor, that I know of.'

'I very much fear,' said Charino, turning towards me, 'that you have been the dupe of a shameless woman, who having no character to lose, has not hesitated to attempt any means of bettering her situation, and has introduced to your acquaintance, as my sister, her own daughter Vitellia, who, I blush to say, has, for the last two years, been the mistress of my deceased father.'

"Had a thunderbolt fallen and crushed me, I could not have felt more misery than I did at the moment of this explanation. Horrid was the reflection, that my affections had been placed on an object deserving only of my contempt; and I was not less hurt at the want of discernment with which I now accused myself, in having been thus duped.

'For God's sake,' I said, 'confess to me instantly, whether she whom you told me was the Signora Lucia is your daughter Vitellia?'

'I did not tell you her name was Lucia,' replied Rodovina; 'you called her so yourself; you must remember I was surprised when I heard you do it.'

'But you had not the honesty to reveal to me my mistake,' cried I; 'thank Heaven that the explanation has been made before it is too late. I have only to beg the pardon of Signor Charino for the confusion I have occasioned in this house, and to quit it, and all it contains, for ever.'

"I addressed some awkward apology to the Signor Charino, and was leaving the house, when Rodovina called out—'Remember you have signed a marriage promise.'

'Do not provoke my vengeance upon you,' cried I; 'be satisfied we part thus peaceably.'

'Our parting will not be for long,' she replied; 'we have a deal of business to settle before we part.'

"I replied to her exclamation with some invectives, which the state of my mind forced from my lips, and rushed into the street.

"I had not been returned to my lodgings a sufficient length of time to have regained any degree of composure of mind, after the unparalleled villany which had just been disclosed to me, when I heard a noise on the stairs, and my name twice or thrice repeated;—before I had time to conjecture what it might be, my servant opened the door of my apartment, and said—'Here is a woman who insists'—he could not finish his sentence before Rodovina burst into the room.

'Have you the audacity,' I exclaimed, 'to appear before me? What is your business here?'

'I am come,' said she, in a cool but decided tone, 'to enquire when and where you design to marry my daughter?'

'Marry your daughter!' I repeated. 'Can you think, that because my heart has been touched by the outward appearance of a woman, my mind is so corrupt as not to recover from its intoxication, now I know her to be a character of shame, and to have used artifice for inveigling me into her snare? Can I continue to love, where reason makes so strong an appeal to my senses against it?'

'I neither know nor care any thing about your love, nor your reason either,' replied she; 'all that I know is, that I have your name signed to a promise of marriage with my daughter, and that all the heroics you can use will not be able to efface it from the paper.'

'The name signed to that paper is Lucia Eldorado,' I returned.

'No, it is not Lucia Eldorado,' she replied, with a smile of triumph, 'it is Vitellia Maritos, the name of my daughter. Your love was so hot a few evenings ago, that you never looked to see what was written by those who signed after you: and pray, can the change of a name have the power of cooling it so suddenly? Or did you only want to marry for what was to be got by it, and not for the sake of the woman, through whom it was to be procured? But you are like all suitors—if a girl be ever so handsome, first the money and then the woman.'

'First character and then love!' I exclaimed.

'Pho,' exclaimed Rodovina, 'face without character is the order of the day; many men have married women in a lower station of life than my daughter, for the sake of what was connected with them. So listen to me; I have your name signed, by yourself, to a promise of marriage with Vitellia Maritos; at eight to-morrow morning I shall call upon you again; if you then marry her willingly, I have it in my power to make your fortune, and I pledge my word to do it, the moment you are her husband; but if you refuse to perform your promise, I shall instantly summon you before the court, which sits an hour after.'

'Leave the room!' I exclaimed, almost maddened by the insolence and artifice of her who addressed me.

'I am going,' she returned, 'and, for the last time, mark my words—at eight to-morrow morning you must either marry my daughter and make your fortune, or appear before the court of justice, and lay aside all hope of what it is in my power to do for you;'

and, with these words, she left me.

"That I had never seen the Signora Lucia, till the moment at which she was led into the apartment by her brother, I wish them both to be called upon to prove; and to the expressions which Rodovina made to me after my discovery of the artifice, which she had practised to draw me into a marriage with her daughter, my servant is a witness; let him, I entreat, be called in evidence for me."

"Proceed first to the end of your story," replied the judge.

"I have nothing more to add," answered Sylvio, "except that Rodovina called upon me this morning, at the hour she had said she would do; and as I still continued firm not to debase myself by a connection with a woman of her daughter's character, I was summoned to meet her in the court where we now stand."

CHAPTER XVII

THE judge immediately dispatched messengers to summon into the court the Signor Charino Eldorado, whose presence, he said, would be sufficient, without that of his sister; and to call hither the servant of Sylvio, who had overheard the conversation which had the evening before passed between him and Rodovina.

During the necessary suspense of the trial which this delay occasioned, Sylvio entered into earnest conversation with the Conte della Piacca and his lawyer; and the innocence of Sylvio, with regard to the charge under which he had just laboured, was so fully substantiated in the opinion of all present, that they were at a loss to guess upon what interesting matter they could be so closely engaged.

Rodovina still kept her seat; no dismay appeared on her countenance, in consequence of the exposure which her villanous conduct had just met with from the narrative of Sylvio; and speaking only to express her impatience at the length of time she was detained in the court.

When the messenger who had been sent to summon the Signor Charino Eldorado returned, he informed the judge that he had brought with him a gentleman, a friend of the Signor Charino, who was empowered to act for him in the business depending.

The judge replied, "that it was impossible for him to take the declaration of any man from any lips but his own, except in a case where the witness was lying on the bed of death; and that as he understood the Signor Charino to be in health, he must appear in person."

Charino's friend bowed to the judge, and begged to be heard. The judge permitted him to speak.

"I am myself," he said, "a practiser of the law in the city of Naples, and it is in my power to acquit this gentleman," pointing to Sylvio, "of any obligation to fulfil the promise of marriage which he is called upon to do by Rodovina Maritos. Her daughter Vitellia, on whose account she has summoned him to the bar of justice, has by the world been believed to be only the mistress of the late merchant Henrico Eldorado; but I have this day discovered amongst his papers, a marriage certificate, which proves her to have been for two years past his wife. Accordingly, as the date of the marriage promise, as I understand, is but a few weeks old, and that of the marriage certificate two years, Rodovina's daughter was at the time of her signing it not Vitellia Maritos, but Vitellia Eldorado; at the moment of her marriage with Henrico Eldorado, Vitellia Maritos ceased to exist; the promise of marriage must therefore be void, as there was no such person as Vitellia Maritos in existence at the time of which it bears the date."

For the first time, the countenance of Rodovina fell; she put her hands before her face to conceal her emotion, and muttered some words, which were intelligible only to herself.

The judge immediately acquiesced in the opinion advanced by the friend of Charino, and requested a sight of the marriage certificate: It was put into his hand, and he read it aloud.

"Your account of yourself, and of the artifices employed against you, have been so clearly and feelingly related," said the judge, addressing Sylvio, "that although I am under the necessity of passing through the forms of acquittal appointed by the law, your innocence has for some time been apparent to me; and although you are released from all unpleasant circumstances by a point of law, it is my duty to remark, that you are equally acquitted by the code of justice."

He then turned to Rodovina—"Have you any thing else to say, before I pronounce this marriage promise invalid?" he asked, holding it up between his fingers as he spoke.

"No!" roared out Rodovina, in a tone of voice which might have been construed into a million of curses, and was beginning to force her way to the door.

Sylvio's lawyer rose hastily, and addressing the judge, said—"I entreat, on the part of my client, that Rodovina Maritos be not yet allowed to quit the court."

The judge nodded his head, and issued an immediate order for her detention.

Sylvio rose and spoke—"I have already laid before this court a brief history of my life; I have already said that I am unconscious of my birth, of my parents, of my rank in life; I have explained that I have no one upon whom, according to the law of nature, I can call for protection; and that thus circumstanced, I am led to believe that I am entitled to the peculiar protection of the law, in the stead of those relatives whom I have never known.—Am I too bold in my opinion?"

"Certainly not," replied the judge; "proceed to what you wish to say."

"At my first interview with Rodovina Maritos, she uttered an exclamation, which I cannot help thinking bore marks of the strongest astonishment at hearing that my name was Sylvio di Rosalva; and when I asked her if my name surprised her, she gave a turn to the expression she had just been using, by saying—'Oh no, it was a very handsome name, and that she thought her lady must be in love with it.'

"This occurrence would probably have made no lasting impression upon me, had it not been for what she last night said to me, and which brought my former observation to my mind, and strengthened my opinion of her being, in some measure, acquainted with the history of my life; her expressions last night were, 'If you marry my daughter willingly, *I have it in my power to make your fortune*, and I pledge my word to do it the moment you are her husband;' and at her departure she added, 'For the last time, mark my words—at eight to-morrow morning, you must either marry my daughter and make your fortune, or appear before the court of justice, and lay aside all hope of what it is in my power to do for you.'

"Am not I, from these declarations, authorized to believe her by some means acquainted with my fate, and to seek the power of compelling her to disclose to me her knowledge?"

The judge replied, that the suspicions of Sylvio were just, and that he considered himself authorized to take the business of inquiry upon himself.

Rodovina was accordingly commanded to stand forth.

The judge began thus:—"Rodovina Maritos, as you have already once this day been proved to have felt no repugnance at the commission of an act from which the hearts of the honest recoil, you cannot be surprised, that where appearances so strongly denote you to be possessed of the secret on which, most probably, depends the happiness of an individual, you will not be allowed to escape the belief of your having such knowledge, except you can acquit yourself of having had any hidden meaning, when you conveyed this idea to him, who is most interested in developing the truth."

"I am not the chronologist of foundlings," replied Rodovina; "what should I know of him?"

"Why did you give him to understand that you had some unexplained means of *making his fortune*, as you termed it?" inquired the judge.

Rodovina hesitated a moment, while the cloud of surliness grew darker on her brow, then said—"I durst not tell him that my daughter was the widow of Eldorado, and would inherit from him as such."

"There could be no reason for your concealing that from him," replied the judge, "as he knew her not to be the merchant Eldorado's daughter; it must, on the contrary, have been in favour of your attempts to win him to an union with her, to have informed him, that instead of having been his courtezan, as he supposed her, she had been his wife."

"I neither know, nor care any thing about him!" exclaimed Rodovina violently; "let him go and make a better match where he can."

"The suppression of the secret which we all suppose to be concealed in your breast, may be the means of preventing him from forming such an alliance as might constitute both his honour and happiness; and as it is the duty of the State to endeavour to promote the well-being of all her sons, it becomes so much more necessary that we enquire with strictness into this affair." Thus spoke the judge.

"And what, if after all, I do not choose to answer?" replied Rodovina.

Which exclamation being considered as an avowal that she was in possession of some secret, if she chose to divulge it, and mocked the power which questioned her, he said—"Recollect that there are punishments adjudged by the law to stubborn hearts, as well as guilty ones."

"Hell shall not make me speak!" cried Rodovina, without the least abatement of her firmness of voice, although a pallid hue stole over her countenance as she spoke.

"You are not alone," replied the judge, "convicting yourself of being possessed of the secret which we demand you to divulge, but laying yourself under the lash of the law, by your insolence to those chosen to enforce its commands."

Again Rodovina started from her seat, and rushed towards the door; Sylvio followed her with his eye, and saw her arrested in her flight by the arm of a man who entered at the moment she was attempting to force her way out; and, in an instant, he perceived it to be the Signor Charino Eldorado who held her.

He led her opposite to the judge, and said—"Now she is secured, I am satisfied, and must retire; my feelings will not suffer me to remain here; what they are you may conceive, when the Signor, who accompanies me hither, shall explain to you why I order her to be detained in custody."

So saying he gave her into the hands of two of the officers of the court, and departed.

The curiosity of all present was now again excited, to learn what new accusation was brought against one whose conduct had already raised their warmest indignation.

The gentleman whom the Signor Charino had deputed to speak for him on the present occasion, was named Sorato, and was an eminent surgeon in the city, well known to all its inhabitants.

He deposed, "that he had for many years past been in the habit of attending the family of the late merchant Eldorado, although he had not been called to him during his last illness; but that the Signor Eldorado having been a man possessed of many strange opinions, had bequeathed in his will fifty zechins to any person who could be found, to separate his head from his body after his decease. As the Signor Charino," he proceeded, "judged that this sum would not prove unacceptable to a man like myself, the father of a large family, he summoned me to the house for that purpose. I have performed the office required of me, and found certain appearances in the blood of the deceased, which I will at any time explain satisfactorily to the court, from which I am convinced that the Signor Eldorado lost his life by having had administered to him a slow poison, which has gradually consumed his existence: and as his son, since his death, has discovered her whom he believed to have been only his mistress, to have been his wife, and seen the impatience of her mother Rodovina to unite her to the Signor Sylvio di Rosalva, the moment the breath had escaped from the body of his father, he is led to judge that she must have been his destroyer, and detains her to take her [to] trial on this suspicion. Her daughter, whom he supposes to have been alike concerned in his death, he has sent in quest of, and ordered to be conducted hither, to share the fate of her unhappy mother."

Murmurs of astonishment and suspicion joined, immediately ran through the whole court.

Sylvio could not forbear fixing his eyes on the wretch in whose heart he supposed the secret of his fate to be hidden, and inwardly returning thanks to Heaven for his escape from the toils which it appeared so fully evident that she had spread for him. He saw her in some degree overcome by the accusation which had just been brought against her, but still her countenance appeared more expressive of regret than guilt.

"Is this the law of Italy!" she exclaimed, "that I, who came hither to seek redress, am to be detained here, in order to be loaded with the monstrous accusations of all those who are uncertain on whom to fix the crimes of the rest of the world?—I myself know sufficient of the law to be acquainted, that this is not a court which can sit upon a crime like murder, which implicates the life of the offender—I therefore demand to be instantly suffered to depart."

"That you cannot be," replied the judge. "You are right in supposing that I am not authorized to try a cause in which the life of the culprit may be involved—that is the office of a higher power; but I am empowered, and commanded by the office I do hold, to detain such as appear amenable to a higher authority, for its inspection; I accordingly command you instantly to be led to prison."

"Beware what you do," said Rodovina; "the eventual proof of my innocence will load your shoulders with the weight of my unjust imprisonment."

"It is an issue," replied the judge, "of which circumstances compel me to take the hazard; it is the business of those in whose happiness the welfare of the whole is entrusted, rather to detain an innocent person for investigation into his conduct, than to suffer the perpetrator of a crime to go unpunished. The innocent only return from the ordeal of the court with increased honour in the eye of society."

Rodovina muttered some half-breathed curses on the judge, and was led out of court by the officers who had for some moments past held her in custody.

Casting an anxious eye upon the judge, Sylvio almost involuntarily exclaimed—"Must I then forego all attempts at discovering the secret of my fate, which appears to be hidden in her breast?"

"For the present you must," returned the judge; "the time for enquiry will come; she cannot fly from our reach."

These words were spoken with a tacit signal to Sylvio's lawyer to take him out of the court, in order to make way for the persons concerned in the trial which was to follow.

The lawyer explained to him the hint which he had received from the judge, and with the Conte della Piacca, they left the court.

As soon as they had quitted it, the Conte Lorenzo addressed Sylvio, by saying—"My dear friend, dispel from your brow the cloud of melancholy which now hangs over it; doubt not, that if the discovery of your birth can give you happiness, but a very short time will intervene before it is made to you. Every circumstance of your acquaintance with the infamous Rodovina, corroborates your suspicion of her being acquainted with it; and that it is of no common degree, you may equally be assured, from her desire to unite you with her daughter; for which purpose it seems more than probable, that she has either herself been the administerer of poison to him who stood in the way of your becoming her husband, or has for that purpose procured the medicine of death to be given to him——"

Sylvio interrupted the Conte—"It must be so:—did you not remark, that in the account I gave of my acquaintance with her, I said that Rodovina had one day told me that the physicians were of opinion that Eldorado could not live out the month; and that she had pronounced, *that he would die on that day fortnight?*"

The Conte and Sylvio's lawyer replied, that they remembered it well.

"And he *did* die on the very day that she had predicted he would," returned Sylvio.

"This is indeed a strong proof of her guilt," said the lawyer, "and must not be forgotten on her trial. She had, beyond all doubt, administered to him the aqua tophana, of which the effects can be calculated to an hour."

"But still," rejoined Sylvio, "There may be mischief to myself in making this declaration against her; if she sees in me a chief instrument of her destruction, she may, from obstinacy, withhold that secret which it may perhaps be in the power of no other lips to reveal."

"For myself," said the Conte della Piacca, "I should have no apprehensions of that nature; few are the sinners so hardened in their nature, especially those of her sex, who do not rest consolatory hopes upon the confession of their crimes, before they yield their forfeited lives into the hands of justice."

"But Rodovina Maritos," said Sylvio, "appears to be a sinner, whose breast is more than commonly fortified with contempt for the opinions of the world, and the punishments which religion denounces against the guilty."

"Which apparently stubborn dispositions," returned the Conte, "frequently dissolve, at the last struggle, with iniquity and life, into a most weak and cowardly exposure of their lives, confessing themselves to have been even worse members of society than they were supposed; and this conduct, it is not unlikely, may be a part of the disposition in which they have lived, and which, at the latest moments of their existence, still takes a pride in shewing to the world, that they do not suffer till their wayward passions have had a free indulgence."

"There is yet," said the lawyer, "sufficient time for deliberation, how it were best to proceed in this case; it will still be at least a week before Rodovina is arraigned upon the charge of the murder for which she is detained a prisoner. But as it is of material consequence to the Signor di Rosalva, that our steps to that end be taken with every possible precaution, that in case of a failure in our hopes, we may not have any blame to lay upon ourselves for having left untried any means which appear to carry hope with them, I shall entreat a few hours conversation with him this evening, that I may, myself, be fully prepared to act in his cause."

Sylvio directly invited his lawyer to go with him to his lodgings for that purpose; and the Conte Lorenzo finding that his presence could not, at the present time, be of any material service to his friend, said that he should prefer returning to his Palazzo, as his Contessa would be anxious to learn the events of the day from his lips.

Sylvio requested the Conte to make his most respectful compliments to the Contessa, and to inform her how highly he felt himself flattered by the interest she was so kind as to take in his fate.

The Conte promised to be the faithful bearer of his message; and obtained from him a promise, that he would dine with them on the following day; upon which they parted, Sylvio taking the road to his Hotel, and the Conte proceeding to his Palazzo, where his Averilla was anxiously awaiting his return—eager not only to hear from him an account of the transactions in the court, but to impart to him some tidings of surprise which had that day reached her, entirely foreign to the occurrence of the day, but of matter equally interesting to her feelings.

END OF VOLUME ONE

The Impenetrable Secret, Find it Out!

Volume II

THE
IMPENETRABLE SECRET

CHAPTER I

THE Contessa della Piacca had already received from the Major-domo Bernardo, an account of Sylvio's acquittal of the charge which had been brought against him.

The moment the Conte Lorenzo entered the apartment where she was awaiting his return, she said—"Well, my dear Conte, Bernardo has already found means of gaining me such intelligence as has satisfied my curiosity with regard to the sentence of our friend Sylvio; he is, I find, as I was certain he must be, acquitted of the accusation preferred against him."

"Oh yes, entirely so," returned the Conte.

"I knew it must be so," replied Averilla. "Bernardo," she added, "has shewn himself very much interested, to bring me all the intelligence he could collect, and therefore I am infinitely obliged to him; but I am sure, that except in the single instance of Sylvio's acquittal, his repetition of circumstances must have been erroneous. Did Sylvio give a narrative of his life in the Court?"

"Yes, he did," answered Della Piacca. "Bernardo was perfectly right in telling you that."

"But he must have been mistaken in telling me what that narrative was composed of," replied Averilla; "pray, repeat it to me; I am very anxious to hear it correctly."

The Conte began to recapitulate, directly, the account which Di Rosalva had given of himself to the Court; and although he perceived that his Contessa endeavoured to restrain herself from speaking till she had heard him out, still, frequently, as by an involuntary emotion, she exclaimed—"Impossible! how very strange! it cannot be!"

To these exclamations she confined herself, till the Conte had concluded his account of their friend; she then said—"I know not that I ever felt so greatly astonished in my life, as I have done during the time that you have been speaking; I can scarcely believe that I have heard right. Did Sylvio say, that from his first recollection of himself till the time of his coming to Turin, about eight months ago, he had resided solely on the mountains of Tortona?"

"Yes, he did," replied the Conte; "and the account surprised me as much as it can do you, as, from your history of him, it appeared to me that he had, for many years past at least, resided at his villa which had borne his own name, in the neighbourhood of Genoa."

"Undoubtedly he did," replied Averilla. "I myself knew him to be a resident there for nearly four years previous to my acquaintance with [him]; you and I had understood, both from himself and the Lady Bianca, his relation, that he had been born on the spot, and had never resided any where else. Did you not mention to him your surprise at hearing him say that he had never lived any where but on the mountains?"

"No, I did not," replied Della Piacca; "I conceived that this false account of his place of residence might be a part of the mystery in which you have told me he is fated to live; and I forbore to infringe upon my promise to you, by hinting at the secret in which he is enveloped."

"But where he has lived," rejoined Averilla, "has no connexion with the secret that he has entrusted to me, no, no, none in the least." She paused. "He said also, did he not, that, until within about a month before his coming to Turin, he had been ignorant of his own name?"

"Yes, even so," the Conte answered; "the old man with whom he had lived on the mountains, disclosed it to him on his death-bed."

"Gracious Heaven!" exclaimed Averilla, "I have for years past heard individuals of every rank call him by the name Di Rosalva, in the neighbourhood where he dwelt. His father, I have frequently heard him say, had lived from his youth upwards in the villa di Rosalva, which was a family estate; but had been dead about ten years when I first knew him; and since the death of his father, he added, that he had never slept a single night away from the villa."

"It is impossible," said the Conte Lorenzo, "that I should be able to guess at the reason for which, in the account of his past life, he deviates so much from fact, as your knowledge of him proves he does, if you cannot yourself devise any motive for it."

"But I still have not proposed to you the question," said Averilla, "in which I most materially wish my doubts to be resolved. Do you really believe that if this Rodovina Maritos had not imposed on him her daughter for the Signora Lucia Eldorado, but that it had been the real

Lucia who had met his addresses, that he intended to have performed the marriage promise to which his name appeared signed?"

"I cannot have the slightest doubt of it," replied the Conte. "If any thing can be gathered from the expression of the features, that of his countenance, while he spoke of his first becoming acquainted with the daughter of Rodovina in the church of Saint Luke, betrayed him to have been most passionately in love with her; and he also confessed to me in the Court, that to have become her husband, had her character been such as a man of honour could have allied himself to as a wife, would have been the greatest happiness this earth could have afforded him."

"Alas, poor Sylvio! unhappy friend!" exclaimed Averilla; "thy misfortunes have touched thy reason! This we have often feared was the case, while I lived at the Palazzo del Alvaretti. Often have we been apprehensive that calamity had bewildered the sense of our friend, and it is now but too evident that such is the case, if Sylvio declares that it was his intention to have become the husband of Lucia Eldorado."

"Of her in particular, do you mean?" asked Della Piacca.

"Of her, or any one," replied the Contessa. "What can I do to serve him?—Something, I am sure, I ought to attempt, to save him from the ruin into which this conduct may lead him. Surely the kind, the affectionate old Bianca, cannot be acquainted that this nervous extravagance, for I will not call it by a harsher name, hangs on his faculties. I think I ought to see her, to explain to her that measures should be pursued for ensuring his safety."

"If his powers of reason are affected," replied the Conte, "he covers the heat of his brain with a composure very unusual to those thus afflicted. His narrative was of the most distinct and interesting nature, unmixed with any starts of passion, or any of those irregularities which scenes, described by persons whose sense is wandering, are ever marked by."

"Nay, nay," returned Averilla, "this idea of marriage is to me sufficient conviction of his reason being disturbed; but can you yourself want a farther proof than that of his addressing the Court concerning a suspicion which he told the Judge he entertained of Rodovina's being acquainted with the secret of his birth, when I have every evidence that he is himself perfectly acquainted with every circumstance relating to it?"

Several minutes passed in silence, during which the thoughts of Averilla and her husband were directed towards the same object, although to different points of it. The Contessa at length spoke:—"I will instantly write to the Signora Bianca; I can express my fears openly to her, without any infringement on my vow."

"You mean her I saw in the carriage with him a few days ago?" said the Conte.

"The same," replied Averilla.

"The hotel of the Good Samaritan, where Sylvio lodges, professes only to entertain gentlemen," said the Conte.

"But it is very unlikely they should be in different lodgings," replied Averilla; "for I, a few months ago, heard Sylvio say, that they had never passed a day asunder since his birth."

"I may be mistaken with regard to the nature of the hotel," rejoined the Conte Lorenzo, "and most likely I am, as it is one I have seldom been in. I think you had better write; it is, at all events, right that a friend, of the nature you describe her to be to Sylvio, should be apprized of your unpleasant suspicions, even if they are false, which I earnestly hope they may be."

"Oh no, no, they cannot be false!" answered the Contessa, and immediately began her letter.

When Averilla had finished writing, she expressed a wish that a trusty messenger might be sent with it, and Bernardo was accordingly summoned for that purpose.

"Go," said the Conte, "to the hotel of the Good Samaritan; enquire for the Signora Bianca di Rosalva, to whom that letter is directed, and give it into her own hands."

During the absence of Bernardo, Sylvio, and the strangeness of his adventures, were the sole topics of the Conte and Contessa; but a retrospection of the past did but tend to confuse their ideas concerning him, instead of elucidating the mystery in which he had heretofore stood enveloped alone to the Conte, but which was now become enigmatical even to the Contessa herself.

At the expiration of rather more than an hour, the Major-domo Bernardo returned. He approached the table at which Averilla was sitting, and laying the letter upon it, which he had received from her hands, he said, "there is no such lady at the hotel of the Good Samaritan."

"You should have enquired of some one belonging to the Signor Sylvio di Rosalva, where she resides, as she is undoubtedly in the city," returned Averilla.

"I did so, Contessa," replied Bernardo, "as I judged her to be a relation of the Signor Sylvio di Rosalva. I desired the waiter of the hotel to request him to send me down information where I might find her."

"And what was his answer?" asked Averilla, impatiently.

"Just as I had said this," answered Bernardo, "he appeared upon the stairs himself, going out with another gentleman, and I proposed my question to him; he replied, that he knew no one of her name, and that I must be mistaken in supposing she belonged to him."

"Unaccountable!" exclaimed Averilla. "Do you think he knew you?"

"I believe not, at least I should guess so, for the stairs were so dark, that I think he could not see enough of my face to recollect me," replied the Major-domo.

"You need not wait, Bernardo," said the Contessa, and the Major-domo left the room.

"Is not this," exclaimed Averilla, the moment she was left alone with her husband, "a confirmation of the sad state of Sylvio's mind, to disavow a knowledge of one who, were his reason still perfect, as it once was, it would be his chief pleasure to acknowledge to the world as his best beloved friend?—Surely, my dear husband, it must be my duty immediately to find her out in person, that I may not only warn her of the malady which has seized upon the brain of our common friend, but also assist her in devising some means for placing a restraint upon his actions, if possible, without curtailing the enjoyments of his existence."

"He comes hither to-morrow to dine, by appointment," replied the Conte; "would it not be better to defer your design till that time? I will leave you alone with him; I will, if you please, be called unexpectedly to dine abroad, and give you the whole day for conversation with him. Perhaps, if you too hastily remark upon his late extraordinary conduct, you may raise his malady to a greater height; if you cautiously proceed to speak of it, you may, by the soothing friendship of your words, bring him to a conviction of the strangeness of his past actions."

"How kind is my Della Piacca," replied Averilla, "in this proposition! Implicitly he relies on the honour of his wife, who will not wound the noble delicacy of his nature, by the paltry assurance that his happiness will be ever the dearest to her, though the ties of humanity appeal to her heart in the behalf of another object. I will therefore, without hesitation, say, that I accept your proposal of being left alone to-morrow with Sylvio. I have reason to believe that in a few hours private conversation with him, I shall have it in my power to relieve his mind from a part, at least, of the burthen under which it labours."

"So it shall be, then," replied the Conte; "Flavia shall ride with me to my farm, and we will return in the evening, and meet Sylvio at supper, without any apparent consciousness of design in having been from home at dinner."

"There is one point in the occurrences of this day," said the Conte Lorenzo, after a short pause, "which I cannot so easily reconcile my mind to, as you appear to do your's: I am convinced that Rodovina Maritos expressed more than a common emotion of features, when Sylvio informed the Court of his suspicion of her having some acquaintance with the secret of his fate."

"And would not you yourself have felt surprised," returned Averilla, "if any one had declared himself ignorant of his birth, and accused you to a public Court of having some concealed knowledge of it?—I do not wonder at even a wretch like Rodovina betraying astonishment at such a declaration being made concerning her."

"Do you think it impossible that she should know any thing concerning him? You are yourself entrusted with a secret by him," said the Conte.

"Which is known alone to me and the Signora Bianca," replied Averilla; "and if he supposed a third person to be acquainted with it, he would much rather use means to procure their silence upon it, than to provoke them to its publication—least of all in a Court of Justice."

A tear had started in Averilla's eye as she spoke.—The Conte observed it, and his feelings gaining warmth from the evident emotion of her's, he exclaimed—"Heaven restore him to happiness!"

"Indeed, indeed, he merits the reward of Heaven!" replied the Contessa; "his unhappiness is one of those mysteries which Heaven conceals from the eyes of its creatures. Were it in any instance allowable to arraign the justice of Providence, it would surely be so in the case of the unfortunate Sylvio di Rosalva, who, doomed from his birth to a life of the most cruel, most uncommon nature, instead of receiving from Providence strength equal to the trials through which he is destined to pass, loses even his reason in a cause, in the producing of which he has himself had no concern. But I am wanton in my speech; Heaven cannot be unjust, and sooner or later the virtues of Sylvio must be rewarded; and great will be his recompence, if the remuneration be equal to the pangs of the sufferer."

The Contessa rose from her seat, and walked about the apartment, in order to stifle the rising emotions of her mind.—After some minutes thus passed, she turned suddenly towards her husband, and drawing a letter from her pocket as she spoke, exclaimed—"In commiserating the lot of one friend, I have entirely forgotten to inform my Lorenzo of the tidings of a more joyful nature, which I have this day received from one who is equally dear to us—I mean of our beloved Felix. Read that letter from the Signora del Alvaretti, and tell me whether we ought to join with her in her present hopes, or to lament that her expectations have more probably been only raised to meet a disappointment, which it had been better to have spared her."

The Conte received the letter from the hand of his wife, and read the following contents:—

"MY DEAREST AVERILLA,

"Not that I am conscious that any pleasurable sensation communicated to the heart of my Felix, or myself, gives equal pleasure to your's, but that I myself experience a double happiness in communicating my joyful prospects to you, I write to you at a moment when trembling anxiety almost unfits me for the task. Oh, my Averilla, the blessing of his sight is promised to our dear Felix! May Heaven look down with pity on the resignation with which he has hitherto borne the darkness of existence, and in its mercy second the attempts of the benevolent being, who has offered himself to me as competent to open his eyes to the light of day! But I will command myself sufficiently to relate to you what has already transpired concerning this event, on which my entire, my anxious, soul is now fixed. This morning I was informed that an aged man, in the garb of a peasant, sought to see me. I went to him, and found him a man of a most mild and benevolent aspect, whose manners were entirely devoid of the usual clownishness of the peasantry, and who spoke in a language both feeling and eloquent.—He informed me that he had, for years past, made the study of physic his favourite pursuit; that amongst other discoveries, he had fallen upon one, with which he had frequently had the happiness of restoring to sight those who had been deprived of that blessing by the inveteracy of disease, or the stroke of lightning; that he had never yet made the attempt upon any one who had been born blind; but that having heard of my son's case, he had come to make me an offer of his endeavours. He judged, he said, that those who had been gifted by Heaven with the power of more acute discernment into the nature of herbs, which were applicable to the purposes of physic, were, of all other men, the most sinful in the eye of Heaven, if they did not, unsought, make offers of their skill to those who stood in need of relief; and, that having heard of the unfortunate situation of the Signor Felix, he had journeyed hither purposely to declare himself willing to exert the utmost of his skill in his behalf. I acknowledged, with all the gratitude I felt towards him, the kindness of the old man's offer, and immediately set before him refreshments, at the same time introducing, by his desire, my son into the apartment; but, ere he entered it, I besought him not to mention to Felix the business which had brought him to the Palazzo, as I could not bear the idea of raising in his breast hopes which might eventually prove futile. He promised me that he would not; and some trivial excuse having been alledged to Felix for the visit of the stranger, the old man, after some time, made the blindness of Felix, as it were, the accidental conversation of the moment, and, as we continued to discourse, he begged Felix to permit him to look at his eyes. This our amiable Felix, with his usual cheerfulness, readily permitted; and the old peasant, after the inspection of a few moments, whispered me in the ear—'I think I can promise to give him sight.' It was, indeed, at that moment, difficult for me to confine my feelings within my own breast; but my resolution did not forsake me. When I had again an opportunity of conversing apart with the old man, he repeated to me what he had before whispered in my ears, and begged me to consent to his process. I told him that I could not give my consent, without I was permitted so to do by my husband, and that I would, for that purpose, immediately send a messenger to Genoa, to request his presence at the villa Del Alvaretti.

I have accordingly dispatched the messenger, and detained the old man as a visitor at the villa. We have told Felix that he was formerly a tenant on the estate, and is come to pay his respects to me as he passed this way. What I have hitherto written I am sure must be almost illegible;[1] but if my dear Averilla can decypher the characters, I am certain she will not quarrel with the penmanship. I have snatched a moment while my unsuspicious Felix, for whom my every nerve now trembles with hope, amuses himself with his favourite flute. I could not defer to write to you till I had seen my husband, because you would have received intelligence a day the later, of this ray of hope which has broken upon us; and that I knew you would chide me for not making you acquainted with it the moment I was myself cheered with its prospect. Farewell, my dearest Averilla; to-morrow I will write again. Oh if I could have to tell you that Felix—but I will not anticipate too warmly, lest the indulgence of hope should render me unable to bear the shock of disappointment. I know you will pray for our success; I will therefore only say, Heaven prosper the prayers of my Averilla; and conclude myself your most affectionate aunt,

"FELICIA DEL ALVARETTI."

"Ah me!" said the Conte, "I have indeed my fears of the disappointment which she dreads; the old man who has presented himself to her, owns that those to whom he had already given sight, were not born deprived of the faculty. I am also, I confess, incredulous of the skill of irregular practitioners of the art of medicine, in cases where able physicians have declared it can be of no avail."

"There can be no doubt but that the consent of the Signor Rossano was easily obtained to the experiment," replied Averilla; "his feelings have always been so much wounded by this calamity being attendant on the sole male heir he possesses, that he will readily agree to any proposal that may promise but the shadow of a hope for remedying the defect. It is therefore by this time, I dare say, decided, whether my poor Felix is ever to be blessed by beholding the light of day, or not."

"The Signora Felicia says in her letter," returned Della Piacca, "that she will write again immediately after she has seen her husband;

---

[1] The text of the first edition reads "ineligible", which does not make sense in this context.

you will therefore, probably, have another letter to-morrow morning, about the time that you received this to-day."

"And to-morrow," returned the Contessa, "is my interview with Di Rosalva to take place. What two unfortunate beings come at this very moment under our confined knowledge of the world's inhabit-ants! and as there can be little doubt that happiness and misery are scattered with an equal hand, over the face of the globe in all its parts, how grateful does it become those, who like ourselves, are unhappy only in sympathy with the distressed, to prove themselves, for the len-ity with which the adverse winds of Heaven blow over them, in their course to their fellow beings!"

"And how eminently do those deserve the protection of Heaven," exclaimed the Conte, pressing his wife to his breast as he spoke, "who are so conspicuously, as yourself, the representative of its celestial pu-rity on earth!"

CHAPTER II

THE following morning, on the arrival of the post from Genoa, the Conte's prediction of the former evening was fulfilled, by a second letter being brought to Averilla; the superscription was in the well known hand of the Signora del Alvaretti. The Contessa hastily tore it open, and read the following lines:

"MY DEAREST NIECE,

"All is still suspense with regard to the light or darkness in which our dear Felix is doomed to pass his future days. Late in the evening, or rather towards the night of yesterday, your uncle Rossano arrived here, in compliance with the message I had sent to him.—Unwilling to be called, without the assignment of a cause attendant on the sum-mons, from his own concerns, he presented himself before me in one of those dispositions which you have often seen check the impulse that I have felt to meet him as the father of my children. I trusted to the communication I had to unfold to him, to soothe his ruffled tem-per, and accordingly, calling him into a private apartment, I, without preface, related to him the offer of the old peasant, who was at that moment an inmate of the Palazzo.—You have ever known what have been his feelings with regard to my Felix being deprived of that most essential faculty of which he has never known the enjoyment; more acute, I fear, from a selfish disappointment in his male descendant, than from parental commiseration for the infirmity of his son. However, in whatever cause they originated, as you are well acquainted with their strength, it is unnecessary for me to expatiate with how great warmth he grasped at the possibility of his release from darkness.

"He instantly commanded the old peasant to be brought into his presence. The old man recounted to him the benevolent purpose of his visit, in the same words which he had done to me; and my husband replied—'Let your experiment take place with the morning of to-morrow, and if you succeed, ample shall be your reward.' The old man returned—'I seek no reward of the nature which you propose to me; the only reward by which my feelings can be gratified is, a promise which you must make to me before I enter upon the attempt of giving your son his sight, and without which I shall not make the attempt at all.'—'What is it?' asked Rossano; 'if in my power to grant, conclude it already yours.'—'Promise me,' replied the old man, 'that if I give your son the use of that faculty of which he has hitherto been deprived, that you will neither oblige him ever to become the husband of any one whom he dislikes to receive as the partner of his life, nor withhold him from forming any connexion which may be eventual to his happiness.'—'These are strange conditions,' replied my husband, 'conditions to which, as the father of one through whom the descent of an honourable family is to be preserved, I cannot agree. What possible motive can you have for desiring I should?'—'My request,' returned the peasant, 'proceeds from the double motives of humanity and justice. Were I to suffer him to remain in the state of darkness he is now in, it is very unlikely that he should ever wish to marry, or that you should desire him so to do; but the moment sight is given to him, it appears probable that you will be eager to connect him with some family which may, by the alliance, add to the splendor of your own, and also that the passion of love may steal into his heart. Therefore, as I may be the means of exposing him to both these contingencies, by opening his eyes to the light of day, I judge myself only to be acting as it becomes me to do, when I obtain a promise from you, not to exact from him any sacrifice which may cause him to repent what my skill has been able to do for him.'

"Here the matter rests; my husband declares himself unable to determine whether it becomes him to make this promise or not. Oh! that it rested alone with me! Can any promise be too great in return for the blessing of our son's sight? I hope, I think, I shall at last induce him to give it; he has taken the day to reflect upon it, and to converse more at large with the old peasant. Almighty Heaven grant that his mind may be won to the proffered good! and may Heaven forgive him if, from any selfish motive, he rejects the blessing which is presented to his acceptance!—Adieu, my dearest Averilla; I am sure that you, like me, will venerate the humanity of the old peasant, in thus providing for the future happiness of one whom his skill is to render a new inhabitant of the world; or, more properly, to make the world a new habitation. Once more farewell; your affectionate aunt,

"FELICIA DEL ALVARETTI."

The Conte and Contessa, especially the latter, read this letter of the Signora Felicia del Alvaretti with an emotion equal to that with which she had written it. They were both so well acquainted with the family pride and avaricious temper of Rossano, that they feared he never would be induced to grant his son the blessing even of his sight, upon the condition of his being unrestrained in the choice of a partner for his future days.

"Pray Heaven he may be won to it!" exclaimed Averilla. "I have a strange, a bewildered idea upon the motive of the old peasant for making this request. I think—and yet it cannot be possible that——"

She was interrupted by a servant announcing to the Conte, that his carriage, which was to carry him to his farm, was ready for his departure.

The ideas which burst upon the mind of the Conte, at receiving this information, rendered him less attentive than he perhaps otherwise would have been to the incoherent exclamation which Averilla had just made with regard to Felix. Sylvio entered his mind, and he said—"The hour is approaching at which you are to expect Di Rosalva."

"I would the hour were past," returned Averilla; "I dread it."

"Do you wish me then not to go out to-day," asked the Conte, "but to remain at home, and meet Sylvio myself at dinner with you?"

"No, by no means," said the Contessa; "let it be as we have before agreed to it."

The Conte and his daughter accordingly departed, and the Contessa continued alone, awaiting the arrival of Sylvio.—The present she considered would be a most favourable opportunity for granting him that conversation apart from the Conte, which in his letter he had requested of her; and she enjoyed the soothing expectation of its being in her power to render him more happy than she had lately seen him.

A few minutes before the appointed dinner hour, Sylvio arrived at the Palazzo della Piacca. The Contessa received him with the utmost friendliness, and having explained to him that her husband was detained from home, she led him into the dining-room, where she continued to converse with him upon different topics, till the repast was placed upon the table; desiring to defer the subject, which she doubted not Sylvio was as anxious as herself to discuss, till the cloth should be removed, and their conversation be free from interruption on the part of the servants, some of whom were now constantly in the apartment, making preparations for dinner.

The meal being concluded, and every servant retired, the Contessa said—"Well, my dear friend, we have now an opportunity for conversing without restraint, an opportunity which, believe me, I have long desired, but from which circumstances have till now withheld me."

"You do me great honour," replied Sylvio.

"Call it not an honour," returned the Contessa, "that is too cold a word between friends like ourselves; call it rather by any name, that will convince you I esteem and respect you."

Sylvio bowed in silence.

"Nay, do not hesitate," continued the Contessa, "to open your heart to me; you can have no cause to blush at revealing its secrets to me. I have never given you reason to doubt my friendship; and if you have argued otherwise of me than as one who feels the warmest interest in your happiness, indeed you have wronged me. Come, explain to me the mystery of the marriage promise, upon which you were yesterday summoned to appear before the court of justice."

"The mystery of it, Contessa!" exclaimed Sylvio.

"Yes," replied Averilla; "what could induce you to give it?"

"Have you not had it explained to you," asked Sylvio, "that I was deceived in the woman to whom that promise was made; that I had believed her as amiable as she was beautiful, till the vileness of her character was revealed to me?"

"Oh, yes, yes, I have," returned Averilla; "but however amiable you might have thought her, there must have been some concealed motive for your giving her a promise of marriage."

Sylvio smiled with an expression of surprise painted on his countenance, and said—"No, indeed, Contessa, I had but the single motive of believing her a woman capable of adding to the happiness of my life."

"Had you then declared yourself to her?" enquired Averilla, with marks of equal surprise on her countenance.

"I had revealed to her my heart, and she had received the confession in a manner that had given me every prospect of felicity," replied Sylvio.

"It was, undoubtedly, very fortunate that you found her thus disposed," returned Averilla; "but still I think there must be much danger, even in the idea of such an union. What necessity could you have to place your happiness in the power of any woman but myself, while we have the opportunity of continuing the friends we now are?"

"As far as friendship can add happiness to life," replied Di Rosalva, "I certainly shall never meet with any who are more capable of administering it to my mind, than the Conte della Piacca and yourself. You are the only friends, except one who is now no more, whom I have ever known."

"You forget your best beloved friend, Felix del Alvaretti," replied the Contessa.

"Felix del Alvaretti!" replied Sylvio; "I am entirely ignorant to whom you allude."

"What!" exclaimed Averilla, "forgetful of Felix!—of that Felix to whom the warmest sentiments of your heart were so lately devoted! You are trifling with me. I entreat you," added she, in a softened tone of voice, for she dreaded that she saw her suspicion of his insanity confirmed in his denial of Felix, "to endeavour to collect your thoughts."

In the earnestness of her mind the Contessa had taken the hand of Sylvio in her's; he withdrew it resolutely from her, and said—"Pardon me, Signora, but from your conduct I cannot help supposing, that the recollection of thought which you recommend to me, is as necessary to yourself."

"Alas, Sylvio," replied Averilla, "it is the malady of your own mind which leads you to believe mine distempered. I do not wonder that the miseries you have been doomed to experience from your cradle, have led you into a conduct unlike your fellow beings; but trust in me, let me find means to sooth your sufferings, to compose your feelings; and, first of all, let me endeavour to convince you that your words and actions do not agree."

The faculties of Sylvio appeared bound up in astonishment, and he suffered Averilla to proceed without interruption.

"Do you recollect," she continued, "that you yesterday declared, in the court of justice, that you never had, till within the last eight months, resided any where but on the mountains of Tortona; that you were ignorant of your parents, and that you had only for a few weeks, previously to your coming to this city, been acquainted with your own name?"

"Undoubtedly I made those declarations to the judge," answered Sylvio.

"If you do remember this," returned Averilla, "let me, by that recollection, endeavour to convince you that your imagination wanders. Look on me; does not my presence recall to your mind scenes and ideas which you must have entirely forgotten to have existed, at the time you yesterday addressed what you called a narrative of your life to the court? Are you not assured that it is Averilla del Alvaretti who at this moment addresses you? Does not her countenance bring with it to your mind the remembrance of the villa di Rosalva?—the good Signora Bianca your aunt?—the poor blind Felix?—the letter which Rossano caused to be written to you when the Conte della Piacca first proposed himself as my husband?—the gladiator from which you fled in alarm in the garden of the Palazzo del Alvaretti?"

"Contessa!" exclaimed Sylvio, "I cannot guess at what you are aiming by these questions, which appear to me the result of a heated brain. Is it a page of romance that you are reciting by rote?—What can be your motive for these unaccountable demands?"

"Oh, Sylvio," cried Averilla, "how it distresses me to see you thus! If every other circumstance has fled from your memory, surely you cannot have forgotten the church of Saint Francis—the vow I pledged to you at the altar of that saint—the secret you then entrusted to my keeping!"

A pause ensued; Sylvio appeared as if undecided whether or not to fly from the presence of Averilla, as one whose reason he supposed to be disordered; and she continued to fix her eyes on him, as if expecting him to recollect the facts she had repeated to him.

"A secret, and between us!" exclaimed Sylvio, appearing at the moment he spoke prepared to burst into laughter.

"Yes, yes!" answered Averilla. "Did you not there confess to me that you were—*a woman?*"

Till this moment astonishment had been the only expression apparent on the countenance of Di Rosalva; his eye now beamed with the animation communicated to it by a heart stung with insult. He darted upon the Contessa a look of fierceness, which she had never before believed him capable of; but appearing suddenly to recollect that the sex of her from whose tongue the insult had proceeded rendered her still secure from active revenge, he replied, in a tone half smothered by the contending feelings of his mind—"For what reason I have been invited hither to-day, to meet this insult from one to whose family accident had rendered me serviceable, I cannot guess; I however can, and shall, take care not to expose myself to a repetition of this degradation."

He moved hastily towards the door. The Contessa followed him, and seizing hold of his arm, exclaimed, "Sylvio, Sylvio, do not leave me thus! That I can be mistaken in what I have said is impossible.— Tell me, only tell me, have you not a scar on the wrist of your left arm?"

With a start, which expressed the greatness of his surprise at the demand which the Contessa now advanced to him, he again disengaged himself from her, and said—"Often have I read of the sorcery practised by your sex, but never till now had a proof of its existing powers; for by sorcery alone it must be that you are informed of my being marked with a scar on the wrist of my left arm; and as this conviction furnishes me with a proof that your intentions towards me cannot be conducive to my honour, and my good, I feel an increased anxiety to fly for ever from your presence!" and as he spoke these words, he opened the door of the apartment. The Contessa endeavoured to detain him, and accompanied her action with words to the same import, but he darted from her; and, before she could sufficiently collect herself to call to any one who might have prevented his leaving the house, he was gone beyond recall.

CHAPTER III

THE Contessa clasped her hands in agony, and continued standing upon the spot where Sylvio had left her with upraised eyes, as if they were directed to Heaven, to implore its explanation of the mystery, which she could not herself develop.

That the ill-starred being, who had ever been believed a male by the world, but who had with tears declared herself a woman to Averilla, in the church of Saint Francis, had told her that at the moment she had believed Sylvio di Rosalva to be seeking her hand, the pretended Sylvio had but been endeavouring to summon resolution to impart to her the secret of her sex, and to implore her friendship; that that being should now fly from her, accuse her of insolence, and disavow a recollection of past circumstances—was an enigma that almost deprived her of reason, as she continued to dwell upon it, particularly as she had discovered too much matter in the replies of Sylvio on that day, to believe his brain affected; and still more as she reflected on the astonishment which he had testified when she had spoken to him concerning the scar which he bore on the wrist of his left arm, and by having avowed himself to be marked with which, he had, beyond all doubt, convinced her that he was the same person whom she had known at the Palazzo del Alvaretti.

She could now only suppose that, from some motive with which she was unacquainted, he had made her the dupe of a false confession respecting his sex; that he was displeased with the chance which had introduced him again to an intimacy with her, and had conducted himself in the manner he had that day done, in order to disgust her, and provoke her to quarrel with him, which would relieve him from the necessity of visiting at the Palazzo. But this supposition was again destroyed by the recollection of the letter which she had received from him, a few days before the present time, at the very hour when he was a guest of her husband's. This recollection again led her mind back to her former idea of his reason being affected.

Restrained by her vow from seeking advice of any one competent to assist her conjectures, she continued to dwell on the strangeness of Sylvio's conduct, till the subject became too painful to be endured, and she resolved to seek the means of liberating herself from the obligation of her vow, a measure which she deemed the recent conduct of Di Rosalva to have rendered essential, both to the peace of her own mind, and the happiness of those with whom she was connected.

When the Conte returned, which he did at an early hour in the evening, Averilla said—"You are, I doubt not, surprised to find Sylvio gone?"

"You mean that he has not been here at all, do you not?" returned the Conte.

"He dined with me," replied the Contessa; "but——"

"But," added the Conte, taking up her words, "it must have been a very late dinner, for we met him and the old lady, whom I once before saw with him, in a carriage coming towards the city, just as we reached a farm house, on the road towards Genoa, where we passed the afternoon. I was so surprised at the rencontre, that I called to his driver to stop, but he did not hear me, or at least did not attend to me, for he continued driving towards the city at a very rapid pace, which probably proceeded from his desire of being punctual to his appointment."

"Did you, indeed, see Sylvio with the Signora Bianca?" returned Averilla; "how strange that he should have denied all knowledge of her yesterday evening to Bernardo, when he went to seek her with my letter. He must have flown to the city," she added, after a pause, "for he arrived here in perfectly good time for dinner."

"Flown, indeed," echoed the Conte, with a laugh; "it is almost an impossibility, from the distance at which I saw him from the city, that he could reach you in any tolerable time for dinner."

"He was, nevertheless, rather before than after his time," answered Averilla.

"And yet you do not appear surprised," rejoined Della Piacca.

"I am stupified with a train of surprises," said Averilla; "but ask me no questions to-night. Let father Philippo be summoned to attend me to-morrow morning; I shall ask his advice respecting the religious propriety of my being released from the obligation of my vow to Sylvio di Rosalva. I am of opinion that circumstances are such as no longer render it a virtue in me to keep it sacred."

"Do you then no longer believe his reason to be affected by his misfortunes?" asked her husband.

"I know not what to think," replied the Contessa; "I am only convinced in my own opinion, that it is for his good and mine, that I be released from the vow which now confines my tongue; and I wish Father Philippo to give me his advice on this distressing point."

"A clock struck four," said the Conte, "just as we saw the Signor in a carriage with the old lady."

"And the clock struck four just as he entered this house," replied Averilla.

"The clocks must differ greatly then," remarked the Conte.

"They must, indeed," replied Averilla, while, for the first time of her experiencing the sensation, a cold trembling stole over her frame, and she almost entertained a doubt, whether Sylvio were not a being of another world, suffered to haunt her existence, and cause her to doubt the impossibility of the occult powers.

At an early hour Averilla retired to rest, anxiously desiring the arrival of the morning, which should bring to her relief the Confessor Philippo. Not less earnestly did the Conte himself wish for the dawn of day; he perceived the agitation of his Averilla's mind to be very great, and he was impatient for the moment at which the voice of religion might permit her to reveal what was passing in her heart, to the sympathy of an affectionate husband.

About nine in the morning the father Philippo arrived; he was a man of the most mild and benevolent manners; with him religion appeared in those alluring points of view, of which the more severe only rob her by their assumed gravity.—He had won the heart of Averilla since her residence in Turin, and she felt no reluctance in opening to him her soul.

He heard her with indulgence and compassion. The case, he said, in which she was involved, was a peculiar one; he would meditate on the consistency and contingent justice of her departing from a vow made at the altar of her tutelar saint, and visit her again when he had formed his opinion.

For several hours the Contessa had been closeted with the Father Philippo. When she met the Conte at dinner, she communicated to him the reply of her Confessor, and expressed her regret at not yet being allowed to impart to him the secret which alone filled her breast;

and her dread lest she should be ultimately withheld from disclosing it to him at all.

"It will not abate my love for you, if even this should be the case," said the Conte; "the attempt which you have made to participate it with me, is enough to free you from every imputation of a selfish or unjust taciturnity towards me."

"But perhaps it is at this moment equally selfish to seek the permission of divulging it, since I confess that it arises from my need of advice, in the strait into which my incautious vow has led me," returned Averilla.

"And when," replied the Conte, "can a wife display a greater reverence for the husband of her affections, than in deeming his advice competent to extricate her from that circle of difficulty, in which every passenger through life is, at some moment of his existence, held a prisoner by the power of destiny?—Come, come, be as cheerful as your sympathy in the fate of the unhappy Sylvio will permit you to be, and if your well disposed intentions have been abused by those on whom they have been conferred, believe that in me you will still find one who will ever applaud the benevolence of your motives, and pity you where their events are contrary to the correctness of your heart."

The Contessa was on the point of replying to her husband, through a mist of tears which veiled her eyes, when the Major-domo entered the apartment, and appeared to wish to speak. He had uttered a syllable or two, but deeming, from the emotion which he saw depicted on the countenance of Averilla, that his intrusion was untimely, he made a hasty apology, and was departing.

"Bernardo," said Della Piacca, recalling him, "what was it you were going to say?—By your manner it appeared to be something of more than common importance."

"I was going to tell you, Signor," Bernard replied, "that as I was, about two hours ago, crossing the square of Saint Gabriel, I saw a crowd at some distance from me. I enquired upon what account it was assembled, and found that the curiosity which most persons feel to behold an offender against the laws had collected it; for that the persons who composed it were surrounding Rodovina Maritos, who was conducting to the Court of Justice, in order to be examined on the accusation which Signor Charino Eldorado had preferred against her, in consequence of the discovery which the Surgeon Sorato had made—

that the old merchant's death had been occasioned by poison."

"And do you know what was the event of her examination?" asked Della Piacca.

"Yes, Conte," replied the Major-domo.—"I was sufficiently curious to wait on the outside of the court, until the sitting should break up, and some one come out who could give me information of what had been passing within. At length one of the officers appeared; I questioned him, and he informed me that Rodovina Maritos had declared that Sylvio di Rosalva had administered the poison to the merchant Eldorado, in order to accelerate his marriage with his daughter, as he had supposed Vitellia to be. The Judge enquired of her if she could bring any witness to prove what she had advanced?—She replied that she could; that her witness was a man named Michael Vivane. The Judge asked where this Michael was to be found, and Rodovina immediately gave one of the officers of the court directions for that purpose. The Judge then broke up the assembly, saying, that he should summon both Sylvio and Michael to meet Rodovina there on the morrow."

"It is impossible that a man like Di Rosalva can have been guilty of a crime of this nature," observed the Conte; "but I am not at all surprised at Rodovina's endeavouring to defend her cause, by charging the accusation brought against herself upon him; and I make no doubt but that the Michael of whom she spoke, is some wretch of an equally despicable character as herself, whose infamy will easily be detected by the court."

"Doubtless so, my Lord," returned Bernardo; "but this is not all I was going to tell you. Whilst I was in conversation with the officer, Rodovina was led out of the court, on her return to prison; and as the way I was going was the same which led towards it, I continued for some minutes to walk behind those who were conducting her. At the turn of a narrow street, where the meeting of several carriages for a short time choked up the passage, I perceived an elderly lady to be excited by that curiosity which was stimulating every other passenger to turn their eyes upon Rodovina, and suddenly I heard her exclaim—'I cannot be deceived! It is, it must be she!' And having uttered these words, she darted through the crowd, and forcing her way up to Rodovina, addressed her by saying—'Do I then again behold you, wicked deceitful woman! I know you well, you are the false Maria Calotti, who—' The clamours of the crowd to endeavour to learn what was passing, prevented me from hearing the conclusion of the sentence, as they did also the reply of Rodovina. But I guess that she disclaimed all knowledge of the old lady, for a momentary silence permitted me to hear her rejoin—'Not know me! Oh, monstrous falsehood! Not recollect Bianca di Rosalva, the nurse, the guardian, the mother of——' Again the confused voices of the populace prevented me from hearing more; the street was now become passable, and Rodovina's conductors led her forward, followed by the old lady, who appeared determined not to lose sight of one, her sudden meeting with whom seemed to have filled her with the most violent emotions."

"Proceed, Bernardo," said Averilla, eagerly.

"I have told you all I know, Contessa," answered the Major-domo; "for as it struck me that the old lady I have seen must be the Signora Bianca di Rosalva, for whom you have lately been making such anxious enquiry, I thought I could not do better than instantly to return home, and impart to you the scene of which I have been a witness."

"Yes, yes," replied the Contessa; "there can, from your description of her, be no doubt of its having been the Signora Bianca."

"And does not this seem to prove," said the Conte, "that Sylvio's reason was perfect, when he informed the court that Rodovina Maritos had some knowledge of his birth?—Shall I instantly go in quest of this old lady, and offer her my assistance in your name, towards the development of that secret, of which it now appears so fully evident that the infamous Rodovina is possessed?"

"No, my husband," replied Averilla, "do not go in quest of her yet; I thank you for your kind intentions towards those in whom I take interest, but put them not instantly into effect. Towards the evening Father Philippo said he would return to me; should he absolve me from my vow, it will then be in my power to give you much clearer instructions how to proceed, in the case before you, than I am now able to do."

"So it shall be, then," replied Della Piacca.

"Would Father Philippo were come!" exclaimed Averilla.—"But then, if on his arrival he should only declare that it will, in his opinion, be an offence against religion for me to break the seal of my vow—"

"I shall still be satisfied," interrupted the Conte, "that my Averilla is at peace with her own conscience."

CHAPTER IV

As the twilight of evening was beginning to fall, the Father Philippo returned to the Palazzo della Piacca. With the mingled emotions of hope and anxiety the Contessa heard of his arrival, and ordering him to be conducted into her closet, she immediately went thither to meet him.

In the course of half an hour the Contessa returned to the apartment where she had left her husband; disappointment was legibly written on her countenance, and her words quickly confirmed that it was the sensation of her mind. "My appeal to Father Philippo has been in vain," she said; "he informs me that he regards the permission I have sought of him, as a point beyond his authority to allow, and that I must seek the grant I ask of the church, from higher authority than his."

The Conte was beginning to reply, when he was interrupted by a voice, exclaiming,—"Help! help! for mercy's sake!—Murder! murder! help!"

The apartment in which the Conte and Contessa were sitting fronted the street; the upper part of one of the casements was open, and through this were admitted the sounds which they had just heard. The Conte ran to the window; it was not yet quite dark, and he exclaimed, as he looked out—"It is a gentleman attacked by bravoes! He runs up the steps of the colonnade, and they are pursuing him!"— And, having uttered these words, he fled hastily out of the room, and calling loudly upon his servants to follow him, he ran to the assistance of the imploring stranger.

Followed by several of his domestics, some of whom had brought lights with them, the Conte hastened along the colonnade which led to the flight of steps he had seen the person ascending. They found a man extended on the ground, from whose side the purple tide of life was gushing, but whose groans bespoke him not yet to have ceased to exist.

The Conte Lorenzo commanded him immediately to be taken into the house, directing, at the same time, others of his servants to go in quest of the first surgeon they could find, and bring him to the relief of the wounded man.

The bravoes, if such had been the two men whom the Conte had seen pursuing him up the steps of the Palazzo, and little doubt could be entertained of their being such, were no longer visible.

The stranger having been taken into the house, was placed upon a couch: his wound was on his right side, immediately under the breast. The Major-domo took a napkin, and endeavoured to bind it up, if possible, to prevent the further flowing of the blood, till the Surgeon should arrive to pursue more effectual measures.

The wounded man did not speak, faint groans alone escaped his lips. The Conte, taking a light, approached him to examine his features, and learn what hope of life they gave him; and scarcely had his eye fallen upon the bleached visage of the sufferer, than he recognised in him Sylvio di Rosalva.

As no surgeon arrived immediately, the Conte went to Averilla, and informed her who was the person that had been brought wounded into the Palazzo. Averilla betrayed more anxiety than surprise at this intelligence, and replied—"Sylvio di Rosalva brought into this house wounded, and under the breast, say you!—then an illucidation of all past mysteries must very shortly take place."

A pause ensued.

The Contessa broke it.—"Much as I lament the injury Sylvio has sustained, I cannot forbear thanking Heaven, after what passed yesterday between him and myself, and the refusal of Father Philippo to absolve me from my vow, that chance has worked the necessity of revealing that which I am withheld from disclosing.—Had not Sylvio conducted himself towards me in the extraordinary manner which he yesterday did, in your absence, I would have suffered any inconvenience, rather than have wished his secret betrayed; but, as circumstances are, it will afford my heart a great relief to be disburthened from it."

Della Piacca could only listen to the declarations of his wife in silence and astonishment, unconscious what to conclude, from the necessity of which she spoke, of Sylvio's wound leading to a discovery of the existing secret between herself and him.

In a very short time one of the Conte's servants returned with a surgeon, the first, as he informed his master, with whom he had been able to meet; and this proved to be no other person than the Signor Sorato, to whom our readers have already been introduced, on the trial of Rodovina Maritos.

The Conte went out to meet him, and conduct him to Sylvio: Averilla followed him, and addressing the surgeon in an emphatic voice, she said—"I intreat you, Sir, if any female assistance be required in the case of your patient, to summon me immediately to his chamber."

Sorato promised to obey, and followed the Conte to the apartment, where lay the bleeding Sylvio.

In about ten minutes time Della Piacca returned to the room where he had left Averilla. He approached hastily towards her, and throwing his arms around her neck, he exclaimed, as he held her to his heart—"Exquisite pattern of exalted virtue, and unbroken friendship! The excellence of your conduct is now explained to me—the virtuous secret which you have constrained yourself to conceal, is disclosed! Sorato has discovered Sylvio to be—*a woman!*"

The tears burst into the eyes of the Contessa, and when she could command her utterance, she replied to the Conte in the same words in which she had before addressed him, on the same subject—"I committed a fault in contracting any promise which bound me to the concealment of a secret from my husband: now that secret is disclosed to him, does he forgive me, that I have forborne to add a vice to a fault, by resolutely forbearing to break through the vow that I had once pronounced?"

"I cannot forgive," replied the Conte, "what I have never considered as an injury; and to a soul so eminently resolute in the exercise of virtue, as yours has displayed itself, the praise of those most interested in your happiness must be a trivial joy, compared with that reward which Heaven instills into your own heart."

"I confess I experience that reward," returned Averilla; "but believe me, even that reward is heightened by the unaltered affection of my husband. But tell me," added she, after a short pause, "is Sylvio's wound dangerous?"

"At present," returned the Conte, "she is very faint, from the loss of blood she has sustained; she has not yet spoken, and Sorato requested that she may not, on any account, be disturbed, lest the exertion endanger her safety."

"I must, I must see her," rejoined the Contessa; "I cannot withhold my attentions from her at this moment: they will, I am certain, be more gentle than those of any other person." She moved towards the door of the apartment, but suddenly stopping, she addressed the

Conte Lorenzo, by saying, "this discovery of her sex is a certain proof of the phrenzied state of her brain. When I yesterday addressed her upon the secret she had confided to me, she denied having entrusted me with it; declared herself not to be a female, and left me in anger, at my having insulted her by the supposition. You now perceive why you found me last night so much disturbed, and why I have, since that time, been thus anxious to be released from my vow. I judged it the only means by which I could convince you of the certainty I have invariably felt of her faculties being deranged, since my being acquainted with her having actually signed her name to a promise of marriage with a woman; and having accused that Rodovina, now in custody, of being acquainted with the secret of her birth, when I am myself so fully convinced that no secret attended it."

"If the necessity she has been under of concealing her sex from the world, has been the cause of her reason being affected," replied Della Piacca, "she is, indeed, an object of pity. But what can be the cause of her having been attacked this evening, by the men whom I saw pursuing her up the steps of the Palazzo, and by whom she was, doubtless, wounded?"

"We will talk of this hereafter," said the Contessa. "I may at this moment be wasting time, which might, perhaps, be employed to her advantage and relief;" and with these words she left the apartment.

The Contessa found her female friend still in a state of insensibility; the flowing of the blood was stanched, but her cheeks were bleached, and her lips, to which the Contessa placed her face, were cold and trembling. The wound beneath her breast having been dressed, Sorato ordered a restorative cordial to be administered to her; the Contessa raised her head upon a pillow, on the bed upon which she had been laid, and introduced the refreshing beverage into her mouth. In a short time after she had swallowed it, the unfortunate Sylvio made an effort to open her eyes, but she closed them again immediately on meeting the flame of the candle. The Surgeon ordered it to be removed to the farther end of the apartment, and addressed to her several questions, which he hoped might excite her attention, but they were advanced by him in vain.

Some time after this she murmured forth the name of Bianca; she repeated it twice, and added, in scarcely audible accents—"Dear friend, are you with me?" The exertion, slight as it was, overpowered her, and she again fainted away.

"Do you think she will die?" asked the Contessa, addressing Sorato.

His answer was of that indefinite nature which expressed the indecision of his own mind, as to the probability of her fate.—Averilla heard it with the most poignant anguish of heart. "Would to God," she exclaimed, "that Signora Bianca were here!" and, leaving the chamber, she went to seek her husband.

"Let us, my dear Lorenzo," she said, "immediately send in quest of Signora Bianca; Sorato has apprehensions for the life of Sylvio; I would not for the worth of worlds that she should die without seeing her; besides, what we have in our agitation and surprise not recollected, consider the misery she must be enduring on account of Sylvio's unexplained absence from her."

"It shall be done," replied the Conte; "I will myself be one of those who shall go in search of her; but where, where shall we first make enquiry for her? where can our applications promise us the greatest chance of success?"

"Suppose," rejoined the Contessa, "they were first directed to the keeper of the prison where Rodovina Maritos is in custody.—Do you not remember that Bernardo saw Bianca following her, as she was leading thither by the officers of justice?"

"Even so," answered Della Piacca; "but my dear Averilla," he added, "even at this important moment I cannot forbear the delay of an instant, to ask you if you are not astonished at the coincidence which there appears between Sylvio's having declared Rodovina Maritos possessed of the secret of her birth, and of her most intimate friend, the Signora Bianca, having attacked Rodovina this morning in the street, as one whose sight appeared both to surprise and delight her?"

"It is," replied Averilla, "an enigma which occupies much of my thoughts, and which I cannot solve. But I entreat you, let us, for the present, think only of such proceedings as the necessity of the hour requires of us."

The Conte immediately sought the Major-domo, and having dispatched him and several of his domestics different ways, in search of the Signora Bianca, he proceeded himself towards the prison of Rodovina Maritos.

CHAPTER V

THE keeper instantly attended to his request to see him, and having heard his inquiries, he replied, that he had seen an elderly lady, of the description he gave, follow his prisoner to the gate that morning, and that she had solicited him to suffer her to enter, and proceed to Rodovina's cell; but that as his office withheld him from granting this permission to any stranger, he had been obliged to shut the door upon her, and had not seen her since.

The Conte hesitated for a moment whether he should visit Rodovina, and repeat his inquiries to her; but very little consideration informed him, that if Rodovina really was acquainted with the person of the Signor Bianca, as it appeared almost doubtless she was, from what had passed in the morning at their unexpected meeting, it was not at all probable that she could inform him where in the city she was to be found, and he therefore forbore to question her.

After having visited most of the principal hotels in the city, and many other places where he guessed it possible the old lady might have taken up her abode, he returned home to his Palazzo. All his servants, except the Major-domo, were come back, with the same ill success that had attended his own inquiries.—In a few minutes after appeared Bernardo; his efforts, like the rest, had been fruitless.

Although the faintness of Sylvio continued as great as when the Conte and his servants had left the Palazzo, Sorato considered her symptoms more free from immediate danger; and as it was now one in the morning, it was judged, on every account, more adviseable that a further search after the lady Bianca should be deferred till the light of day; Averilla consoling herself in the hope, that Bianca was so situated as to be ignorant of Sylvio's absence from her lodging, wherever that might be.

The Contessa expressed a desire of watching by Sylvio during the night; the Conte raised no objection to her request, but entreated Sorato to remain her companion. This he readily agreed to, and of the rest of the family, except a couple of attendants, who were stationed in an adjoining chamber, retired to bed.

Sorato said, that quiet was the best medicine which could be administered to his patient; an uninterrupted silence was therefore preserved in the apartment.—Towards the dawn of day Sylvio began to breathe more audibly than she had yet done, and Sorato, regarding this symptom as a proof of her having derived some small portion of strength from the medicines which he had administered to her, ventured to address her.

"Where am I?" she inquired, raising her head as she spoke.

"With me, with your friend, with your Averilla!" said the Contessa.

"With Averilla!" she returned; "oh Heavens, give me your hand, and let me kiss it!" She drew it to her lips, and then again sunk down upon her pillow.

This was the first time, during the many months that they had been in the habit of frequently seeing each other, since Averilla's residence in the city of Turin, that Sylvio had, by any single word, acknowledged the friendship which they had vowed to each other at the altar of St. Francis, in the village Del Alvaretti; the Contessa therefore believed the words she had now uttered to be a proof of her returning reason, and dreaded that it might be the forerunner of her death.

She imparted her fears to Sorato, and he was compelled to confess that her apprehensions were similar to his own. On receiving this conviction of her fears, the tears burst into the eyes of Averilla; but Sorato begged of her to retain her composure, assuring her that if the danger of Sylvio were even confirmed, which was not yet the case, the termination of her existence could not by any means be so near as she apprehended it to be.

Two hours passed in silence; Sylvio did not again attempt to speak, but it was evident that she did not sleep. At the expiration of that time, she said—"My dear friend, Averilla, are you still with me?"

Averilla went to the side of the bed, and received her extended hand in hers.

"How infinitely happy I am," said Sylvio, "in being with you in my present wretched situation! I now perfectly recollect the occurrences of last night, and cannot sufficiently bless my fate for having given me to your protection."

Averilla replied by pressing the hand of Sylvio, which she held in hers. Sylvio continued thus:—"Oh, my friend, how often have I desired again to clasp you to my breast! have not you thought the same of me?"

"Yes, indeed, I have," answered Averilla; "can you need to be told so, after what I said to you the day before yesterday? Oh, Sylvio, why did you then disavow all former recollection of me, and of your friend Felix? why deny to me the secret of your sex, which you had voluntarily entrusted to my keeping?"

"How strangely you talk!" replied Sylvio; "I know not what you mean by what you mention of the day before yesterday." She paused a few minutes, then added, "I am not able to converse now; my ideas are confused, and will not let me collect for utterance, what I would say.—Do not talk to me at present." Her eyes confessed the bewildered state of her brain, which Signor Sorato observing, administered to her a composing draught, in a second portion of the restorative cordial, and in the course of another hour, he pronounced her to be sunk into a slumber.

About the time Averilla conjectured the Conte to be risen, she went to his chamber; he met her at the door, and after she had replied to his inquiries concerning Sylvio, she informed him of the letter which she had received from Sylvio, on the day that he was dining at the Palazzo, during her confinement to her chamber, and telling him that in this letter he had directed her to send her answer to the hotel of the Holy Virgin. She asked him whether he did not judge it most probable that he might there be furnished with some intelligence of the Signora Bianca?—"This circumstance," she said, "had entirely escaped my recollection, till you had for some hours been retired to rest last night."

"There then, indeed, it appears most probable that I shall be able gain the information we desire," returned the Conte. "I did not go to that hotel in my rounds yesterday evening, because it is one of little note, in the suburbs of the city, and I judged it unlikely to be the abode of any persons of condition. And still," added the Conte, "as her letter to you can be considered only as an additional proof of her insanity, at the time she wrote it, it appears an even chance whether she knows more of this hotel than its name, or if ever she sent to enquire for your answer, directed for her at it."

"It is, however, in the present state of things, worth an inquiry," replied Averilla.

"It is, undoubtedly," returned Della Piacca: "and I judge it of so material consequence that we endeavour to find the Signora Bianca, that to insure the inquiry being made with exactness, I shall go to the place myself."

The Hotel of the Holy Virgin was at the opposite extremity of the city to that at which stood the Palazzo della Piacca. The Conte having accordingly taken a hasty breakfast, previously to his departure, set out on his errand of inquiry.

During the absence of the Conte Lorenzo, several of his friends, who had heard the rumour of a Signor that had been attacked and wounded by the bravoes, having been received into the Palazzo della Piacca on the preceding evening, called to inquire into the truth of the report. The Contessa resolutely confining herself to the chamber of Sylvio, sent Bernardo to answer their inquiries, instructing him to reply solely to their questions concerning the event, and to say nothing of the discovery of Sylvio's sex, which had followed it.

About an hour after she had issued these commands, and before the Conte was yet returned, the door of the chamber where she was sitting, by the bedside of Sylvio, was opened, and, as she looked towards it, she perceived Flavia, who, with a countenance of unusual earnestness, was beckoning to her to come out.

Supposing her husband to be returned with the desired intelligence concerning Signora Bianca, or perhaps to have brought her with him, she directly complied with the signal of Flavia. As soon as she was in the gallery, and the chamber door shut, Flavia exclaimed, in a tone of voice that betrayed her to be violently agitated—"Pray tell me, did not papa say it was the Signor Sylvio, who saved my life, that was desperately wounded last night on the steps of our Palazzo, and who now lies at the point of death in that chamber?"

"Yes, my child, yes," replied Averilla, "it is the same."

"No, no, indeed; it is not," returned Flavia; "look at him again, and convince yourself."

"I am already convinced," answered Averilla; "it is the same, I assure you."

"Oh mercy, is it indeed!" exclaimed the child, throwing her arms round the waist of the Contessa, and clinging to her as she spoke, "then I have seen a ghost!"

"What, my love!" rejoined the Contessa; "what do you mean, Flavia!"

"Yes, indeed, it is now sitting in the breakfast apartment," replied Flavia: "I was going into the room just now, but seeing something there so very like Sylvio, at the moment I knew him to be in bed up stairs, and almost dying, I ran away again as soon as I had caught a glimpse of it, for I thought it could be nothing alive; and you see I was quite right, was not I?"

"My dear child," answered the Contessa della Piacca, "you must have been mistaken; your hasty view of the person, whom you believed to be the Signor Sylvio, has deceived you. For the sake of your future peace of mind, I must go down with you, and convince you of your error."

The child persisted in her tale, and was extremely unwilling to return to the apartment, from which she had just fled in alarm; but the Contessa, fully conscious of the mischief of suffering the mind of youth to go unconvinced of the fallacy of its childish conceits and apprehensions, insisted on leading her down.

When they had descended the stairs, and were arrived within sight of the door of the breakfast apartment, the Contessa was startled by seeing several of the domestics on the outside, whose looks were little more composed than those of the trembling Flavia. She could not forbear conceiving that others had been alarmed in the like manner as Flavia had described herself to have been; but convinced, by the reason of her own mind, that every foolish terror and idea of such a nature can be explained, by those who have courage to investigate their error, she said—"Bernardo, what is the matter here?"

"Signora—Contessa," replied Bernardo, stammering, "there is an occurrence which—which——"

Averilla was on the point of turning into the apartment, round the door of which the servants were collected, without waiting for the conclusion of Bernardo's sentence. He caught her arm, and withheld her from entering:—"Pardon me, Contessa," he said, "but do not enter; a prognostic of the death of the Signor Sylvio di Rosalva has just appeared to me in that apartment."

"It rang at the gate, as naturally as if it had been the Signor himself, instead of his ghost!" exclaimed one of the servants; "and I, Heaven help me! durst not shut the door in its face, for fear it should owe me a grudge in the next world."

The Contessa resolutely disengaged herself from the hold of Bernardo, and entered the apartment, where, seated on a sofa, she beheld a figure, which, had she not known Sylvio di Rosalva to be at that moment too ill to move, and in bed in the chamber which she had just quitted, she must have pronounced to be Sylvio di Rosalva herself.

Involuntarily she started at the sight.—Flavia shrieked, and snatching away her hand from that of Averilla, fled from the apartment; the servants echoed her cry, and likewise ran from the spot of terror.

The Contessa herself certainly felt surprised, but she did not attempt to leave the apartment. The figure rose, and with a slight inclination of its head, said—"I do not wonder, Signora, that you are surprised at seeing me here again, after the strange method which you took the day before yesterday, to inform me that my visits here were unpleasant to you. But as I still feel an esteem for the Conte della Piacca, and have been informed that he has been wounded by bravoes, my visit is to him. I am happy to find that it is not so; but the conduct of your servants towards me has so much resembled what yours was the other day, that I must suppose they are authorized in it by their master; and I shall, therefore, await his return home, to inquire how I have provoked him, and his family, to offer me these insults."

Abstract ideas the Contessa had at this moment none; a chaos of undigested visions filled her imagination, and she had not the power of utterance, could she have resolved what to say, which she found impossible.

The figure was preparing to speak again, when the Conte della Piacca entered the room, with Signora Bianca leaning on his arm.

"Thank Heaven you are come!" exclaimed Averilla, addressing the Conte Lorenzo.

"Dear lady, what do I not owe to your kindness," cried Bianca, catching hold of Averilla's hands; but no sooner had she spoken these words, than her eyes falling on the figure resembling Sylvio, she added,—"What do I see! my child already recovered!" and saying this, she darted towards it with open arms.

"Your child!" exclaimed the figure.

"Are you not my Sylvio di Rosalva?" asked Bianca.

"I am Sylvio di Rosalva, most undoubtedly," replied the stranger; "and if you know me to be your child, why have you thus long deserted me?"

"Deserted you, dearest child!" exclaimed Bianca; "what can you mean?"

"You are in error, we are all in error," said the Contessa, moving up to Bianca, and addressing her; "this is not the Sylvio di Rosalva who was brought hither yesterday evening wounded; this is not the Sylvio di Rosalva to whom I bound myself by a vow of secrecy on her sex, in the church of Saint Francis, at Alvaretti.—Who or what it is that usurps her likeness, and her name, I have yet to learn—guess I cannot."

"Heavenly God!" cried Bianca, "and are you, indeed, called Sylvio di Rosalva, and yet do not recollect ever to have seen me before?"

"Sylvio di Rosalva is my name," replied the figure; "and yet do I not recollect ever to have seen you before."

"Blessed be Heaven!" exclaimed Bianca, flying round his neck as she spoke, "he is found!—he is found! he lives—he lives!—Oh God, accept our thanks!—You are the brother of my Sylvio, the twin brother of that Sylvio whose necessity of disguising the softness of her sex, beneath the habit of yours, ceases, now you are restored to us."

The various emotions of the persons who formed this interesting groupe may be easily imagined; broken exclamations of joy and astonishment was all they were, for some time, capable of uttering.

Bianca was the first who spoke collectedly.—"Yes, yes, you are indeed the lost Sylvio," she said; "the resemblance you bear to one another is a sufficient proof of your affinity. From the hour of your birth, you were distinguishable from each other only by your sex; so strongly alike, that you both bear a scar on the wrist of your left arm.—Am I not right? have you not that mark?"

Sylvio drew up the sleeve of his coat, and displayed the scar; which done, he was beginning an apology to the Contessa, for having construed her friendship for his sister into an insult intended to himself; but the Contessa enjoined him to immediate silence on that head. She said, that the circumstances in which fate had placed him, and those connected with him, were apologies, she hoped, for the misconception of the past, in his sister's friends, as well as himself; and that, after so much sorrow and misfortune as they had both known, it was just that no subject should be admitted to their thoughts, but the means of rendering their future lives happy.

CHAPTER VI

When the agitation of mind into which every one present had been thrown, by the unexpected existence of two Sylvios, had in some measure subsided, and a few observations had been made upon the various errors which had arisen from the concealment of the female Sylvio's sex, and the recently acknowledged Sylvio's ignorance of his birth, he entreated to be immediately conducted to that sister, whose breast he had never folded to his own; but as the Contessa learnt that her slumbers still continued, she besought him not to disturb her repose, promising, that if she was sufficiently refreshed by her sleep, for no danger to be apprehended from the discovery being made to her, he should visit her as soon as she awoke.

The Conte della Piacca had found the Signora Bianca at the hotel of the Holy Virgin, her mind upon the rack for the fate of her dear child, as she called Sylvio, whom she had not seen, or been able to hear of, since the hour of six on the preceding evening. In her way to the Palazzo, she had told the Conte of her desire to obtain an interview with Rodovina Maritos, and had entreated his assistance to that end, which he had promised her.—Hitherto she had only said, that she trusted such an interview, if she could obtain it, would lead to a discovery of material consequence to the happiness of Sylvio; and the discovery of the existence of the twins being now made, she requested him to attend to the history of their births, and to give her his advice for bringing the offenders against their peace to justice.

The Conte and Contessa were little less eager to hear the detail of those events, which had led to the disguise of the female Sylvio's sex, and her brother's removal from his family, than was the newly-discovered Sylvio himself; and as the surgeon Sorato announced his patient still to be asleep, the present was judged a favourable time for the explanation from the lips of Bianca, which she gave in the following words:—

"I am myself distantly related, by marriage, to the family Di Rosalva. The father of those whose story I am about to relate, was himself the last descendent of his house, the nearest relative which he could trace being a cousin, several degrees removed, whose estates lay in the Dutchy of Parma.

"A few weeks after the Signor di Rosalva had completed his twenty-seventh year, he married a very beautiful woman, with whom he promised himself every earthly happiness. She was an angel in disposition, and he loved her with the utmost tenderness.—I was an eyewitness of their felicity, for my kind relative had, some time before his marriage, offered me his house as an asylum, when I was left in circumstances of distress by the death of a profligate husband; and his wife kindly insisted that I should not quit it, because she was become its mistress.

"For two years nothing occurred to be a momentary drawback upon their comforts or enjoyment.—At the expiration of that time the Signor Sylvio began to grow impatient for an heir; he could not bear the idea of his name dying away, and his estates being transferred to persons who were to him utter strangers; and his prayers were constantly offered up to Heaven for a son.

"His wife grew uneasy because she saw her husband so; and the cloud of disappointment hung on both their brows, although their mutual affection was not diminished by the cause of their anxiety.

"Nearly eight years passed without one ray of his favourite hope cheering the heart of the Signor Sylvio. About this time the Signora declared herself in a state of pregnancy, and the raptures of her husband were only equalled by his attention to the health and happiness of the object to whom he was to owe the gratification of his most ardent wish.

"The hours passed anxiously on between the extreme of joy, hope, and apprehension, till the moment arrived at which the Signora di Rosalva was to be released from her burthen.

"When she was about three months advanced in her pregnancy, she had been alarmed by seeing a man in the streets of Genoa, from her carriage, who had been wounded in the wrist with a stiletto; the circumstance had dwelt very forcibly on her mind, and some alarm was entertained lest this accident should have affected the perfectness of the child in her womb.

"After a day of pain, the Signora gave birth to a girl. I conveyed the intelligence to Di Rosalva, and easily discovered that the sex of the child cast a damp upon the pleasure which its birth gave him; but there was a second piece of information reserved for me to convey to him, of which I had not formed the slightest suspicion. On my return to the chamber of the Signora, I found her agony by no means abated, and the surgeon who attended her said, she was as yet released from only half her burthen.

"Pray Heaven this second prove a boy," I exclaimed to myself, and my prayer was propitious, for in little more than a quarter of an hour, the second child was born a male. Never shall I forget how extravagant was the ecstacy of the Signor di Rosalva, when I bore him the tidings of his being become the father of a son; and equally imprinted on my memory is the sad reverse of feeling he experienced, when it became necessary to inform him that his beloved wife, in giving existence, had herself lost the bliss of life.

"The dead we can only bewail, the living require the exertion of our active services in their cause; accordingly, while the thoughts of all the household of Di Rosalva were in the tomb with the lamented mother, the universal care of all who were its members were directed to the rearing of her babes.

"The twins were of remarkable beauty, even at the very period of their birth, when there is usually very little to be admired in infants, and so exactly alike, that some little difference in their dress alone rendered them distinguishable from each other; and on the wrist of the left arm of each of a scar, exactly on that part where their late mother had seen the man wounded in the street, and it was deemed providential that her children had incurred no greater calamity from her fright.

"On the third day of their birth they were baptized; the girl was called by her mother's name of Rosabella, and the boy was named Sylvio, after his father.

"I had at this time, in some measure, the power of returning to my relative the benevolence which he had exercised towards me; for he believed his children only to be safe when under my immediate inspection, and I endeavoured to repay to them the loss of their mother, by every tenderness and attention I had the means of bestowing on them; and, at such times as I left their nursery, I applied myself to prevent their father from sinking into that lethargy of grief, of which the effects are more to be dreaded than those of violent sorrow, and to which I saw him most inclined to become a prey. Di Rosalva had an insuperable aversion to the idea of his children sucking food from the breast of any woman but a parent; and as hers had been denied to them by that regulator of human events, whose ordinations are not to be questioned, he determined that they should be nourished by the milk of goats.

"Upon this arrangement I took upon me the sole care of the twins, with the assistance only of a young woman who had attended on the late Signora, and been a favourite with her, and whose parents were peasants in the neighbouring village, and tenants of Di Rosalva.

"When my charges were rather more than five weeks old, I was one day informed that there was a woman below in the hall, who desired to speak either with the Signor di Rosalva or myself. As I knew that the least exertion was painful to him, in his present state of affliction, I went down myself, and found, expecting me, a middle-aged woman, whose appearance denoted her to have been reduced from a state of some condition in life, to recent poverty. Her dress it was that so forcibly conveyed this idea, being composed of garments that had once been rich and ornamental, and which, in their present tattered and soiled state, were emblems of the most pitiable indigence.

'Do I behold the Signora Bianca?' she said, as I approached her.

'Yes,' I replied, 'Bianca is my name.'

'Alas, Signora,' she returned, 'my visit is a sorrowful one! I have walked hither from Genoa, to implore some little charity from the lady whom I still believed to be the mistress of this house, and my misery is now complete, in finding her to be no more. Oh Heaven, what will become of me, wretch that I am!'

"Her spirits and strength seemed equally exhausted; the dust upon her shoes and stockings confirmed her having come on foot from Genoa; and the compassion I felt for any object, thus sinking under fatigue of body, and affliction of mind, caused me to invite her to take a seat, and to order some refreshment to be set before her.

"When I had given her a glass of wine and water, she appeared in some degree refreshed, and said—'It is impossible, Signora, to express the wretchedness of my situation; complicated misfortunes have driven me out of the house which the excellent Signora di Rosalva had, in her humanity, provided for me. I am cast a beggar upon the world, and in this painful dilemma I have directed my steps towards her mansion, that I might, in person, explain to her the calamities I am suffering under, and I now find her dead—no longer able to offer her consolation or support to an unhappy woman, who has so long existed on her bounty alone.'

'If this is the case,' replied I, 'if you are one whom the deceased Signora thought worthy of her countenance, there is no doubt but that, from affection for her memory, not less than a reverence for the dictates of humanity, the Signor di Rosalva will afford you some relief.'

'He must, I think, know who I am,' she replied; 'I am, wretched and humble as I now appear before you, a distant relative of his angel wife. Tell him, I entreat you, Signora, that the unfortunate Maria Calotti begs to fall at his feet.'

"I undertook, without hesitation, to carry her message to Di Rosalva.—'Poor woman!' he exclaimed, on receiving it, 'although I have myself never seen her, I know her well, from the report of my beloved, my departed wife, to be an object of pity and charity; she has seen better days; she has two unhappy sons, who are the causes of constant affliction to her; but it must be some excessive calamity, I think, which brings her hither, and on foot. Tell her I will come to her immediately.'

"When I returned with the Signor's answer, she expressed great joy, and began to inform me that one of the sons, whom he had mentioned to me, was just returned from sea, and had, with a most abandoned courtezan, who was attached to him, driven her out of her house, and seized upon what little property she had been possessed of, to supply themselves with the indulgence of all kinds of extravagant pleasures.

"When the Signor di Rosalva came to her, she recounted to him, with a fresh flood of tears, her accumulated misfortunes, and said that she had walked hither from Genoa, in order to entreat the only relative of whom she was now possessed, with the exception of her unnatural sons, to afford her the means of a present subsistence, and to gain her redress, for the injustice practising against her.

"Di Rosalva assured her, that one like herself, who had not only been accustomed to find a friend of the most liberal kind in his deceased wife, but who was also her relative, should never sue in vain to him; and he invited her to remain a few days in his house, during which time, he said, he would write upon the subject to a friend of his in the law at Genoa, and desire such steps as her case required, to be pursued in her favour.

"For this kind assurance, on the part of Di Rosalva, she expressed most unbounded gratitude; and would have burst into a string of united encomiums on the virtues of the deceased Signora, and lamentations at her untimely loss, had not I, by a look which I gave her, restrained her from proceeding on a subject so heart-rending to the senses of the Signor Sylvio. In his presence, accordingly, she forbore to speak of her; but no sooner were we left alone, than she began to enquire of me all the particulars of her death, and to pour forth praises to her memory.

"I gratified her in answers to such questions as she advanced; and, in my turn, asked of her, how she had become acquainted with the death of her benefactress, as, from her own account, she had been ignorant of it when she had set out from Genoa?

'I learned it,' she said, 'of a peasant whom I joined on the road, near the avenue leading to this house, and who informed me that it was the Palazzo of the Signor di Rosalva. The good man came with me all the way to the house. He said he had a daughter, a servant here, and that her mother being very ill, he was come to fetch her home for a short time, to see her, as he believed her to be lying on her deathbed.'

'Indeed!' cried I; 'there is no other servant in this house whose father is a peasant in this neighbourhood, except a young woman who relieves me from the more laborious part of the attendance, which the dear babes of our deceased friend require. You must excuse my leaving you for a while; I must go and enquire whether she wants to be absent for any time from her duty.'

'Permit me,' said my new acquaintance, 'to go with you: next to the gratification I should have reaped from beholding my lost relative, will be that of contemplating her innocent babes. Pray let me go with you.'

"I readily consented, and we went together into the nursery, where I found Lauretta impatiently waiting my coming, to request that she might be permitted to go and see her dying mother.—'Theresa or Antonia,' she said, 'would readily take her place for a night.'

'You cannot,' said Maria Calotti, 'confer a greater happiness on me, than to suffer me to be the substitute of this young woman for the night of her absence; I shall experience such pleasure as I have long been a stranger to, in watching over, and attending to the wants of the children of one for whom I have ever felt the affection I did for the Signora di Rosalva, and to whose family I owe every service of which

I am capable.'

"I had some hesitation in accepting her offer; but she argued it so strongly, that I deemed I should not only be acting wrongly myself, but offend her, by refusing to accept it. I accordingly yielded to her entreaties, and Lauretta directly set off to visit her mother, with permission to remain out until the next day at noon.

CHAPTER VII

"In the evening, as we sat together, Maria said, she hoped that on the following day she should be permitted to visit the spot where her deceased relative had been buried, that she might, by the side of her tomb, offer up her prayers for the soul of one whose existence had been so great a comfort to her. I told her that she lay interred in the Church of Saint Francis, hard by, and that I would find her a proper conductor to it in the morning.

"The children slept in adjoining apartments, in each of which there was a bed, besides those in which they slept, one for me and one for Lauretta. As I had not for an instant been able to leave my charges in her absence, Maria and I had sat together in one of the chambers. When we were about to retire to bed—'They are excellently quiet children,' I said to my companion, 'and scarcely ever awake between the last time of my feeding them before I go to bed, and the hour of six or seven in the morning.'

'And yet, I warrant me,' returned Maria Calotti, 'that anxious as you must naturally be about the welfare of the important charge you have so humanely taken upon you, you wake at least a dozen times every night, whether they do or not.'

'No, I do not,' I replied; 'I very seldom wake, except they cry; but the least noise on the part of either of them rouses me instantly.'

'Except I am indebted to the length of my walk to-day for sleep,' she rejoined, 'I dare say I shall not enjoy much of its refreshment; for I am at all times a very bad sleeper, especially in a strange bed. At night too my afflictions all pour into my thoughts, and keep me awake; and when I have not them immediately to distress me, I am subject to violent pains, which often oblige me to leave my bed, and wander about my chamber for hours together.'

"I desired her to make no scruple of calling to me, if she should want any thing before morning that I could supply her with. She answered that she should not do that, and begged, if she was restless, it might not disturb me, as she was quite unaccustomed to have any one near her during the hours devoted to sleep; and upon this we bade each other good night.

"Between five and six in the morning I awoke with the cry of the infant whose little bed was placed by the side of mine. I arose, and taking her in my arms, for it was Rosabella, I went to get her some milk. In my way to the closet where it stood, I was obliged to pass the bed of my new acquaintance. I perceived that she had left it, and was not in the room. I looked into the bed of the infant Sylvio, and, to my utter astonishment, found that he was gone also.

"For a few moments I knew not what to believe; I thought that Maria must have risen, and taken the child with her into the garden. I ran to the window, in the hope of seeing her from it. A thick rain, which was falling, convinced me this could not be the case; and I now first supposed that the child had been carried off by design.

"Conscious of nothing but the loss of the child, I ran wildly into the chamber of Di Rosalva, and bursting into tears as I spoke, informed him of the discovery I had made.

"It must be unnecessary to describe the agony of an affectionate parent listening to the information I was doomed to convey to him. He sprang frantically from his bed, and throwing around him his night-gown, he ran into the gallery, calling aloud upon his servants to arise, and go in pursuit of his child, who had been stolen.

"In a few minutes most of the family were gathered round him. The agitation of his mind rendered his commands unintelligible, and I was obliged to explain for him to the domestics, the disappearance of the child, and of Maria Calotti, whom I could not but suppose to have taken it away.

"Every male servant was directly sent out in pursuit of Maria and the child; and these were ordered to communicate the intelligence to the peasantry on the estate, and engage their services likewise in the search.

'Bianca,' said Di Rosalva, addressing me, 'you now hold to your breast my only hope: grant me the single consolation my present affliction admits of; promise me, that, for the present at least, it shall not pass from your arms to those of any other individual.'

'It shall not, it shall not,' I replied; 'whatever is in my power, you know you have only to command.'

"The intelligence was quickly spread abroad; and the gentlemen whose estates were contiguous to that of Rosalva, came almost immediately to him, and made an offer of their services in his present distress. He related to them the story of Maria's arrival, as composed as he was able, and of her subsequent disappearance with the child.

'Have you not sent to Genoa,' asked one of the gentlemen, 'to learn whether she is returned to her own house, and to have her detained by the hands of justice, if she has?'

"This had, in the confusion, been omitted; and the same gentleman who had advanced the question, kindly set off for the city in person for the purpose.

"None of the servants or peasantry could gain the slightest information on the desired point; not one individual they had met with, had seen either the woman or the child; every habitation for leagues around had been searched, but without success. At length the gentleman returned from Genoa, and the information he brought opened our eyes to the atrocity of the affair. He had enquired for the house of Maria Calotti, and on reaching it, had learned from a friend who had resided with her, that she had for three days past been a corpse.

"It was now plain that some wretch had assumed her name, in order to procure herself an introduction into the house of Di Rosalva, for the infamous purpose of stealing one of his children."

"And this infamous wretch, I trust," said the Conte, interrupting Bianca, "was no other than that Rodovina Maritos, whom you so unexpectedly met yesterday in her way to prison."

"Yes, yes, the same, the same," exclaimed the Signora Bianca. "Heaven be praised that I have at length found her!"

"This explains her conduct towards me," said Sylvio.

"Towards you, my dear Sylvio!" exclaimed Bianca; "do you then know her?"

"But too well," answered Sylvio; "but indulge us by concluding your narrative, and I will then give you mine in all its particulars."

Bianca complied, and proceeded thus—

"The agonies of Di Rosalva's mind, it may be easily imagined, were such as to render him entirely unfit for the task of deciding what steps were proper to be taken for the recovery of his infant. His friends kindly took upon them the office, they promised with the morning to visit the Doge, and ask his advice upon the conduct which it was becoming to pursue in this unparalleled perplexity.

"It was late in the evening when the friends of Di Rosalva quitted his villa to prepare themselves for the business of the succeeding day, and left its unhappy possessor alone with me. We sat for a considerable time in silence. His burning head rested on my shoulder, and one of the hands of his remaining infant was held in his.

"At last, starting up, he spoke with a wildness that alarmed me; he exclaimed—'Great God! Bianca, that I should not yet have enquired which of my children it is that remains to me!'

'It is your Rosabella,' I replied.

'And is it then my Sylvio, my boy, my dear boy, who is torn from me?' he cried. 'Oh Heaven! be merciful, and restore him to the arms of his distracted father!'

"Another silence ensued, which he again broke.—'I must go to bed, Bianca,' he said. 'I am too ill to sit up.'—He took the child in his arms, and fervently kissing it, he added—'How blessed is thy state, to be unconscious of the pangs which rend thy father's heart! Selfish is my prayer, when I desire thy preservation, for thou art now my only blessing, and, without thee, the world would be a void.'—As he returned her to my arms, he addressed me—'Remember, you have promised to trust her with no one but yourself, Bianca,' he said.

'I will instantly retire with her to our apartment,' I replied; 'no one shall even accompany me to it.'

'Bear with me, I entreat you,' he said, 'for I am almost mad, and account you alone fit to be trusted in this world of treachery and crimes.'

"I would have entreated him to endeavour to tranquillize his mind, but I considered how unfeeling would appear these admonitions, which it requires a stoical apathy to follow; I therefore parted from him in silence, and locked myself within my chamber, with the infant Rosabella.

"I now, for the first time, gave vent to my own feelings. During the day I had imposed on myself the restraint of controlling them as much as lay in my power, in order that my tears might not still more unstring the nerves of the unhappy Di Rosalva; in the solitude of my chamber they flowed freely; while the innocent cherub, to whom all my attentions were directed, lay smiling in the placid lap of sleep, unconscious that an only brother had been so mysteriously snatched from her.

"About two in the morning, as I was first sinking into a disturbed sleep, I heard some one rap with their knuckles upon the door of my chamber, and at the same moment a voice without repeated, 'Bianca, Bianca!'

'Who is there?' I asked, rising up in my bed.

'It is I, it is Di Rosalva,' replied the voice, which I immediately recognised to be his. 'Pray admit me into your chamber; I have something of the most immediate consequence to communicate to you.'

'I hurried on my clothes, and opened the door to him. He came in, and shutting it again after him, he said—'Let me sit down, and endeavour to collect myself for conversation; I have a great deal of important matter floating in my brain, that I wish to communicate with you upon.'

"For a few moments I was not thoroughly convinced that affliction had not given a temporary incoherence to his mind, and I placed myself in a chair by his side, while I kept my eyes employed in watching his countenance, of which the expression very soon convinced me that my apprehensions had been groundless.

'I do not recollect,' he said, 'that you left me yesterday for a moment, after the time that my poor boy was taken from us.'

'No, I did not,' I answered.

'Nor did you, I think,' he went on, 'give Rosabella from your arms, even for an instant, into the arms of any other person?'

'You desired I would not,' I replied, 'and I felt it a pleasure in obeying you.'

'I was the first person to whom you mentioned the disappearance of my beloved Sylvio—was I not?' he asked.

'Yes,' was my reply. 'I came immediately to your chamber, on making the discovery which now afflicts us.'

'Do you not then, my dear friend,' he rejoined, 'think it probable that, all these points considered, no one but ourselves is acquainted which of the two babes it is that is taken from us?'

'I should suppose so, indeed,' I returned; 'for I perfectly recollect that you only told your servants and friends, that one of your children had been stolen, and did not say which. The confusion occasioned in the house by the event, I imagine, prevented enquiries from being made on the subject; for none were advanced relative to the sex of that which was spared us.'

'And as Rosabella was in her night dress the whole of yesterday, she wore nothing upon her to distinguish her sex by?' he continued.

'No, she did not,' I answered; 'but why such earnestness relative to this circumstance?'

'Because, with your assistance,' returned Di Rosalva, 'I intend so to use it, that, if it does not lead to the recovery of my boy, it shall, at least, foil the views of those who have stolen him. The recovery of my boy! did I say?—Oh, Bianca, I dare not flatter myself with a hope of his recovery! he has been taken hence—never to return; and I must derive the only consolation his murder, for such I know it is, can afford me, from the consciousness that his innocence must send him, an angel, to the bosom of his sainted mother.'

"The tears, for some moments, interrupted his utterance; when again capable of articulating, he proceeded thus:—

'To you, who have been almost the constant companion of my life, it must be unnecessary to repeat the anxiety that preyed upon my mind during the first years of my marriage, while my beloved wife gave me no promise of an heir. You have also, I think, heard me repeat, that, should I not be blessed with a son, my estate, in which consists nearly all my wealth, must descend to my next male heir, and that this relative is a cousin several times removed: I have scarcely ever seen him—but, from an unerring report of him, I know him to be a man of an evil disposition, who has, for many years past, been desiring my death, in order to become the possessor of my property. Assist me then, my dear friend,' he added, in the most persuasive tone of entreaty, 'assist me to bring up my Rosabella, in the eye of the world, as the male descendant of my house. As we alone, and those who have stolen from me my boy, are acquainted which of my children is now remaining to me, those who have done me this wrong cannot bring proof of the feminine sex of my present heir, without declaring themselves the perpetrators of a crime, for which the law of justice would award them the severest punishments; and if this plan does not restore to me my Sylvio, and lay open to me a knowledge of my enemies, it will, at least, have the good effect of preserving to my daughter that inheritance of which it has been their aim to deprive her.'

"I perfectly comprehended his feelings upon the subject, and I was not surprised that the unparalleled calamity which had fallen upon him should impel him to strange methods of redressing, as far as lay in his power, the evil which had been intended to his family; but I could not, at the same time, avoid foreseeing the many unpleasant situations in which a disguise of sex would place the unhappy being condemned to practise a deception which would, probably, end only with her life—and I told him, that, in my opinion, the price of her inheritance would be too dearly paid by the many unavoidable straits that the terms upon which she enjoyed it would force her into—and that, I conceived, it would be infinitely more for her happiness and his own, to suffer the event of his misfortune to weave itself out in its natural course.

"He undoubtedly heard my arguments, but they produced no change in his sentiments: his idea had been taken up with a kind of frantic resoluteness, which he deemed it cruel and unfeeling towards him, in me, to dispute; and I was constrained to become the instrument of Rosabella's sex being disguised to the world; for which purpose the clothes of her lost brother were, on the following morning, put upon her, and she was, from that time, addressed only as Sylvio."

"Unfortunate sister!" exclaimed Sylvio, "how much greater have been thy torments in inheritance, than mine in the privation which I have experienced of my rights."

"Great, indeed, have been the sufferings and conflicts of her mind," replied Bianca.

"I shall not, at this moment," she continued, "enter into a minute detail of the various feelings which have rent her innocent heart, but merely speak of such matters as tend to the elucidation of other circumstances, which it is now becoming that all here present should be made acquainted with."

CHAPTER VIII

AFTER a short pause, Bianca proceeded thus:—

"Every enquiry after the pretended Maria Calotti, and the lost Sylvio, proved in vain. For a time Di Rosalva was inconsolable, and I had very great apprehensions of his life, so strongly were the marks of heart-corroding grief stamped on his features; but time, the most efficacious of medicines in the diseases of the mind, gradually produced a change in him—and, as Rosabella grew up, his thoughts turned from the child whom he had lost, to the one which still remained to bless him.

"Arduous was, at this time, the task which my affection both for the father and the child imposed on me, of concealing the sex of the heir of Di Rosalva—a task of a much more difficult nature during the extreme youth of Rosabella, than I found it when she was become capable of comprehending those admonitions which were daily poured into her ear by her father and myself.

"Thus passed on eight years; Di Rosalva satisfied with the conduct he had pursued for preserving to his descendant that inheritance, of which a selfish enemy would have deprived his family; but still dreading that the step he had taken might have caused his enemies to revenge themselves upon him, for the subtilty he had practised towards them, by the murder of his child.

"The thought was horrid; but it was now too late to retract the action which might have been the cause of it, and he endeavoured to drive it from his mind.

"When Rosabella was on the point of completing her ninth year, Di Rosalva, who had for some time past been extremely unwell, conceived a presentiment that the hour of his death was not far distant.

"One evening, which succeeded an unusual gloomy day, and which had been rendered still more melancholy by the disquietude of mind and lowness of spirits, which the reflections of Di Rosalva, added to his ill health, had brought upon him, he called to him Rosabella, and having for some time caressed her on his knee, during which time he had more fully explained to her, than he had ever done before, the loss of her brother, and the cause for which she had been bred to the outward assumption of his sex—he took her in his arms, and moving with her along a gallery in his mansion, requested me to follow him.

"The child had listened to her father's account of her brother's disappearance with a wicked woman, who, he told her, he feared had been employed to steal him by some vile man, who intended to kill him as soon as they had got him into their power, till her little heart, which had, for the first time, been swelled with a sense of sorrow not her own, had relieved itself in tears, with which her face was still wet, when Di Rosalva carried her into an apartment at the extremity of the gallery, which was seldom in use.

"It was a room dedicated to the purpose of evening entertainments: the furniture was antique and heavy—the walls were covered with a dark-coloured silk, with which the furniture corresponded—and the only relief throughout the gloomy sameness of the whole, were large mirrors, which, at the present moment, appeared placed there solely to repeat the gloomy scene in various points of view. Di Rosalva opened the shutter of only one of the windows; its aspect was western, and it admitted those faint and watery rays of a departing sun, which do not unusually burst from the clouds for a few moments before it retires from the world after a day of rain; they fell immediately on a picture of large dimensions, which I found had been lately, and unknown to me, introduced into the apartment. To this Di Rosalva directed the attention of his daughter.

"The scenery of the piece was a wild and rugged cave, through a chasm, in the rocky substance of which, darted one ray of light, which seemed to render the surrounding gloom more awful; and this ray fell on the countenance of a beautiful girl about the age of Rosabella herself, who was seen upon her knees, in the midst of a group of men, with countenances descriptive of every cruelty, the most savage of whom was on the point of thrusting his sword into her breast.

'What think you of that picture, Rosabella?' asked her father.

'Horrid! dreadful!' she exclaimed.

'How should you feel,' he rejoined, 'if you were in place of that unfortunate child?'

"A faint 'Oh!' escaped Rosabella's lips, and she clung to me, shuddering at the idea.

'I have caused this picture to be fixed here,' Di Rosalva continued to say, 'that, by contemplating its horrors, you may learn to avoid being placed in a situation of equal misery with the child whom you there behold; regard this as a picture of your own fate, should you ever divulge the secret of your sex.'

'Fear me not—indeed, indeed, I never will,' replied Rosabella.

'It is for your own sake I caution you, my dear child,' returned her father: 'let not one rash moment of your life explain to your enemies a secret which I have, for so many years, succeeded in preserving sacred from all the world; should they discover it, doubt not that their vengeance will be to you more cruel than the swords of these assassins whom you are now contemplating. Should you, therefore, ever feel your heart inclining you to betray the secret on which your happiness depends, visit this apartment, contemplate this picture, and impose silence on your lips; and if, when absent from this spot, you should ever feel the disclosure of your sex rising to your tongue, check the impulse, by concluding that an assassin, armed for your destruction, hovers near you at the moment.'

"A silence of some minutes ensued. When Di Rosalva believed her sufficiently impressed with the horror of the subject she had been contemplating, he said—

'We will now quit this object; but fail not, Rosabella, to remember the purpose for which it is placed here.'

"The sound of his voice aroused her from a trance of thought, into which the subject had thrown her: she turned hastily round, and the reflection of the picture, in one of the large mirrors, met her eyes; she started at the sight, and, exclaiming—'Oh, mercy, there again!—I shall never forget it!' ran out of the room.

"After we had been a short time returned to the apartment where we usually sat, she addressed her father, by saying—

'Tell me, pray tell me, do you know my enemies?'

'By name only, my love,' he replied.

'Tell me their name, then,' rejoined she, 'that I may always avoid them.'

'They are called,' he answered, 'Della Piacca.'

'Then from all who bear the name of Della Piacca,' said Rosabella, 'I will ever fly, to keep myself safe from such horrid assassins as are represented in the picture."

"Della Piacca! said you?" exclaimed the Conte Lorenzo, interrupting Bianca in her narrative.

"Yes, Signor—yes, Della Piacca," replied Bianca, "the same from whom you inherit your title and your name; but suffer me to proceed to the sequel of my explanation—

"Di Rosalva's presentiment of his death was a just one: in the course of three months he paid the debt of nature; his last breath was emitted in prayers for the preservation of his daughter, and the restoration of his son to happiness, if his existence were still granted him.

From this time Rosabella and myself continued to reside at the villa, with very few acquaintances, and without any intimate friends, till she, by accident, gained a knowledge of the family Del Alvaretti. To this amiable Lady," pointing to the Contessa Averilla as she spoke, "it is needless for me to repeat how soon a friendship was contracted between them; I have only to add, that it was a friendship which formed the greatest happiness of my unfortunate Rosabella's life."

"But recollect that neither my husband nor the Signor Sylvio have heard the particulars which ensued from our introduction to each other, although they are known to us," remarked Averilla.

"Will you, my good Lady," said Bianca, hesitatingly, and casting a look of meaning at the Contessa as she spoke, "here take up the thread of my narrative for me?"

Averilla understood the delicacy of Bianca's idea, and said—

"It is immaterial which of us relates it. The Conte is already acquainted that Rosabella imposed herself on me, with so great success, for one of the sex whose habiliments she wore, that——"

"The Signor Sylvio cannot want any farther explanation of your error," interrupted the Conte, smiling; "and I cannot be sufficiently thankful to my propitious stars, that it was the *sister*, and not the *brother*, who was the object of my Averilla's first love."

The Signor Sylvio heard these confessions, with a countenance that bespoke him fully to comprehend the nature of past occurrences, but forebore to offer a single remark upon them, which might create the Contessa a momentary feeling the reverse of satisfaction.

"You cannot now want, I think, Contessa, to be told," said Bianca, addressing Averilla, "that at the moment you believed Rosabella to be on the point of making you a confession of a passion for you in the garden Del Alvaretti, you had so far won upon her feelings and her heart, that she had come to the resolution of imparting to you the secret of her sex, and that she was withheld from it by casting her eyes at the instant upon the statue of the Gladiator, which so strongly brought to her mind the words of her father, when he shewed her the picture—'If you should ever,' he had said, 'feel the disclosure of your sex rising to your tongue, check the impulse by concluding, that an assassin, armed for your destruction, hovers near you at the moment.'—And you cannot be surprised that a female, placed in the unparalleled situation she was, should have been affected by a circumstance at which any other individual would have been unmoved.

"It is impossible for me to describe," continued the venerable Bi-anca, "what were the emotions of Rosabella, when the unexpected visit of Felix, which you cannot but remember, to the villa Di Rosalva, informed her that your uncle Rossano had selected for you a husband, and first explained to her that you had regarded her friendship for you to be of a different nature to what it really was. The discovery com-municated to her heart the keenest anxiety; she dreaded lest your still supposing her to be a male should withhold you from an alliance with a man calculated to ensure your future felicity; and she now feared to make the confession of her sex to you, lest you should entrust it to your husband, and it should, through his inadvertency, fly into the world. In this perplexity of mind she determined to meet you in the church of St. Francis, at the hour of your attending mass, and, having requested your attention to a matter of importance which she should tell you she had to communicate to you, to disclose the secret of her life, and implore you to bind yourself, by a vow at the altar of your tutelar saint, not to repeat her confession to any individual being. She judged the avowal of her sex now to be necessary to your happiness, and therefore, even with a degree of hazard to her own safety, she resolved, from her high esteem for you, that no consideration should deter her from the disclosure; and the event has justified her opinion of you—she has found you a friend worthy of the most unlimited confidence."

"But why," said Averilla, "on the very day that I had pronounced this vow of secrecy, and immediately after my procuring her a recon-ciliation with the Signora Felicia and her son, did Rosabella, secretly as it were, leave the Palazzo del Alvaretti, without bidding farewell to any one of us—and on what account, I may also ask, did yourself and she so suddenly quit the Villa di Rosalva?"

"When you and your aunt," returned Bianca, "had that morn-ing quitted the apartment, and left her alone with Felix, she, for the first time, heard from his lips the name of your intended husband. The sound of Della Piacca struck terror to her heart: breathless, she instantly returned home, and seeking me, declared to me her inten-tion of flying to some distant part of the country; and I confess, that knowing such to be the name of her enemies, I felt no small degree of anxiety myself to remove to some distance from our present abode;

We accordingly left the Villa di Rosalva that very evening, and have ever since been wandering over various parts of Italy."

"You then, doubtless, supposed me the old Conte Roderigo, who has been dead many years," said Della Piacca, "and whom I myself never saw—nor did I know that I was the heir to this title, till I received information of it through the channel of the law?"

"Even so," replied Bianca; "he was the most dissolute of men, and aimed at the life of this youth," casting her eyes towards Sylvio, "that he might secure an inheritance to a son, equally profligate as his father, and whom I have, a few days since, learned to be dead as well as himself; at which time I also became acquainted that his name and title had descended to a very distant branch of his family."

"You came to Turin the day before the last—did you not?" said the Conte; "I met you on the road, at the distance of about a couple of leagues from the city."

"Yes we did," returned Bianca.

"And you and Rosabella have also been in this city once before, since the time of your quitting the Villa di Rosalva—have you not?" asked Averilla.

Bianca fully comprehended that, in this question, Averilla referred to the letter which she had received, dated from the hotel of the Holy Virgin, during the time of her confinement to her chamber, and replied—"It is very true, Contessa; but I cannot speak of that visit to Turin; Rosabella must herself inform you of our motive for that. Pardon me; but I do not feel myself at liberty to disclose *one secret* which still labours in her breast."

"To this secret," she continued, "was owing our arrival in this place on the evening before the last. My meeting with Rodovina Maritos, as I now find the wretched woman who imposed herself upon me and the late Signor di Rosalva, for Maria Calotti, to be named, you are already acquainted with. Rosabella's sole reason for coming hither had been to seek an interview with the Contessa: throughout the whole of the day my rencontre with this woman, and its consequences, had detained her from putting her design into execution. In the evening she set out from our hotel for that purpose; and as her enemy, the late Conte della Piacca is now no more, I cannot guess on what account the poniard of any assassin can have been aimed at her innocent breast."

"Was it not, perhaps," said Sylvio, "rather intended to have pierced my heart than that of my unfortunate sister; and that the resemblance we bear to each other, of the strength of which the errors that it has led the most intimate friends of us both into, is an undeniable proof, may have deceived those who were employed upon my destruction?"

"Have you then enemies, whom you suspect of this treachery towards you?" asked Bianca anxiously.

"That Rodovina Maritos," replied Sylvio, "who stole me from the protection of my parent, is accused of the murder of a merchant, named Eldorado, lately dead in this city. In her examination yesterday, before the court of justice, she charged the accusation brought against herself upon me, and mentioned one Michael Vivane, as a witness that I had committed the crime. I had, accordingly, last night information brought me, that I must appear to-day in the court at a certain hour, to confront this Michael Vivane. About three hours ago, fresh intelligence was brought me that Michael Vivane was not to be found; and that the process, of course, must be delayed till he could be made to appear. Does it not, from these circumstances, strike you as probable that no such person as Michael Vivane exists? that she mentioned him as a witness of the crime, which she knows not to have been perpetrated by me, merely to gain herself time? and that she has used that time in employing some of her vile accomplices to take away my life, in the hope that my death would free her from the charge of Eldorado's murder, and equally spare her a confession of such knowledge as it has already appeared evident that she is possessed of concerning my fate?"

The Conte Lorenzo immediately replied, that he judged Sylvio's conclusions to be drawn with much appearance of their being just.— "I will, without delay," added he, "set on foot an experiment, by which we shall, in a very short time, discover whether those villains, who last night attacked your sister, were the accomplices of the infamous Rodovina. If they are such, nothing but the temptation of reward could have linked them to her service; a stronger temptation will as quickly convert them into her enemies. I shall, therefore, instantly publish the reward of one thousand zechins for the apprehension of either of the two ruffians who last night pursued your sister up the steps of my palazzo."

Sylvio was beginning to pour forth the gratitude of his heart to the Conte, for the interest he manifested in the happiness of himself and his sister; but the Conte stopped him by saying—"Not another word, or I must call in Flavia, to convince you how much I am still your debtor. I shall go immediately, and take the proper steps for putting my design into execution. In the mean while, do you compose yourself to meet your sister, and use a few minutes of the intermediate time to convince Flavia that you are the same human being to whom she owes the preservation of her life;" and with these words the Conte departed, to execute the purpose of which his mind was now full.

CHAPTER IX

IT must easily be imagined how many interesting subjects Bianca and Sylvio had to discuss, and with what avidity they seized the first moment that offered itself to their acceptance for that purpose.

But the privilege of conversing together was not long allowed them after the departure of the Conte; for Sorato entering the apartment, informed them that Rosabella was awake, much refreshed and amended by the sleep she had enjoyed, and anxiously enquiring for the Contessa.

Averilla immediately replied to the summons by rising to leave the apartment, and the Signora Bianca rose to follow her, saying—"I am sure she will be the happier for seeing me; I cannot, therefore, delay to visit her; and you, my dear Sylvio, shall soon be introduced to the sister whom you have never known. I shall have no apprehension in shortly disclosing to her the happy intelligence of your being restored to us; it will relieve her mind of a weight of anxiety, that must accelerate the return of her health and strength."

When left alone in the apartment, Sylvio's mind rested upon the events of his infancy, which had just been made known to him, and as he dwelt on the destruction which had, at that early period of life, threatened him, and compared it with the felicity for which the beneficent hand of Providence had reserved him, the mingled sensations of his soul drew the tears into his eyes, and as he wiped them from his face, he exclaimed—"Oh, my dear father! that thou wert still alive, to witness the happiness of thy children! My mother too, would thou hadst also been spared to bless us with thy presence!"

As he uttered these words, he felt a hand placed upon that which he was holding before his eyes, that drew it gently from his face, and on turning round his head, he observed that it was Flavia, who now held his hand in both [of] her's.—"Don't cry, Signor Sylvio," she said, in a tone of voice that bespoke her scarcely able to restrain her own tears, "don't cry because you have no mamma alive; my poor mamma has been dead a long while too; but I don't feel the loss of her now, the dear Contessa makes me so excellent a second mother; and I am sure she will be equally kind to you, and make you a second mother too, for she told me long ago she pitied you, and she pitied me at first, and very soon after she loved me, and so she will you, depend upon it."

When the heart is swelled to a certain pitch of tender feeling, one added particle of sympathy, poured into the vein of joy, causes it to overflow. The tears which had before started singly into the eyes of Sylvio, now burst, united, from his heart, and he clasped the little Flavia to his breast, with feelings of unutterable love and gratitude.

Flavia, who had not been perfectly convinced, till within a few moments before the Conte left the room, that Sylvio was not the ghost which the servants had supposed him, and still unable to suppress her curiosity to learn whether he was of this world or not, had been standing behind a silk curtain, which, in the summer months, was the substitute of a door that opened from this apartment into the garden. From this covert she had heard the whole of Sylvio's story, and being rather ashamed of confessing herself a listener, she intended to have left the place of her concealment, without entering the apartment, by the way she had reached it; but Sylvio's address to his deceased parents had struck so forcibly to her heart, that she could not resist the desire she felt of offering him consolation.

Whilst Sylvio still held Flavia in his arms, the Conte, returned from the city, entered the apartment. Flavia ran to him, and exclaimed—"Papa, won't you be the Signor Sylvio's father, and allow my second mamma to be his mamma too? Do say you will: you once told me it was my duty to confer the greatest happiness in my power on him, as the preserver of my life; and I am sure, if I judge of him by myself, he cannot be more happy than in being allowed to have the same excellent parents that I am blessed with."

The Conte uttered an affirmative from his heart to the request of

Flavia; and the present moment cemented, by the most sensitive ties, a friendship commenced under the most interesting of circumstances.

In the afternoon, Rosabella was so much restored, by the joint efforts of Sorato's care and the nursing of the Contessa, as to be able to leave her bed; and as the first subject upon which she attempted to address her friend Averilla and the Signora Bianca, was to explain to them the uneasiness which she had experienced from a knowledge of the discovery of her sex having been made to Sorato and the Conte della Piacca, Bianca judged that she could not act more wisely, in the case of her niece, than gradually to reveal to her, that the necessity of her appearing in a male habit had ceased.

The task is sometimes difficult, to communicate an event of excessive joy, in such a manner that it may not produce on the hearer an effect of an opposite nature; but Bianca so adroitly conducted the discovery of Sylvio's being restored to his family, that Rosabella suffered as slightly as possible from the unexpected intelligence.

But those feelings which had been controlled while his idea alone was present to her mind, she could no longer repress when he stood before her. With a wild shriek, she attempted to spring into his arms, but sunk back upon her chair, overpowered with the exertion; while Sylvio stood utterly unable to afford her assistance; every sense was deprived of its power, save his eyes, and they fastened themselves upon his sister with a gaze of astonishment, which bespoke him almost incredulous, that it was not the reflection of himself upon which they were fixed.

At length the charm, which held the senses of each in subjection, died away. Rosabella revived to an easy composure of mind; and the surprise of Sylvio yielded to the joy he experienced at folding a long-lost sister to his heart: it was a moment of transport that exceeded any emotion which they had hitherto felt.

In the course of the evening it was explained to Rosabella, that the poniard from which she had been a sufferer, had doubtless been aimed at the breast of her brother, the leading events of whose history were, in as few words as possible, made known to her, with a promise that the particulars of his life should be recited to her on the morrow, after a night of rest should have better enabled her to give her attention to them.

The wound which Rosabella had received was not very deep; it was from loss of blood that she had most materially suffered; thus weakness was at the present moment her chief cause of indisposition.

To her brother's questions, of when she had first been assailed by the bravoes, and whether she thought she should know either of them again? she replied, that at some distance from the palazzo della Piacca, she had on the preceding evening seen two men in masks, whom she had remarked to be observing her, but of whom she had entertained no dread, till they had pursued her up the steps of the colonnade; and that, although their countenances had been concealed from her by their masks, still there was something so striking in the figure of him who had given her the blow, that she thought she could not fail to recognise him, should she ever again behold him.

The Conte informed her of the reward he had published for their apprehension, and with a fervent wish from the lips of all, that the succeeding day might throw some elucidation upon the past mystery, they left the chamber of Rosabella.

The Conte remarked, that till the enemies of Sylvio were detected and brought to justice, it would not be safe for him to appear in the streets by night, and therefore insisted on his taking a bed at the palazzo. The Signora Bianca he also entreated to consider it as her home for the present; and the happy circle assembled beneath its roof, in a recapitulation of past events, heightened the enjoyment of the present hour.

CHAPTER X

ABOUT the fall of twilight, on the following evening, the Count Lorenzo was informed that there was a man at the gate of the palazzo, requesting to be admitted to his presence. Not doubting that the person was one of the confederates in the villany to which Rosabella had so nearly fallen a sacrifice, he imparted his suspicion to Sylvio, and they retired to a private apartment, into which they ordered the man to be brought to them.

In a few minutes he appeared. He was tall and handsome; in age, he seemed at most twenty-seven years; his countenance was expressive of contending despair and satisfaction; and his dress such as bespoke him necessitous, without being the garb of one in a very inferior situation of life.

"Do I," he said in a faltering, but still impressive tone of voice, "do I, in either of these Signors, behold the Conte della Piacca?"

"This is the Conte," said Sylvio.

As Sylvio spoke, the stranger, for the first time, turned upon him his eyes, which had before been directed towards Della Piacca; he started, and exclaimed—"Thank God! thank God!"

Sylvio hastily demanded an explanation of his emotion.

"I thank God," replied the stranger, "that you are unhurt, that the poniard which was the evening before the last directed at your heart, missed its aim!"

The Conte comprehended that Sylvio was still mistaken for his sister, and said—"Are you then acquainted who it was that attempted his life?"

"I am," replied the stranger; "say but that the thousand zechins you offer for his detection shall be mine, and I will make him known to you—deliver him up into your power."

"Doubt me not," returned the Conte; "the proclamation which I have made to that effect is your security for the performance of my promise. Tell me then who is the villain."

"Myself," replied the stranger.

"You!" ejaculated Sylvio.

"You!" echoed Della Piacca; "and are you come hither voluntarily to expose yourself to the vengeance of the law?"

"Even so," returned the young man. "My life has been a series of infamy, not from choice, but because I found the hardened nature of the world to be such, that by the pursuit of virtue, I could not procure bread for an aged parent, whose sole dependence for support was on me; for her, therefore, and not for myself, have I been a villain. The moment is now arrived, at which I may expiate my crimes, by the punishment which is due to them; and by the same act ensure to my parent comfort and independence for the remainder of her days. Conduct me, therefore, to prison; but ere I die, grant me the satisfaction of knowing my mother possessed of the thousand zechins which you have offered for my apprehension."

With equal astonishment did the Conte and Sylvio listen to this declaration on the part of the stranger; the confession he had made of the atrocity of his past life, and his heroic intention of sacrificing his own existence to secure the independence of a parent in want, appeared to them irreconcileable contradictions.

"Who are you?" exclaimed Della Piacca; "what is your name?"

"Michael Vivane," replied the young man.

"Michael Vivane!" repeated the Conte. "Have you then any knowledge of a woman named Rodovina Maritos?"

"Knowledge of her!" exclaimed Vivane; "fiend of hell! it is to her that I owe my fall from those principles which can alone render man happy and respected; by being a witness of her atrocities, by listening to her unwholesome precepts, and following her vicious examples, I have sunk gradually into error. But the hour of delusion is past; my resolution has not forsaken me with my honour, and I will expiate my crimes with death and ignominy in this life, in the hope of forgiveness being granted to me in the next."

The young man's case appeared interesting to the Conte and Sylvio, not only on account of his connection with the vile Rodovina, but also from the sentiments of repentance which seemed to flow in sincerity from his heart; and they requested him to relate to them such particulars of his life as were connected with Rodovina, and her designs upon Sylvio.

Vivane readily complied, and spoke thus—

"My father was once a creditable tradesman in this city. On the day that I compleated my seventeenth year, he died. I was his only child, and so great had been the repute of wealth and worth that had ever been attached to his name, that my mother believed she should find herself in possession of an ample fortune at his decease; instead of which, picture to yourself her disappointment, her misery at finding that her husband had died insolvent, and that nothing was left her which she could now call her own, except a few articles of wearing apparel, and some ornaments of trifling value.

"The sudden and unexpected discovery of the wretched situation to which she was fallen, produced so great a shock upon her frame, that it, in some slight measure, affected her reason, and reduced her to a state of nervous weakness and ill health, from which she has never recovered.

"I alone appeared to her the single comfort which Heaven had spared her in the midst of all her calamities. But, alas! her hopes in me were visionary, at least as far as they had referred to the future honour and credit to which I might rise in the world.

"My mother had had the principal direction of my education, and relying on my father's being possessed of a sufficient fortune to enable me to live without the drudgery of following any trade, I had been left uninstructed in such branches of knowledge as might, at the time of his death, have led to my advancement in life.

"How melancholy an example is my case, of the necessity of every man being made acquainted with those branches of useful knowledge which cannot burden the understanding of the richest, which are serviceable to the lowest orders of society, and of which the most preeminent quality is their power of extricating, from the gulph of misfortune, those who are doomed by fate to slip in their passage through life from the eminences of fortune, on which they had believed themselves to be securely treading!

"Totally unacquainted how to render myself useful in trade, I found no one willing to take upon himself the pains or the humanity of becoming my instructor; and every application I made for the purpose of procuring myself a situation, was attended with a negative, that every time discouraged me more and more from renewing it in any other quarter.

"Driven from our home by my father's creditors, I took up my abode, with my remaining parent, in a mean dwelling in a back street of the city, where we subsisted on the sale of such articles as had been her own private property in the life-time of her husband. My constant thoughts were placed upon the beggary to which we must inevitably be reduced when they were all gone, if fortune did not favour me, in presenting to me the means of averting the evil from my parent and myself. She appeared as if she had lost the faculty of thinking, partook sparingly of such food as I provided for her, without any comments or enquires how it was procured, and continued to weep almost incessantly. Thus, by the melancholy state into which she had fallen, I was deprived of the only counsellor upon whose advice I could have relied in my present forlorn situation.

"False shame for a long time prevented me from offering myself to perform those menial offices by which I saw many lads of my age, who had been brought up differently to myself, earning a livelihood. At length the necessities of my mother overcame my delicacy, and I presented myself at one of the travelling waggons, for the purpose of either assisting in carrying the luggage of the passengers, or shewing the way to those who were strangers to any part of the city where their business might lie.

"The first man to whom I acted in the capacity of servant, was a priest. He gave me a small trunk to carry, and ordered me to follow him. As we went along, I told him that I had been reduced from a very different situation, to the one he now saw me in; that I had a mother ill, and hoped, for the love of humanity, he would reward me generously. He did not reply, and when we reached the gate of the monastery to which I found he belonged, he stopped, and receiving the trunk at my hands, said—'God bless thee and thy mother,' and entered the gate.

'Will you not reward me for my trouble, father?' exclaimed I.

'Prayers,' replied he, 'are the only rewards our fraternity ever bestow; those thou hast had;' and with these words he disappeared.

"What were my feelings at that moment it is impossible for me to describe! I could have rushed upon any vice, to relieve the necessities of my suffering mother—lied, stolen, nay, even murdered, so inexpressible an effect had this mark of inhumanity, from one in the habit to which I had ever been taught to look up for the example of my life, produced on my mind.

'Is not this,' I exclaimed, 'an authority for criminality in me, when I observe one whose office it is to preach the duties of charity, thus making a mock of affliction in his actions? If this is the conduct of the world at large, if the ministers of religion can reconcile it to their consciences to bestow only prayers on those who stand in need of actual relief, can it be a sin in me to feed a hungry mother by any means which present themselves to my hand?'

"It was at this moment that the advice of a truly well-disposed heart would have convinced me of my erroneous judgment, and led back my heated imagination to the path of rectitude, from which it was now straying; but no such counsellor presented himself to my ear. It was my fate to meet with a being of an exactly contrary disposition, whose frail arguments at this moment fixed my ideas in the horrid channel they were roving in—and this being was no other than Rodovina Maritos.

"She lived in the neighbourhood where my mother and myself resided. She had before spoken to me, more than once, on the subjects of the day; and now chancing to meet me on the way home, after the disappointment which had attended my first attempt at service, she addressed me, enquiring what was the matter with me, that I looked so angry and unhappy? In few words I explained to her my case.

'You have met with nothing uncommon to those who are acquainted with the world,' she answered. 'Those who are most able to afford relief to such as stand in need of it, are always the most backward in its performance—and men who set forth doctrines of goodness, like priests and orators, are always found to be satisfied with moving others to virtue, without practising it themselves. If you are in the needy situation you say,' she continued, 'come and be occasionally at my house—I have many little offices wherein I can make you useful, and with much more ease to yourself than the slavery of a porter's business; you were not born to work, I am sure.'

"I confessed such to be the case.

'Nor shall you work, at least not in any way that shall fatigue you,' said she, 'if you will come and be at my house. Walk with me, and I'll shew you where it is.'

"I complied—and not to detain you upon this part of my narrative, I found her house handsome and well furnished; her daughter Vitellia, and another young girl, whom she called her niece, resided in it, beside herself. She told me that they were both unfortunate in not having a brother, which frequently exposed them to rude attacks from young men of quality without morals; and that if I would act the part of a protecting relative to them, she would, in return for my kindness, consider me, and treat me, as her son. I suspected no ill of one who spoke so fairly, and procured myself apparel suitable to the appearance of her son, for which she provided me with money—and I was at her house as much as she desired my company.

"In a short time I discovered that both the young females had lovers, at whose visits I was seldom admitted to their presence, but regularly detained there when any other men came to the house; and, in a few months more, my eyes were opened to the real nature of every thing which I saw. But Rodovina had so far inveigled me into her toils and her opinions, that I saw it not in the light of disgust and horror, with which it would have inspired me had I been less ably trained than I had been during my noviciate in her service.

"At the end of about a year, reflection began to steal into my mind;

but as my mother's faculties continued as incapable of argument as they had been from the few first days after her present misfortunes had fallen upon her—and as I had no acquaintance beside herself, but such as were living in situations similar to my own, the ideas which one hour of solitude would give birth to, were ever dispelled by the conversation of my associates.

"Thus passed on four years, during which Rodovina Maritos had twice changed her habitation, and her daughter and pretended niece had twice as often transferred their favours, from one object to another; and, during these years, the most arduous task which had been imposed upon me, had been that of representing the husband of Vitellia, to an old Nobleman, on whose purse the keen-eyed Rodovina had fixed her desires. The plan succeeded, and I had a share, although a limited one, of the spoil, with which I encreased, to my unhappy mother, such comforts as she was capable of tasting.

"Time moved on in a monotonous round of disgusting similarity—I felt my trammels more keenly every day, and every hour I wished more ardently to be freed from them; but I felt, also, that I had entered upon a plan of life which must have cut off from me the possibility of ever being admitted into an honourable employment—that, if I should quit my present means of existence, I could not hope to procure any other except of the same nature—and thus I must either continue to pursue a life, which I abhorred, or see my mother reduced to want for the gratification of my feelings, which it would be in vain for me to attempt to explain to her. She would judge me cruel, unfeeling, unnatural, if her comforts were curtailed to her; and only be able to comprehend that it must be to some fault of mine that the change was owing.

"In this conflict of mind, months and years passed on, till Vitellia was taken into the house of the merchant Eldorado to reside, and contrived that her mother should also be admitted as a resident with her. Rodovina told me of her good fortune, and added, that as I had been docile and attentive while in her service, as she now plainly called it, and as it was very possible that the wheel of fortune might quickly revolve, and she might again be glad of me for one of her household, she would continue my friend.

"Not having, now, her house to resort to, I was entirely at my own disposal, and had more leisure for my reflections; and I had actually come to the resolution of quitting my present mode of life, when Rodovina, calling on me one day, as she had frequently done, with small sums of money, since her residence in the merchant's house, informed me, that her daughter Vitellia had wheedled the old miser into marrying her, and that she was, on the following day, privately to become his wife—'After his death, therefore,' added she, 'we shall have a round sum at our disposal, and I will then find you an honourable situation in my daughter's family, as a reward for your past adherence to our interest.'

"This intelligence gave me some satisfaction. I hoped that both mother and daughter would now abjure their former habits, and that it would not, at the time she had mentioned, be any disgrace to me to be one of their family.

"On the day that she announced to me her daughter's marriage with the Signor Eldorado, she made me a handsome present; for her exultation at the success of her plans had opened her heart—and I saw her no more for nearly two months.

"When we met again, her countenance was not, by any means, so expressive of pleasure as it had been when we had last parted. She said, that, in her eagerness to procure her daughter an alliance with the Signor Eldorado, she had not so fully considered, as she ought to have done, the importance of compelling him to fix on her a handsome settlement at his death; and that now he had, by marriage, obtained the possession of her daughter's person, which she had artfully instructed her to withhold from him for some weeks previous to the time of his making her his wife, as a stimulus to urge him to the action, she could not succeed in inducing him to alter the will, which she knew to have been, for some time past, made by him solely in favour of his children.

"However chagrined as she might be herself, she abated not of her usual generosity to me, probably dreading that the time was near at hand when she might again feel the want of my services.

"Some time after she had given me this unsatisfactory intelligence, she again sought me out, at her accustomed hour in the evening. Fortune, she said, had once more smiled upon her: a gentleman, whom she had, in the most unexpected and strange manner, discovered to be heir to an immense property, had seen her daughter at mass—had fallen violently in love with her—and requested an introduction to her, through her, whom he supposed to be her *governante*. The gentleman to whom she was alluding, she proceeded to say, had fallen into the error of believing her daughter to be the child of the merchant Eldorado—that she had encouraged his idea—and having found that the tongue of rumour had informed him that the merchant would not allow his daughter to entertain a suitor during his lifetime, on account of his aversion to portioning her off before his death, which was the actual truth, she had taken advantage of this circumstance, for acting with such pretended caution as should prevent him from being seen by the father, by which means she had also prevented him from seeing the Signora Lucia, the real daughter of the merchant. All, she said, had prospered hitherto under her management, and she doubted not but that immediately on the death of the Signor Eldorado, the gentleman of whom she spoke would marry Vitellia, and carry her to the estate to which he was heir, at a great distance from hence, which would effectually prevent him from ever discovering that it was not the daughter of the deceased miser whom he had taken to wife.

"You, Sir," said Vivane, interrupting himself in his narrative, and addressing Sylvio, "are the gentleman on whom she had fixed to execute this vile deception."

"I am!" replied Sylvio.

"You cannot, Signor," continued Michael, "imagine how eagerly I desired to know your name, that I might have informed you of the toils that were spreading for you, and trusted to the generosity of your nature to have placed me, as my reward, in a situation no longer to need those wages my soul abhorred to receive from the hand of Rodovina; but she had, doubtless, sufficient cunning to fear that such might be the issue of her entrusting me with it—for she tenaciously withheld from me that, and every particular by which I could have guessed at the person whom she had marked out for her dupe."

CHAPTER XI

Michael Vivane proceeded thus:—

"Would that the discovery of your name had been permitted me by the kindness of fate, I had not then stood accursed, as I now do, in the eyes of heaven and of man."—His voice faltered; he endeavoured to collect his fortitude, and continued speaking thus—"When she summoned you into the court of justice, on her accusation of your having refused to fulfil a promise of marriage which you had made to her daughter, she sent to call me to her, and informed me of what she had done, telling me, for the first time, your name, and adding, that she made no doubt but that the law would award her daughter so heavy a recompense, as would immediately impel you rather to take her to wife, than submit to so great a diminution of your property.

"In the evening of the same day, the report of the city informed me what had been the event of the trial, and also of Rodovina's having been detained a prisoner, on suspicion of her having been the murderer of the merchant Eldorado, who, it was discovered, had died by poison. Scarcely had this intelligence reached me, ere she sent to summon me to her in the prison where she was confined.

'I have much business, and business of importance, for you to perform,' she said, the moment she saw me.—'I am accused of having been the murderer of the merchant Eldorado; they have already discovered that he died by poison.'

"I started and shuddered. She did not appear to notice my emotion, but added—

'I shall foil their plans with regard to myself, and, at the same time, gain revenge on Di Rosalva: I shall accuse him of the murder of Eldorado, which I shall make it appear that he perpetrated, in order to accelerate his marriage with her whom he supposed to be his daughter.'

'Horrid idea!' I exclaimed; 'but how can you expect to gain belief to this assertion?'

'You,' she replied, 'must ensure me that, by appearing in my favour as a witness to the deed.'

"Her words struck me with so great horror, that I trembled at every joint, and was unable to speak.

'Not only this,' she continued, 'but you must also render it impossible that this Di Rosalva should appear to confront my declaration—and his not appearing in the court will immediately give colour to my fabrication, by rendering it believed that he is fled, under the alarm of justice overtaking him for his crime, which will at once absolve me of suspicion.'

'I will sooner die!' I exclaimed, 'than become accessary to a plan of this heinous nature.'

'Many men,' she answered, 'can talk calmly of death, who have not the fortitude to stare him in the face. You will be put to the test,' she continued; 'for, unless you comply with my proposals, you *must* die yourself.'

"Again I fixed my eyes on her in silence, unconscious whether or not I heard her right.

'Shall I explain myself?' she said.—'Thus then—if you refuse to make it impossible for Di Rosalva to contradict the charge which I shall refute upon him I will bring into court satisfactory proof of *your* having been the administerer of the poison to Eldorado.'

'Almighty Heaven!' I, with difficulty, articulated, 'can there be such wickedness in the breast of a human being?'

'Is there any human being,' she returned, 'who will not put in practice any measure to save his own life?'

'However guilty,' I replied, 'I may, from your instruction and ex-ample, have been in other respects, you know me entirely innocent of the merchant Eldorado's death. How can you talk of bringing satisfac-tory proofs against me into a court of justice?'

'Do you not,' she returned, with the malicious smile of a demon seated on her lips, 'recollect my one night employing you to fetch me a drug from an obscure vender of medicines in a retired part of the city?—that was the draught which sent old Eldorado to his account. I feared Di Rosalva's patience would be worn out, by his being so long kept in expectation of the hand of the supposed Lucia, and I, there-fore, accelerated the event which was to give her him to wife.'

'Heaven and earth! was I made the instrument of procuring you an accursed draught, which has curtailed a fellow-being of his allotted portion of years?' I rejoined.

'Have I not paid you handsomely,' she cried, 'for the utility you have been of to me?'

'Were you to crush me beneath the weight of your gold,' I re-plied, 'you could not reward me for the loss of that guiltless mind I possessed when you first knew me.'

"She increased her smile, as it were with the satisfaction which she experienced from the assurance I had now given her, of my ruin being chargeable upon her, but spoke not.

'Equally,' said I, 'do I defy you to bring a proof that I have been the monster your baseness would assert me to be.'

'Do you?' she cried, with a serenity of tone and countenance which I believed to be assumed, till she added—'Advance, my better friend.'

"Her eyes, as she spoke these words, were turned towards a door in her cell that stood open, and from which immediately issued, in compliance with her call, a needy, mean and squalid male figure, which I instantly recollected to be the indigent wretch at whose miserable shed I had, according to the direction of Rodovina, bought that drug, of which I had never, till this fatal night, suspected the nature."

Vivane paused a moment, then said—"I am sensible how repugnant to the feelings of men like yourselves must be the description of scenes, which display the most wretched depravity of human nature; I shall, therefore, hasten to the conclusion of my account.

"The vender of the drug, whose name was Iago Zincti, I found to be a wretch of such abject necessity, and so devoid of every pretension to those qualities of the heart which alone do honour to the name of man, that he was entirely at the disposal of Rodovina, and ready to act his allotted part in any villany of which she might command the perpetration.

"A few minutes conversation with this Zincti convinced me, that, if I did not agree to enter into the diabolical plan of Rodovina against your existence, my own life would immediately pay the forfeit of my refusal. In this case my wretched, my necessitous parent, would be left alone in the world, without one consoling hand to relieve her wants; the reflection was insupportable—maddening; it drove me to the resolution of making any sacrifice of myself, rather than condemning an aged parent to die deserted and in want.

"How dreadful were the pangs of thought which I endured, when, at the dead hour of midnight, I quitted the prison, and the infamous woman whom its walls inclosed! How did I curse the first moment of my acquaintance with her! How did I lament that I had not exerted my resolution to free myself from her toils, when I first began to perceive the banefulness of her character! One moment I had half resolved to fly from the city; but, in this case, the same calamities would overtake my mother as in that of my death, as she was incapable of moving with me. The presence of the villanous Zincti, also, who refused to leave me till we should have perpetrated the deed required of us by

Rodovina Maritos, would have rendered this step impracticable, had there been no other obstacle to it in my own mind.

"No consideration could, that night, have induced me to have returned to the habitation beneath whose humble roof slept my mother. Strange it is, that, when the mind is perplexed by the dread of horrors attendant on conscious criminality, its greatest torture should frequently arise more from concomitant circumstances, than from the contemplation of that act from whence they spring.

"Zincti led me to his own home—the wretched habitation where I had so innocently made the purchase commanded me by the vile Rodovina, and upon which she had doubtless employed me, with an artful view to the emergency in which she might be placed by its use, and the hold it would, in such case, give her upon my services; as Zincti being, to every appearance, as intimate with her as I was, there could have been no necessity for her sending me to fetch it from his shop.

"Zincti placed liquor before me, and endeavoured to reconcile my mind to the business which my soul abhorred to think upon, by recounting to me the various acts of a like heinous nature in which he had been an actor. I listened to him, but was not moved by his arguments. I drank, almost unconscious of so doing; and, having swallowed a greater quantity of liquor than the harassed state of my brain was able to bear, I fell asleep in the chair where I sat. My mother had been the constant object of my waking thoughts, and she continued so, now they were lodged in sleep: I dreamt that I saw her lying on a miserable pallet, more pale and emaciated than she really was, her eyes dim, her lips quivering—'Where,' I imagined she faintly pronounced, 'is my son, that he brings me no food to save me from death?'—So forcibly was the idea of her voice impressed on my senses, that I awoke at the supposed sound, and was surprised to find that I was not by her side.

"Zincti had thrown himself upon a bed, and called to me to come and take part of it. I felt faint, sick, and trembling; I staggered to the bed, and fell down upon it. Zincti soon slept again; for myself, my thoughts, horrid as they were, were less painful than the dread of a repetition of my soul-harrowing dream, and I forbore to close my eyes again. When the morning came, Zincti did not attempt to open his shutter. The day passed in a kind of awful stillness, which I was constantly wishing to have broken, and still the slightest noise made me start and tremble violently. Towards evening Zincti produced the masks and stilettos, which were to be our only equipment for the deed of horror. Zincti had seen you, and was acquainted with your person; for myself, I knew you not. We were to lurk about the places of evening resort for gentlemen, he told me; and when you left any of these, in which we might happen to find you, we were to follow you, and, at the first convenient and private moment that should present itself to us, effect our purpose.

'Come,' said he, 'take your mask and stiletto—by the Holy Mother, it is time for us to be going.'

"The word *mother* brought to my mind afresh a train of sensations, which finally resolved me to become the wretch I hated.

"It is unnecessary for me, Signor," continued Vivane, addressing Sylvio, "to repeat to you in what part of the city we first found you; for I am conscious that you saw us observing you, which intimidated us from attacking you for a long time. At length you ascended the steps of this palazzo. I had the villanous courage to point my stiletto at your breast—but I had not the courage of a practised villain, for my hand lingered in its purpose; and, although you fell beneath my stroke, I still entertained the consolatory hope, that the feebleness of my resolution had been your safeguard from death.

"The moment you fell, Zincti fled. I returned instantly to the habitation of my mother, whom I had not visited since the preceding afternoon, and there I passed the night and the present day, in a state of inexpressible torment of mind; one moment I hoped that the blow I had given you might not prove fatal to your life, and that I should thus be spared the curse of a murderer—at another, I dreaded the vengeance of Rodovina, which, I could not doubt, would fall upon me, if she discovered that you were still in existence.

"Zincti did not approach me, nor did I receive any message from Rodovina herself.

"About two hours ago, as I sat by the casement, which I had opened for air, for air had been the only refreshment which I had felt myself capable of tasting throughout the day, I heard a proclamation pronounced, which awarded one thousand zechins to him who should discover either of the two villains that had, on the preceding evening, attacked a gentleman on the steps of the Palazzo della Piacca.

"I instantly conceived the idea which I have just imparted to you, of delivering up myself to justice, on the certainty of the promised sum being settled upon my unfortunate mother; and thus, by one action, rendering her future days independent, and atoning for my past crimes; and for this purpose am I now come hither."

Here Vivane paused.

"How strange a contradiction does this man display!" said Di Rosalva.

"It is true," replied the Conte, "but I believe him to be possessed of a mind of much feeling; and such dispositions frequently combine in them contradictions, which few but those feel their existence can believe ever to unite in the human heart."

"Rodovina Maritos," continued the Conte, addressing Vivane, "has already mentioned you to the court, as one able to prove Sylvio di Rosalva to be the administerer of poison to the deceased merchant Eldorado; and you were yesterday sought for that purpose by the officers of justice."

"This I supposed," replied Vivane. "Why they found me not, is explained by what I have told you of my having throughout the day remained in the house of Iago Zincti."

"I shall now immediately," said the Conte, "dispatch a messenger, with information to the officers of justice, that Michael Vivane is found, and will to-morrow morning appear in court."

"It is my desire you should do so," returned Vivane; "let me till that time be led to prison."

The unparalleled instance of conduct to which parental affection had driven Michael Vivane, had created for him an interest in the hearts both of the Conte and Sylvio, which even the recollection of his crime could not entirely divest them of; and the Conte said—"The sense of repentance which you now display raises you above the rank of the stubborn criminal; you shall therefore not be exposed to the rigours of a prison during this night, but remain beneath the roof of my palazzo."

Vivane acknowledged that he heard the Conte's indulgence with gratitude, but he did not appear to receive it as a mark of favour which was acceptable to his feelings; his whole soul seemed intent on the voluntary death to which he had delivered himself up, and the benefit which was to accrue from the act to his parent.

Sylvio and the Conte continued in conversation with him for some time, and the subject of their discourse leading them to mention Rosabella, Michael Vivane was informed that it had not been the Signor Sylvio, in whose presence he now stood, but his unfortunate sister, whose breast his stiletto had on the preceding evening pierced, and who was still suffering from the wound.

The sorrow and contrition which Vivane had already expressed, at the detestable deed which his hand had attempted to perpetrate, were feeble emotions of regret, when compared with those which now burst from his lips, on learning that an innocent female had been the victim of his diabolical act. "I now insist," he exclaimed, "on being led to prison; the rugged flints which compose its pavement are the only bed worthy to bear a wretch like myself, till the hour arrives at which I shall stretch my sinful frame upon the wheel; summon the officers of justice; lead me to the dungeon that I merit!"

The Conte and Sylvio were so strongly moved by the agonies of remorse under which they saw him suffering, that they could not forbear offering some consolation to his mind; but he received it with entire apathy.

The Conte had reasons for not choosing to deliver him up to the custody of the officers of justice till the following morning, and made arrangements for his being retained at the palazzo that night.—Vivane was accordingly obliged to comply, but he appeared to consider himself sinful in accepting the slightest mitigation of a murderer's fate, during the protracted period of his present existence.

CHAPTER XII

ON the following morning, at a proper hour, the Conte della Piacca, and Sylvio di Rosalva, proceeded to the court of justice, whither they had caused Michael Vivane to be conducted before them.

Previously to their setting out, they had promised him to use all their interest in his favour with the judge, in order to procure a mitigation of his punishment; but Vivane had, as on the preceding evening, heard all their promises with indifference: his desire still was to expiate the crimes of his existence by condign punishment from the hands of the law.

Rodovina entered the court with an air of firmness and insolence; she had heard that Michael Vivane was already there, awaiting her coming; but not having entertained the most remote idea that he was there in any character but that of her sworn friend, she had gathered courage from the information.

The judge had been made acquainted with the circumstance of Vivane's confessions, on the preceding night; he accordingly proceeded, upon that information, to the examination of the culprits before him.

Amazement is a weak term to express the horrors of surprise which were pourtrayed on the countenance of Rodovina, when she heard herself accused of the murder of Eldorado by Vivane; and there are not words of sufficient strength to convey an adequate idea of her feelings, when she beheld Iago Zincti, whom the Conte della Piacca had taken means to have apprehended, led into the court, pale and trembling, and immediately accused by Vivane as the man who had been an accomplice in her crime, by having sold her the drug of death, with a certain knowledge of the use to which it was her intention to apply it.

The courage of Iago Zincti was of that nature, of which it usually is in depraved hearts, insolent and confident in security, trembling and fugitive when it meets danger;—he fell on his knees before the court, and, urging his poverty as the plea of his crime, supplicated for mercy.

With his courage fell the last hope of the frantic Rodovina; she sunk upon a bench before which she had been standing, and uttered a groan, which was by many believed to be her last. Restoratives were called in, and a few minutes proved it to have been only the effect of the stifled rage and disappointment which were rending her heart.

Still one last attempt at self-preservation remained to her; she again rose, and was endeavouring to prove to the court that Vivane and Zincti had been bought to work her destruction, by the revengeful Sylvio di Rosalva;—to this accusation it became his business to reply—and having acquainted the court that Rodovina had, on one of his visits to the house of the late Eldorado, informed him that the physician had said that the old miser would not live out the month, and that she had pronounced that *he would die on that day fortnight*, on which very day he had breathed his last—which facts the Conte della

Piacca and Sylvio's lawyer both vouching for his having declared to them to have taken place long before he knew such persons as either Michael Vivane or Iago Zincti to be in existence—he concluded by saying—"that he thought the judge could not for a moment hesitate to admit the evidence of Vivane."

Iago Zincti was immediately questioned by the judge, whether the drug which he had sold to Vivane, and which he had conveyed to Rodovina, for the purpose of producing the death of the merchant Eldorado, had been the aqua tophana?

Every one present was well acquainted that it must have been from the administering of this drug alone, that Rodovina could have ascertained the exact period of her victim's death:—on Zincti's answer, therefore, to this demand, seemed to depend the decision of her fate and criminality.

Rodovina saw Zincti hesitating how to reply,—and a spark of hope once more warmed her breast.

"You had better answer at once," rejoined the judge, addressing Iago, "As I know you to have been concerned in this criminal transaction, from your own confession—your obstinacy in withholding any part of it from me, will but provoke me to command it to be wrung from you by torture."

At the mention of the torture, the coward heart of Zincti sunk still lower in his breast.—"Have mercy on me," he said, "and I will confess;—it was—it was the aqua tophana which I sent to Rodovina Maritos, by the hands of Michael Vivane."

"Hell blaze for thy reception!" shrieked Rodovina; and all sense fled from her.

While restoratives were again used to recall her to life, the judge made enquiry of Vivane, and the abject Zincti, whether they believed Rodovina's daughter, Vitellia, to have been a confederate in her mother's crime? and as they both declared their opinion of her innocence, she was not summoned to witness the dreadful scene of her mother's condemnation.

While Rodovina was yet so far senseless as to be unable to comprehend the words of the judge, the Conte della Piacca explained to him the unexampled conduct and situation of Vivane: "he had also," he said, "taken the most satisfactory means for ascertaining the truth of the account he had given of his respectable birth, and the wretched state of his mother; and he hoped, on these considerations, mercy would be extended towards him."

These words on the part of the Conte Lorenzo, were spoken in the ear of the judge; Vivane, therefore, was not conscious of their passing, and, of course, prevented from seconding or contradicting the petition of the Conte, which latter, in the present wretched state of his mind, it is most probable that he would have done. He sat await-ing his sentence with a resolute composure, which bespoke the most praise-worthy repentance; while the meanly-minded Zincti stood in the trembling suspense of a child, who dreads the correction of an offended superior.

When Rodovina Maritos again expressed signs of life and intel-ligence, the judge addressed her, inquiring if she had any thing to say in her own defence, in contradiction to the charge of which she stood convicted?

"I fall," she said, "by the malice of my enemies; may the pangs which I now endure be delight, when compared with the agonies in which they quit life!"

To this exclamation the judge returned an address, which exhort-ed her to calm the turbulent passions of her mind, and to exert the only virtue which was now left her to perform, that of meeting the fate, which justice was about to award her, with a tranquil and sincere repentance; that in dedicating her last hours to the purpose of dying a Christian, she might quit life with some expectation of receiving forgiveness in a future state.

She had a cross upon her neck—for the most vicious deceive the world, and even themselves, by the outward forms of virtue; she caught hold of it, gazed upon it for an instant, and again letting it fall from her fingers, shuddered, and cast down her eyes.

Her action evinced that the judge's exhortation had not passed unheeded through her senses, but that she had omitted to be devout, till she feared to pray at all.

"You then have nothing to urge in your defence," said the judge, after a short time which he had given her for reflection.

Upon the repetition of this question, the blood, in the course of the same minute, several times fled away from, and again returned to, her cheeks; and her lips were as frequently seen to move, but without sound: at length a faint—"No," audible only to those who stood near her, proceeded from them.

The most awful moment of the criminal's life was now approaching;—that, at which the administrator of justice, whose voice speaks collectively for every honest heart, declares him no longer worthy to exist in the society of man, into which his Creator originally sent him, free from vice, and for which his own frail passions have unfitted him.

Even Rodovina trembled when the judge rose to pronounce her fate. His words were few, but impressive. On the second day from the present he condemned Rodovina Maritos, convicted of the wilful murder of Henrico Eldorado, to die upon the wheel: the interval he once more recommended to her to use in attempts to make her peace with Heaven.

Her sentence being pronounced, she was conducted to her cell.

To Iago Zincti, as a willing accomplice in the deed, the punishment of death was also adjudged, but with the indulgence of not expiring beneath the tortures of the wheel.

Michael Vivane was lastly placed opposite the judge.—In an address of feeling, humanity, and strong sense combined, the judge called the attention of the whole court, to observe how conspicuously, in the instance of the culprit now before them, the evils of pride, indolence, and disgraceful connections, had driven him, in whose heart they had insensibly taken root, even to the dreadful act of raising his hand against the life of a fellow being. He next represented to Michael Vivane himself, the manifold mischiefs of which the death of an individual being, setting aside the heinousness of the crime itself, which cuts him off from life, might be productive, and which all naturally tend to swell the account of him at whose hand he receives his unfair death.—"You are repentant," he added, "and I rejoice to behold you so;—trusting that the penitent atonement of your future days may prepare you to die in the purity of heart in which you entered life, your existence is spared you; the law does not consider the attempt, and the perpetration of a crime, as the same; your punishment is, therefore, confined to three years of imprisonment. Again I exhort you to employ your time in making your repentance worthy of the Divine acceptance."

"Notwithstanding the resolution I had formed of dying," said Vivane, as he was led from the court, "I rejoice in the lenity of my sentence:—my mother will not now descend to the grave the parent of an executed criminal."

Sylvio and the Conte directly followed him to his cell, where they congratulated him on the lenity of his sentence, and promised that every attention should, through their means, be paid to his mother. Of the thousand zechins, which were his due, he refused to accept the smallest share, for the purpose of providing himself any comfort in his imprisonment, but insisted on their being all appropriated to the use of his mother.

CHAPTER XIII

BEFORE they left the prison, the prediction which the Conte della Piacca had made to Sylvio, that the dread of futurity would open the lips of Rodovina, concerning what was known to her of his fate, was verified; she sent to request their presence in her dungeon.

The apprehension of death had humbled the hitherto strong mind of Rodovina, and the moment she saw them, she exclaimed—"If I confess to you all I know concerning Sylvio di Rosalva, will you, for my reward, exert your influence with the state for the preservation of my life?"

"You merit no reward," returned Della Piacca, "for a confession of circumstances, which it has been a crime in you, hitherto, to have concealed;—nor will I flatter you with any promise, which it is not my intention to fulfill. I conceive your sentence to be just, and, therefore, cannot act against my own conscience, by any attempt at getting it revoked."

"Must I then die!" shrieked out Rodovina, and sunk upon the straw, which had been placed for her bed, in one corner of her dungeon.

At this moment entered Vitellia, who had brought with her a priest; she started at the sight of Di Rosalva, and flew to her mother.

"You have nothing to fear from me," said Sylvio; "the accomplices of your mother's infamy have declared you innocent of her most atrocious crime;—let her fate be a warning to yourself, to pursue that course no longer, which, if persevered in, may ultimately lead you to her misery and disgrace: if you have any interest with her, exert it to procure from her a confession of such circumstances as she is acquainted with concerning my history, and your recompence shall be the means of reform, without indigence, after her death."

The tears were streaming down the cheeks of Vitellia—"O mother! mother!" she said, "for your own sake confess, and save your soul from perdition."

"Confession before death," added the priest, "is your only hope of averting, from your sinful soul, the wrath of God in a future state, which has already fallen upon you in this life."

Rodovina fixed her eyes upon him with a frenzied stare.

The priest requested the Conte and Di Rosalva for a few moments to quit the cell; whilst he represented to her the awfulness of her present situation.

They complied, and entered the courtyard of the prison. In about a quarter of an hour the priest recalled them to the dungeon;—his arguments had prevailed;—her fear of death was now lost in her apprehensions of the state beyond that of dying; and, with a mistaken energy, she was, with wild shrieks, calling for mercy upon the Son of God!

When the frantic emotions of her mind were, in some measure, appeased, she said—"I was born in sin, may it prove an atonement for my having lived in it!—Oh, that I had never lived, thus to die!—Pray for me, that I may escape the eternal fire of God's retribution!"

She fell upon her knees, and her eyes appeared fixed, by the agony of her mind. Her daughter prevailed on her to drink some water, which she held to her lips—it seemed to cool the fever of her soul.

The priest and Vitellia raised her between them, and placed her on a stool. Clinging round her daughter, for support from falling, she turned her eyes upon Sylvio, and spoke thus—

"My brother Julio and myself were the natural children of a man of the first distinction in Parma, by a peasant girl, whom he seduced. For eight years she enjoyed, in his protection, all the affluence and affection to which the title of a wife could have given her claim; but, at the end of that period, he died suddenly, and his affairs were discovered to be so much involved, that there was not even enough left, after the expences of his funeral were defrayed, to pay the legacies which he had bequeathed to my mother and her children; and from that time she was obliged to owe her own subsistence, and ours, to the wages of the profligate.

"At the time she died my brother had just completed his nineteenth year, and I my eighteenth. My brother had already passed through various scenes of life;—he had lived in the service of a courtezan, had thence been a bravo, and, at length, was become one of a gang of pirates.—I had been initiated by my mother into all the mysteries of her profession, and was now left to pursue my way through the world, without any hand to guide my steps.

"For ten years I experienced a variety of fortune, in which adversity bore the greater share;—with the eleventh circumstances changed materially in my favour.—I became acquainted with a gentleman, some years older than myself, who placed me in a house, which he hired for my accommodation, and conducted himself towards me, in every respect, with the greatest liberality. For some time he concealed from me his name; but when I had lived with him about three years, and given birth to Vitellia, for she is his child, he informed me that he was the Conte Roderigo della Piacca, and that the reason of his having thus long forborne to let me into the knowledge of his name and rank, had been his consideration for the feelings of his wife, who had died within the last few days.

"Another year passed on like the former ones. At the expiration of this time, he one day came into my apartment, with a visible dejection hanging over his countenance. I enquired the cause of it, and after some hesitation, he replied to my enquiries by saying, that he had an only son, whom he had suffered to be as expensive in his pleasures as he was himself; that he had never curtailed him of any enjoyment which money could purchase him, because, although his own private property was, from this indulgence, fast decreasing, he had, till within the few last days, considered himself secure of inheriting considerable possessions, from a distant relative, which would repair his own broken fortune. This relative, he said, was named Di Rosalva, and lived upon his estate in the neighbourhood of Genoa; he had no personal knowledge of him, but was merely acquainted that, in case of Di Rosalva's dying without a son, his landed property must, in the course of law, descend to him.

'About eight years ago,' he continued, 'this Di Rosalva married; my apprehensions were then great, lest a nearer heir than myself should appear to claim the possessions which I coveted. Seven years having passed away, during which no sign had appeared to give Di Rosalva the expectation of becoming a father, I considered myself once more as his undoubted heir: but a cloud has overcast my hopes; I have received intelligence from a friend, who has for some time past been my spy upon Di Rosalva's conduct, that his wife is pregnant.'

"Having thus explained to me his cause for anxiety, our conversation hereafter was scarcely on any other subject, and I endeavoured to console him in his disappointment, by representing to him that the sex of the child might prove feminine, which would exclude it from the inheritance, and that, at all events, there was an equal chance of its life and death.

"At length he brought me information that the Signora di Rosalva had given birth to twins, a male and a female, and that, in the extremity of the moment, she had expired."

Here Rodovina discontinued speaking. The Conte della Piacca urged her to proceed.

"I cannot," she said, "in the present wretched state of my mind, dwell minutely on the events of my past life; the leading circumstances of the explanation you require, I will endeavour to impart to you. Suffice it then to say, that knowing at that time no interest but that of the late Conte Roderigo, he easily won me into a promise of employing persons to steal Di Rosalva's male child, which stood between him and his inheritance.

"In order to devise means for the performance of this act, he immediately transported me to Genoa, and left me with my brother Julio, who was at this time one of a company of pirates, who sailed from that port. I imparted to my brother my business in Genoa, and informed him that the reward attached to the stealing of the child was two thousand zechins. On the fourth day after my arrival, my brother said to me—'If you will entrust me with the child, and pay me the reward offered for its death, I will put you into an easy method of serving your friend, by stealing it yourself, without employing any one in the business, who might hereafter be tempted by a reward from Di Rosalva to betray you!' I liked the nature of his argument, and desired him to tell me his plan.

'One of my fellow-pirates,' he returned, 'is the son of a woman named Maria Calotti, who is distantly related to the late Signora di Rosalva, and who has for years past been in the habit of receiving from her acts of kindness. This Maria Calotti, I have positively learnt from her son, is not known, except by name, either to the Signor di Rosalva, or to his aunt, the lady Bianca. Personate her, therefore: go to the villa Di Rosalva, in pretended ignorance of the death of the Signora, and excite the pity of the Signor, by a tale of the ill-treatment you are receiving from one of your sons: so great is his character for benevolence in the world, that he will, doubtless, detain you an inmate of his house, not less out of respect to your misfortunes, than your affinity to his late wife, while he makes an investigation into the merits of your case; and this opportunity you may employ to carry off his son.

"After some hesitation, I agreed to the plan; and having disguised myself in a dress, such as was worn by the real Maria Calotti, I set out on foot for the Villa di Rosalva. On arriving there, the Signora Bianca"—"We have already heard from Bianca," said Della Piacca, "an account of your nefarious proceedings, whilst beneath the roof of your hospitable entertainer, to whose peace you were devising the means of becoming a serpent. Proceed to the moment of your quitting it with the child."

"My brother," rejoined Rodovina, "had accompanied me a part of the way from Genoa towards the Villa di Rosalva; we parted at a mean hut on the road, the owner of which he bribed to tenant him till my return; thither I immediately sped with the child; he instantly came out to me, and we proceeded to the first post-house, where he procured me a conveyance to transport me towards Parma, and another for himself, into which he ascended, after having received from my hands the child and the bag of gold; and since that time I have never seen him.

"On my return to the Conte Roderigo, his transports exceeded all bounds, on learning that I had succeeded in the enterprise upon which his soul was placed: but in a very short time, the same spy who had given him intelligence of Di Rosalva's becoming a parent, informed him that the female twin had been stolen, and that the male still lived beneath his father's roof. At first he believed his spy to have committed an unconscious error in the statement of the fact, and wrote to him, enquiring if he had not been guilty of a mistake, in regard to the sex of the child which had been stolen? and to this enquiry an answer was quickly returned, confirming the account which the former letter had brought.

"In the first tumult of his feelings, the Conte knew not whether to believe that I had deceived him in carrying off the girl instead of the boy, or that Di Rosalva had conceived the intention of repairing to himself the injury which had been done him in the theft of his child, by giving to his daughter, in the eye of the world, that sex which would secure to her the inheritance of her father's possessions.

"At length I convinced him that I had been true to the trust he had reposed in me, and had executed it faithfully. His rage was then all turned against Di Rosalva and his brain racked with plans for publicly exposing the sex of his remaining child; but Di Rosalva, he found, had been more subtle, in stratagem, than himself. Reflection taught him that it would be impossible for him to give evidence, in a court of justice, of the sex of the remaining child, without exposing, by the same means, that he was acquainted with the sex of the one which had been stolen, and, consequently, a party in the theft.

"It is not an uncommon instance to behold, that when the project upon which any man has placed his hopes and his desires, falls to the ground, that his spirits, his resolution, and his health fall with it.—Such was the case with the Conte Roderigo; all his enjoyments in life appeared from this moment to cease; and although he lived several years after the time of his experiencing this disappointment, they were years of melancholy sadness;—they were years, during which he bore about with him, in his own heart, the punishment of the wrong he had done to a fellow being, who had never offended him.

"At his death he divided, between his son and myself, what property he had to bequeath; and, with my share, I shortly after removed to this city, for reasons which it is unnecessary for me to state to you.

"The son, I have learnt, survived his father but a few years."

"And here," said the Conte, "your acquaintance with Vivane and Iago Zincti commenced?"

"Iago Zincti," replied Rodovina, "was a member of my family, for the first year of my residence here; when he left me to pursue a separate avocation, I invited Vivane to my house, to supply his station."

"At my first interview with the Signor Sylvio," she continued, "I was not less surprised to find that he had mistaken my daughter for the Signora Lucia, than I was at his informing me that his name was Sylvio di Rosalva. I had, from the first moment of my hearing this, my suspicions of his being the very Sylvio whom I had stolen from his cradle. But I had no confirmation of my opinion, till in a letter which he wrote to Vitellia, he gave a short sketch of his history, exactly similar to that which he delivered a few days ago in the court, except that it mentioned the old man, with whom he resided on the mountains of Tortona, to have been named Julio. The name of my brother being that of his protector—my brother never having been heard of by me, since the moment of his receiving the child at my hand, and his having declared to Sylvio that he had been hired to murder him, all tended to convince me that he must be Sylvio, the heir of Di Rosalva. Thus convinced, I determined to remove every obstacle which presented itself to his immediate union with my daughter, and to declare him to the world for the person he really was, the moment I had bound her the partner of his good fortune.—To this end—Merciful God, forgive me for the deed!—I administered the aqua tophana to the merchant Eldorado!"

Her narrative concluded, Rodovina again burst forth into exclamations of horror, occasioned by a sense of her past crimes, and the expiation of them to which she was condemned!—Violent convulsions followed those shrieks of terror, which she had mingled with frantic appeals to Heaven for mercy; and nature being exhausted within her, she sunk down upon the ground, where a faint trembling, which shook her joints, alone expressed her to be in a state of existence.

Having given orders that she should receive every necessary attention that her situation required, the Conte della Piacca and Sylvio left those gloomy walls, which in the persons of the culprits whom they enclosed, contained a warning lesson to the guilty to sin no more.

CHAPTER XIV

WHILE the circumstances just recorded were passing in the prison of Rodovina Maritos, and her associates in iniquity, an explanation, not less interesting to the feelings of those concerned in it, took place at the Palazzo della Piacca.

It was late in the afternoon when the Conte Lorenzo and Sylvio returned from the prison; and entering an apartment in the palazzo, adjoining to the bed-chamber of Rosabella, where they expected to see the family assembled, and awaiting their return, they were surprised by finding it vacant, and by observing a servant, who was leaving the bed-chamber adjoining to it, to shut the door with the utmost caution, as if afraid of disturbing the repose of some one within it.

The soul of Sylvio was immediately filled with apprehensions for his sister, and he hastily demanded an explanation of what he saw. The surgeon Sorato directly appeared to give it, with a smile on his countenance, which relieved the mind of Sylvio before he spoke.— "Your sister," he said, "fainted away about an hour ago, and I have since ordered her to be kept perfectly composed upon her bed, as the emotions of joy, if indulged, are sometimes as powerful as those of grief."

"Joy!" repeated Sylvio.

"Even so, Signor," returned Sorato; "but here comes one who will explain all to you better than I am able to do."

The Contessa entered as he spoke, and immediately satisfied their curiosity by an account of the transactions of the morning; which, as her spirits were at the time violently agitated, may, perhaps, be more incoherent and diffuse than would agree with the impatience of our readers;—we will, therefore, give the explanation in as few words as possible.

It will be remembered that the Signora Bianca had said, that Rosabella had still *one secret* lurking in her breast, which no tongue but her own should reveal. At the moment of her making this declaration, Averilla was silent, but she believed herself to be perfectly acquainted what that secret was. On the morning of the present day, Rosabella had appeared so much recovered from her wound, that the Contessa felt no reluctance to indulge her in a recapitulation of the past events of their lives. When they had conversed for some time, Averilla said—"Bianca tells me that you have yet one secret labouring in your breast;—I think I am prophetess enough to divine what that is. When you mentioned to my aunt Felicia an alliance with her family, was it not your desire to declare to her your sex; and having done this, to avow to her an affection for the poor blind Felix, whom every other woman disregarded, on account of his infirmity of person, and to whom your generous heart allied you, for the virtues of his mind?"

"Oh my friend," returned Rosabella, "you have penetrated into the inmost recesses of my heart!—To you I blush not to confess that my affections are placed on the amiable Felix; but had he been possessed of that faculty, which would have permitted him the blessing of a free choice, never should I have entertained the presumptuous idea of making that election for him; and should he now gain the blessing of his sight——"

"You have then heard of the peasant, who is, at this moment, a visitor at the Palazzo del Alvaretti?" said Averilla, interrupting her.

"Heard!" exclaimed Signora Bianca, with a smile; "it was she who sent him thither. A few days after we had quitted the Villa di Rosalva, chance introduced us to an object who had just recovered his sight, after having been for eleven years deprived of it. Eagerly she inquired who had been the happy instrument of restoring it to him. He informed us that it was an aged peasant, who resided on a small farm, in the duchy of Tuscany, and who was at that time gone into France, in compliance with the intreaties of a lady of distinction, whose only daughter had been struck blind by lightning. Instantly she resolved that Felix should enjoy the benefit of his advice. We accordingly went into Tuscany, and took up our abode in the neighbourhood of his dwelling, where we awaited his return home.

"At length he came; we visited him, and with a most gracious humanity, which marks his character, he promised to comply with our entreaties, and go with us to Genoa.

"No sooner had she obtained his consent, than she felt a reluctance to appear in the business herself. After the violent anger, which Signor Rossano had manifested, at the idea of your forming an alliance with the supposed Sylvio di Rosalva, she could not hope that he would ever permit his son to receive the hand of that same individual in marriage. Uncertain how it became her to act, she resolved to ask your advice for her conduct; and for this purpose, having sent forward the peasant Morano to Genoa, where we directed him to await our coming, we entered this city. We had not at that time heard that the Della Piacca, whom Rosabella dreaded, was no more; accordingly, fearing to be beheld by your husband, and yet unwilling to forego the desire of asking your counsel, in her present embarrassed situation, she sent you the letter, which you received from the hotel of the Holy Virgin. Your reply to it announced you to be confined to your chamber, and unconscious how soon it would be in your power to quit it. We had promised to meet Morano in three days, at the longest, in Genoa, and, therefore, were obliged to leave this city again without seeing you.

"We found Morano true to his appointment, at Genoa. Every hour since our acquaintance had first commenced with him, had given us additional proofs of his great benevolence, and excellent sense;—and, at my persuasion, Rosabella entrusted to him the secret of her heart and history.

"He listened, and replied to them in a manner that shewed him to be sufficiently interested in her cause, to act with all due regard to her happiness; and promising not to inform the family Del Alvaretti, by what means he had gained a knowledge of them and their son, he left us to proceed on his humane errand.

"A few hours after he had set out for the Villa del Alvaretti, I learnt, by a most unexpected accident, that the Conte Roderigo della Piacca, and his son, who had been the enemies of the family Di Rosalva, had, for some years past, been dead; that the Conte, your husband, was their very distant relative, and that to him the title and name had descended.

"With ecstacy Rosabella received this intelligence from my lips, and instantly she determined again to return to Turin, and, under the consolation of your friendship, to the enjoyment of which there now, no longer, existed any obstacle, to await the issue of Morano's visit to the family Del Alvaretti. Her resolution was no sooner taken than put into effect. We quitted Genoa that very hour. With what has occurred to us since our return to this city, you are already acquainted."

"But I can give *you* some information," returned the Contessa. "I have already received two letters from the Signora Felicia, concerning the benevolent peasant, who is arrived at the Villa del Alvaretti, and the occasion of his visiting it;"—and as she spoke she drew them from her pocket, and put them into the hands of Rosabella, at whose request the Signora Bianca read them aloud.

When the second letter had been read, "Kind, benevolent Morano!" exclaimed Rosabella, "the interest which he feels in my happiness is the only motive from which he proposes to the Signor Rossano, as the price of his son's sight, that if it ever be granted to him, he shall be unrestrained in his choice of an alliance. But, alas! Rossano hesitates to agree to this. Thus should he ever seem to acquiesce, and should Felix judge of me in my present character, as he did of me for a friend, there is no doubt but a father of this description will place some impediment in the way of our happiness."

The Contessa was beginning to reply, when a servant, who entered the apartment, brought her a letter.—"Whence comes this?" she asked; "it is not the usual hour of the post."

"It is brought by a courier, who says he comes from Genoa," answered the man.

Averilla tore it hastily open, and read the following words:—

"Oh, my beloved Averilla! In what terms of sufficient gratitude to Heaven shall I inform you that my beloved Felix beholds the light of day?—Yes, Averilla, Felix possesses the faculty of sight!—My husband was, yesterday morning, prevailed upon to consent to the conditions of the worthy peasant. The operation was successful, and Felix lost in ecstacy and wonder.—I scarcely know what I write, only this, that Felix implores to see Averilla; and that his mother entreats her to come directly to this scene of joy. Hasten hither, with your husband, and bless, by your presence, your affectionate aunt,

"FELICIA DEL ALVARETTI."

Having heard that the letter came from Genoa, it was impossible long to secrete, from Rosabella, its contents. The moment they were imparted to her, a faint shriek announced the effect which the intelligence had produced on her mind; and having uttered it, she sunk senseless into the arms of Bianca.

Such was the account of the transactions of the morning, delivered by Averilla to her husband and Sylvio, to which she added, that the violence of Rosabella's emotions had been softened, by a medicine administered to her by Sorato; and that she trusted to find her composed, when she should awake from a slumber into which she had now fallen.

During the explanation given by the Contessa, Bianca entered the room, and joined her in expressing eagerness to learn the events of the trials which the Conte and Sylvio had just returned from witnessing.

With the omission of such circumstances as might shock the delicate feelings of their auditors, they recounted the awful scenes which had passed in the court of justice; and, subsequent to them, those in the prison, to which the unhappy victims of iniquity had been conducted, after the voice of the law had pronounced judgment upon them.

In the evening Rosabella informed them, through Sorato, that she felt a wish to join their party for an hour or two at the least; if he did not judge it advisable for her to leave her chamber for a longer time: they accordingly met her in the apartment contiguous to that where she slept.

"In the letter which the Contessa received this morning from Genoa," said Rosabella, when they were assembled around her, "the Signora Felicia particularly mentions that Felix desires *to see* Averilla; this request I am certain she will not fail to comply with; and I think, if she would delay setting out till the day after to-morrow, I should be able to travel at the same time. I am extremely anxious to shew my brother the inheritance out of which he has so long been kept, and I should like to perform the journey in the company of friends whom I so much esteem, as those who would compose our party."

Every one present looked at Sorato for his reply to this proposal.

He said, "that the only complaint under which his patient now laboured was weakness; and that its most efficacious remedy was frequent indulgence in such points as the mind was warmly set upon, provided too much exertion was not used in their accomplishment; and that, upon this consideration, he believed, that if they would resolve not to perform their journey with too great rapidity, it would be more beneficial to Rosabella, to accompany them at the time she had mentioned, than to be left where she was, merely to repine that she was not with them."

Rosabella heard his decision in favour of her petition with the most heartfelt joy; and the day after the next being, accordingly, fixed upon for the commencement of their journey towards Genoa, she promised, till the arrival of that hour, implicitly to obey the regulations of Sorato, that she might, by attending to them, render herself more adequate to the undertaking.

CHAPTER XV

THE morning appointed for the party assembled at the Palazzo della Piacca to begin their journey towards Genoa, was that of the day on which Rodovina and her accomplice, Zincti, had been condemned to suffer.

The Conte desiring that neither his wife nor Rosabella should experience any unnecessary anxiety, by being acquainted with the exact time of their death, recommended to them to begin their journey early in the morning, which he said would allow them more time for rest during the day, and favour Rosabella's weak state of health. They agreed unsuspiciously to his proposal, and set out, after an early breakfast, accompanied by the Signora Bianca, Flavia, and their attendants.

The Conte judging that reasons might occur to require the presence of himself or Sylvio, in the city, during the course of the day, promised to overtake them in the evening, at the village where they had agreed to repose that night.

About three hours after their departure from the city, the impatient crowd was collected round the platform of death, on which the culprits were to expiate the crimes of their past lives by the forfeiture of their existence. The buz of expectation sounded on every side. The hypocrite was drawing a comparison between his own heart and that of the criminals; the mind of benevolence expressed its hope of their punishment ending with their existence; the unfeeling rejoiced only that the case was not their own; and a tribe, still more senseless than these, were expressing their impatience for the sight.

At length the door, which opened from the prison upon the scaffold, was thrown back upon its hinges. The moment this was witnessed by the crowd, the single words of "Now! now! There! there!" burst from every mouth; and the awful silence of dread, and expectation mixed, then prevailed.

First was led forth to the public gaze, Michael Vivane, a part of whose sentence it had been to witness the sufferings of his less fortunate accomplices. Next appeared Iago Zincti, with his neck bared for the rope, a deadly paleness overspreading his features, which were rendered so inanimate by apprehension, that he already appeared a corpse.

Lastly came forth Rodovina Maritos. From the moment at which the Conte della Piacca and Sylvio had left her dungeon, two days before, the frenzy of her soul had been encreasing with every instant. The more strongly the priest, who attended her, had represented to her the offences she had been guilty of to her Creator, by the conduct of her past life, the more she had dreaded to pray for mercy to him whom she had offended. "I am lost! eternally condemned and lost!"

was the only sentence which had proceeded from her lips. Great as had been the exertions of her agitated mind, still her strength had not deserted her; and, at the foregoing midnight, whilst the priest and her daughter had believed her occupied in silent prayer, with a sudden start she had dashed her head against the stone wall of her prison, with the intention of ending her existence.

The blow had not been so effective as she had desired it should; but it had been sufficient to deprive her of all sense, and to throw her back inanimate upon the floor of the prison. Vitellia had called for assistance, and means had been used for recalling her into life. The flowing of the blood had been stanched by bandages; and some drink, of a restorative nature, had been poured down her throat.

As sense returned, the frenzy of her mind had entirely evaporated; she was now become calm, and obedient to the instructions of the priest. Thus she continued till the moment arrived at which she was call[ed] to her fate. When she heard the summons, a silent struggle, between fortitude and weakness, appeared to pass in her breast;—her resolution conquered, and she sprang up from the bench on which she was reclining.—"My child!" she said, throwing her arms round the neck of Vitellia, "take thou warning by the fate of thy wretched mother! it is not yet too late for thee to repent. I charge thee, sin no more; it is the only blessing I am capable of tasting at this miserable moment." She impressed on her lips a fervent kiss, and repeating, in a most emphatic tone, "I charge thee, sin no more!" she suffered herself to be led to the platform.

The instant she arrived upon it, probably conceiving that the pain with which her head was bursting was occasioned by the bandages which encircled it, she tore them off, and threw them from her. The blood began immediately to flow from the wound, and the ghastly horror of her countenance was increased by the unchecked current.

While Zincti was undergoing the performance of his sentence, at the hand of the executioner, she knelt in prayer by the side of the priest. At length the executioner awaited her;—raising her hands to Heaven, as she fixed her eyes on the wheel, she exclaimed—"O God, that my death were past!" She paused an instant, and advancing a few steps, towards the edge of the scaffold, she said—"Mothers, save your daughters from the fate to which you see me condemned; teach them that the greatest virtue of a woman's life is *modesty*; my deviation from it was the first step which has brought me to this wretched end; teach them to be *modest* and you will save them from *criminality*."

This said, she suffered the executioner to place her upon the wheel. The priest knelt in prayer by her side. Once more she directed her eyes towards the populace—"Pray for me!" burst from her lip, and in a few instants she emitted her last breath, in the midst of unsatisfactory repentance and bodily tortures.

Intelligence that the dreadful ceremony of the hour had taken place having been conveyed to the Conte Lorenzo, he dispatched a message to Michael Vivane, assuring him that he had placed his mother in a situation of comfort, where every attention should be paid to her till the term of his imprisonment was expired; at which time he would lend his assistance to him, in procuring him some creditable employment for the remainder of his days.

Vitellia was the next object of his care.—He had gained permission for her to become an inhabitant of a mansion, supported by the contributions of the benevolent, for the reform of the profligate; and to this he had her immediately conveyed.

These matters having been attended to, no further cause existed to detain the Conte della Piacca at Turin; and, therefore, with his friend Sylvio, he immediately left it.

On overtaking their travelling companions, they found that Rosabella had borne her day's journey with very little fatigue, and was in excellent spirits; which no one doubted to be produced by the pleasure she anticipated at again beholding Felix. But there was a new sensation attached to this pleasure, which might either heighten or depress the expected joy.—She was *again* to behold Felix, but Felix was to behold her for the *first time*; and it might be possible that the charm of friendship, in which she had held his senses, might fade under his newly-acquired power of beholding her person.

In the presence of the Conte and Sylvio she forbore to introduce the subject which filled her heart; but when alone with Averilla and Bianca, she spoke freely of all her apprehensions and all her wishes.

There is nothing which affords so great delight to the love-devoted heart, as to unburthen its feelings to the bosom of sympathizing friends. It is an indulgence which not only robs doubt or absence of half their power to wound, but which carries with it a double sensation of delight, by imperceptibly fixing the ideas more strongly on the object of adoration.

Towards evening, on the third day of their journey, they arrived at the precincts of the village del Alvaretti. Rosabella had already expressed her earnest desire to be permitted to proceed with her brother and the Signora Bianca to the villa Di Rosalva; as she wished the particulars of her history to be communicated to the family del Alvaretti by the friendly tongue of Averilla, before she was introduced to them in her real character. Here they, accordingly, parted, with a promise of meeting again on the following day.

Felix had now enjoyed the blessing of his sight for nearly six days; and was, therefore, become, in some measure, able to calculate distances, and to distinguish between substance and shade; but he was not yet deemed sufficiently acquainted with the use of sight, by the kind Morano, who still continued with him, to be allowed to move about unled.

When Averilla entered the Palazzo del Alvaretti, Felicia met her, with Felix leaning on her arm. For a minute they were all silent; during which the features of all were animated with the warmest expression, except those of him by whom their emotions were caused.—"Felix, it is Averilla whom you behold," at length burst from the lips of the Contessa. The sound of her voice was an instant conviction to his senses.—"Dearest Averilla!" he exclaimed, and clasped her in his arms. The tears fell from the eyes of both. After having, a second time, pressed her to his heart, he released her from his grasp, and said—"Oh, Averilla, I never murmured at the imperfect state in which it pleased Providence to send me into life; and it has rewarded my patient endurance, with feelings of that exquisite nature which it is impossible for those to conceive, who have not wandered in the darkness I have done!"

CHAPTER XVI

HAVING thus far deduced our history according to the plan announced in the preface, of awarding to vice its due punishment, and bestowing on virtue its merited recompence, our readers will, doubtless, guess that we shall not transgress our rule with the long-suffering Rosabella, and the exemplary Felix; and that, were it from no other cause than that of conformity to our system, we should render them the greatest degree of happiness in the possession of each other.

If thus they have divined, they are true prophets. No sooner did Felix become acquainted with the sex of that friend whom he had before called Sylvio, with the real cause of the error into which himself and his family had all fallen with regard to his supposed affection for Averilla, and, above all, with the interest Rosabella had taken in his happiness, in becoming the instrument of bringing him acquainted with that benevolent man to whom he owed the blessing of his sight, than his friendship was converted into the most perfect love; and as we have already been admitted to the cabinet secrets of Rosabella, it is almost unnecessary to say that she did not frown on his hopes.

The Signor Rossano, and his daughter, the Marchesa Hyppolita di Bivelli, alone, did not smile on the proposed alliance so cheerfully, as every one else allied to the parties whom it concerned. But Rossano had pledged his word to Morano, not to restrict the inclination of his son in marriage, as the condition of his gifting him with sight; the word of a merchant is sacred, and therefore it was impossible for him to endeavour to retract his promise; and his dislike was also considerably softened by a dower of ten thousand zechins, which the Conte della Piacca insisted on presenting her with on the day of her marriage.—"My name," he said, "has been instrumental in adding to the unpleasantness of your past life; it is therefore but just that it should, like all your other enemies, make you some remuneration for its offences."

Peace now smiled on the house of Di Rosalva, the lowering clouds which had for some time past obscured its happiness were dispersed, and the union of Felix with Rosabella was the golden sun that cast a joyful splendour over the scene.

At the wedding festivities of Rosabella, Virgilia della Bagua again beheld the beautiful peasant, who had fascinated her heart on the mountains of Tortona; and as the knowledge that we are beloved, frequently leads us to contemplate with affection an object who would, perhaps, never else inspire us with passion, Sylvio became first flattered by Virgilia's opinion of him; and thence, passed through the intermediate steps of her friend and lover, into her husband.

Having proved the excellence of the hearts of Felix and his Rosabella, it is unnecessary to say, that the gratitude which they so eminently felt for the chief instrument of their happiness, the worthy Morano, they returned to him in the most grateful coin in which it is possible to reward a mind of feeling—that of their friendship and their love.

That Averilla and her husband enjoyed that felicity in the marriage state which can alone be the result of the exemplary virtues they practised, of the pure affection which reciprocally warmed their breasts, and of the unlimited confidence which they placed in the hearts of each other, we have already fully shewn; and we shall conclude with hoping that all married couples, into whose hands our *secret* chances to fall, may so benefit by this part of our moral, as to render it *a secret worth its weight in gold.*

FINIS.

NOTES

4   *league*: a unit of distance equal to 3 miles or 4.8 kilometers.

45   *Po*: the longest river in Italy; it passes through Turin on its way to the Adriatic.

51   *Cicisbeo*: in Italy, the gallant of a married woman.

64   *Riquet with his Tuft*: a fairy story about Prince Riquet who has not a head of hair, but only a tuft of hair on his head. At birth Prince Riquet is so ugly that his mother describes him as looking like a monkey. But as the tale unfolds and Prince Riquet, endowed with extraordinary gifts and wisdom, grows into maturity, his life and the love he feels for a beautiful princess turn into a moral fable about how ugliness can be transformed into beauty and stupidity into brilliance while under the spell of love.

79   *zechin*: taken as a monetary unit that later in the novel is identified as gold; from the Italian "zecchino", "a sequin."

102   *aqua tophana*: More commonly spelled "aqua tofana", a poisonous arsenic solution.

115   It is clear that the Conte is fearful of quacks and mountebanks, with cause. The trade was widespread in eighteenth-century England and already hawkers of a range of powders and nostrums had found magazines and bills as ready sources for advertising their wares.

200   *cabinet secrets*: may or at least obliquely refers to cabinets or closets of curiosities, the most famous of which during the eighteenth century belonged to one Mother Bunch. Mother Bunch offered watered-down philosophy and secrets (in the manner of helpful hints from Heloise), especially to women, on the ways of getting good husbands.